THE GENOA FERRY

Books by Ronald Harwood

THE
GENOA FERRY

Ronald Harwood

SECKER & WARBURG
LONDON

First published in England 1976 by
Martin Secker & Warburg Limited
14 Carlisle Street, London W1V 6NN

Copyright © 1976 by Ronald Harwood

SBN: 436 19123 7

Printed in Great Britain by
Richard Clay (The Chaucer Press) Ltd,
Bungay, Suffolk

For
Gillon Aitken

Death, in itself, is nothing; but we fear
To be we know not what, we know not where.

DRYDEN

PART ONE

PART ONE

When the ferry from Genoa docked the sun had not yet risen; the light belonged neither to night nor day; there was no visible horizon; sky and sea were one. From the deck Fisher could vaguely discern the grey outline of the city divided in two by the straggling ruins of a fort or castle bleak against the sky : to the west, on a gentle hill, a pyramid of crowded structures relieved by scattered minarets; to the east, the taller, sleeker buildings of the modern city, imposing in the haze. The wind was sharp, insistent, beating from the north across the water. Fisher was shivering a little by the time the gangplanks were secured, and from the moment he stepped ashore he became uneasy : he didn't know why : there was nothing in particular to which he could attribute his disquiet, just a nagging sensation that all was not well. He stood on the quay listening to the lapping water, the creak of ropes, the early morning murmurs of passengers and Immigration Officers, an occasional cry of a gull, and he was convinced that something dreadful was about to happen.

He was among the first to land. Six or seven Japanese youths had preceded him and formed an orderly line at the door of a long shed guarded by a policeman. All of them wore identical American baseball caps with upturned peaks; they were, for the most part, silent and watchful; one, however, laughed frequently, high-pitched and, Fisher thought, nervously. Soon, the other passengers disembarked in a slow but continuous flow : Arabs mostly coming home, Fisher supposed, and British businessmen in crumpled suits, Italians in shirtsleeves, Americans smelling of after-shave lotion. The ship had been packed to overflowing : the Colonel had closed his airspace as a protest – Fisher didn't learn against what – and as a result, hundreds of travellers converged on Genoa where the fortunate ones found places on the ferry. Fisher had slept the two nights of the crossing in reclining seats called sleeperettes; the days he passed in the main saloon watching old Doris Day films maniacally dubbed into Italian; he wanted to read but the perpetual babble made concentration impossible; he saw no one aboard in the least attractive, so he kept to himself, drawn to the ship's rail to gaze at the patterns of the sea, hoping that Gerald had written, 'I must see you. I *need* to see you,' because he wanted to forgive Fisher.

Motor-car engines started up inside the ship and a procession of vehicles emerged driven at breakneck speed down the ramps on to the quay. All pretence of a queue vanished. Fisher found himself pressed into the long, narrow shed where four Immigration Officers waited in a cubicle with semi-circular open windows numbered 1, 2, 3 and 5, echoing the disorder in the shed itself; the passengers, now a rioting mob, waved their passports desperately, shouted and shoved and pushed towards the windows where the officials selected documents at random, and dealt with them at speed. Fisher, who had an over-developed sense of smell, was grateful that the throng was, at least, odourless. He began to push and shove, too, and when at last his turn came, the Officer scrutinised his passport and face with exaggerated and insolent caution as though deliberately to aggravate his anxiety. And after his documents were finally stamped and returned to him, Fisher was consigned to struggle through a single narrow door into the Customs Hall: again, the examination of his baggage seemed to be more thorough and painstaking than that afforded to others. Was it because his hair was too long, he wondered? Or because he wore faded blue denim? Or because he carried a shoulder-bag? The police officer in Accra had said, 'We don't want any ageing hippies, thank you,' and laughed. Here, his pockets were searched, parcels unwrapped, his suitcase lining patted and kneaded; even a bottle of cologne was uncorked and sniffed. 'Any alcohol?' he was asked.

'No, no alcohol.'

'It is forbidden.'

But by the time he stepped out into a large forecourt where the taxis and buses waited his feeling of disquiet had subsided. Premonitions of disaster, he told himself, belonged to darkness and were always worst at the moments before sunrise. Now,

4

the lights of the ferry, which had glowed so brightly when she docked, lost their brilliance as dawn yielded to day and Fisher experienced a faint excitement at the prospect of seeing his half-brother again after so long. The thought of their reconciliation warmed him and, eagerly, he scanned the faces of the waiting groups for Gerald, but Gerald wasn't there.

Fisher sat astride his battered suitcase and waited. The ferry had the deserted look of an empty tin can. Deckhands stood at the ship's rail like customers at a bar waiting to be served. The Captain, a short, hunched figure with a scowl and bloodshot eyes, marched down the gangplank gripping a black plastic briefcase. He gave the impression of carrying an intolerable burden and during the crossing Fisher had christened him Charon, the surly ferryman of the Styx. A policeman on the quay saluted him as though he were an admiral. Fisher lit a cigarette but the early-morning taste was bitter; he tossed it into the breeze and watched it carried away.

The buses set off bulging with passengers, and, soon, there were no more taxis. Fisher could see them making their way towards the city along the perimeter road like a funeral procession. The forecourt was almost deserted now, but for two policemen in pale blue uniforms with matching berets, looking ridiculously adolescent like boy scouts. They leaned against a wall, gossiping, one buttoning and unbuttoning his holster. Time passed reluctantly.

It became noticeably warmer. A fishing smack unloaded its cargo encouraged by an ecstatic chorus of gulls. The boy-policemen wandered off arm in arm. Fisher looked at his watch. He had been waiting almost two hours for Gerald, and there was still no sign of him. From his shoulder-bag he took Gerald's letter and re-read it, to reassure himself. There was no greeting or word of endearment:

I must see you. I *need* to see you. Come at once, if you can. Just cable time of arrival and I'll meet you. You can stay with me. I'll pay you back your fare and all expenses when you get here.

G.

In the bottom right-hand corner he gave his address, a

transliteration of the Arabic. Typical, Fisher thought, to write after fifteen years' silence and not turn up to say welcome.

He was about to replace the letter in its envelope when he was surprised to see inside the photograph of Anne because he couldn't remember putting it there. He looked at her face: too plump to be beautiful, but expressive eyes and a determined chin though the cheeks were inclined to puffiness. He wished she was with him now; he wished he hadn't caused her pain.

He tried to find a smile from somewhere. To Fisher, a smile was a sort of signature; he noticed it as a response in others, when and how frequently it was used and what it revealed: politeness, anxiety, self-deprecation, pleasure. His own smile, Anne once said, was hopeful. He remembered smiles as a way of remembering people: Gerald, who smiled with his lips, never showing his teeth, knowing and disapproving; Anne, who squeezed a smile and closed her eyes at the same time, modest and indulgent; Mother, too much pink gum above the upper teeth, ugly, forced, manic. And his father? Fisher couldn't remember; perhaps his father hadn't smiled much.

A solitary taxi, like a bee that had lost the swarm, buzzed into sight. Fisher stood and waved; the taxi nosed towards him.

Fisher read Gerald's address off the letter. 'Do you know it?' he asked.

'Oh yes,' said the driver and smiled with bad teeth. 'One pound.'

Fisher nodded. He had very little money left and badly needed Gerald to reimburse him for the fare. But Gerald had failed to appear. All sorts of doubts plagued Fisher: had his cable been delivered? had he read too much into Gerald's letter? After all, there was no mention of reconciliation. But Fisher knew perfectly well that he wanted to believe in Gerald's charity, wanted his forgiveness. He wasn't ashamed to acknowledge that Gerald was still important to him, the only person he had ever known whose censure he feared, and whose approbation he sought. Why? Authority was a mystery. Yet, once, Fisher had defied Gerald's authority.

The driver loaded the suitcase into the boot and, with Fisher seated beside him, set off. They travelled at speed. Fisher leaned back, cool air rushing at his face, and was assailed now by irritation and resentment. He knew there would be no apology, no explanation. Gerald would greet him as if it was yesterday

6

they'd last seen each other, and then play his secretive games, not revealing at once his reasons for writing, not letting on how he'd found out Fisher's whereabouts, but at some unexpected moment telling just enough to whet the appetite for more. What would he say? 'Oh, by the way, you're forgiven'? And yet, Fisher was reluctant to admit, Gerald's letter could not have been better timed: how like him to use the words 'I need to see you' at the moment Fisher himself was in need. He glanced over the rim of the windscreen and began to make out heavy traffic; he could distinguish the squat houses and shops of the old town dominated by a mosque on the waterfront. He could see distinctly the ruins of the Spanish castle now, built of golden stone, as they made their way towards the modern city where trim minarets sprouted everywhere like cultivated flowers in a garden run wild.

And then, for no apparent reason, Fisher remembered an incident from childhood, to do with Gerald. The business with the tree-house: he must have been ten, eleven at most; Gerald would have been in his late teens? early twenties? 'Gerald's coming home for the weekend,' Mother had said. The tree-house – it had taken Fisher a month to construct – rested across two sturdy branches of a tall maple on the Common. He used it at first as a place to re-enact the adventures he saw in the cinema or read about: Mowgli's jungle hide-out, or the bridge of the *Hispaniola*, or a coral island. One day, Fisher had overheard his Aunt Rosa, who was visiting, proudly telling a friend that her nephew had built a sanctuary in the trees. Sanctuary. The idea stirred Fisher's imagination and, gradually, the re-enactions ceased; instead, he took there treasures and mementoes more personal, solemn and expressive. The memory was all so harmless now, like the history of someone else in another time. The photograph of T. E. Lawrence in his desert robes, the framed account of Haliburton swimming the Panama Canal, the bust of Shakespeare with the broken nose, a print – cut from a schoolbook – of the Death of Nelson, black-and-white photographs of the stained-glass in Chartres, the cross made of two horse-chestnut twigs strung together and nailed to the wall. He could no more explain the reason for each childish fancy now, than he could then. And Gerald came home that weekend, as he had promised, and set fire to the

7

sanctuary, surrounded by jeering boys, raked it down out of the branches and stamped in fury on the embers. Why? Mother had asked with interest, not reproach. And Gerald had answered, 'Because I don't approve of shit.' Was it then, Fisher wondered, that he'd learned to smile? Don't let him see that you're hurt, Aunt Rosa had said. (In secret, pain, if it was pain, began in emptiness, a weightless state connected in his mind with a sense of loss – but of what?) And it struck Fisher as ironic that although he could point to countless similar cruelties, it was he who sought Gerald's pardon.

The taxi braked. They had come to a modern apartment block which looked as though it was still in the process of being built: scaffolding clung to a side wall, and the pavement in front was being re-laid. The driver carried the suitcase into the entrance lobby, took his payment and departed. The vestibule was cool and shadowy. A row of wooden letter-boxes lined the left-hand wall, and Fisher bent over to study them: Gerald's visiting-card had been stuck to one with a drawing-pin: G. A. MATHER – and in pen had been added, Flat 8, 3rd Floor. Fisher took the lift, which ascended in spasms and came eventually shuddering to a halt.

There was no one about, and it was dark on the landing. Fisher peered at each door in turn until, at last, at the end of a short corridor he found the one numbered eight. He knocked. There was no reply, but somewhere behind him another door shut.

2

The photograph of the Queen, smiling, was unexpectedly reassuring.

A tall, flat-chested girl with spindly upper-class legs showed Fisher into a waiting-room on the ground floor of the Embassy.

She said, 'Mather, Mather. Rings a bell. I'll go and find someone who knows *all* about it. Do sit.'

The room had a high, white ceiling bordered with gold leaves, an imposing marble chimney-piece which seemed out of place, polished floors, claret rugs, a Louis-Quinze sofa, an ornate desk – and the Queen, smiling. Fisher waited half an hour before an earnest man in his early thirties carrying a

8

plain buff file cover took up a position behind the desk, his fingers spread wide on the virgin blotter like a schoolmaster about to admonish a class. He had a pinkish complexion that you knew would blister in the sun; he wore rimless glasses and his hair was immaculately combed with a side-parting. He said, 'My name's Wirrel. I believe you're making enquiries about a Mr Gerald Arthur Mather. May I ask in what connection?' His tone gave nothing away.

'I'm his half-brother. My name's Fisher. Martin Fisher.' Involuntarily, he produced his passport and offered it to the man.

'His half-brother? I see,' Wirrel said, glancing cursorily at the passport but not taking it. Slowly, he opened the file.

Something terrible is about to happen, thought Fisher, and closed his eyes as though to shut out the light prevented also the possibility of disaster.

Wirrel cleared his throat and when he next spoke, his voice was softer, kindlier. 'Mr Fisher,' he said, 'your half-brother is dead. He was killed in a – in a motor-car accident.' He looked up at the ceiling, unused to breaking bad news.

Fisher tried not to smile: the news did not shock him: he'd been prepared. 'When did it happen?' he asked, thinking: there is worse to come.

'Last Tuesday. Shortly before dawn.'

'I'd only just received his letter. I've been living in Rome. I cabled to say I was coming. It was to have been a reconciliation.' The words tumbled out faster than he intended: why tell the man these things, he wondered? 'How did it happen?'

'The police –'

'Yes?'

'He committed suicide.'

'Gerald?'

'Yes.'

'How?'

'He drove his car straight off the Old Quay into the water. Strapped himself in. Drowned, in fact.'

A fierce, uncontrollable longing to see Gerald took hold of Fisher. 'Where's he now, his body, I mean?'

'In the morgue. But he's been cremated. As a matter of fact, he's to be buried tomorrow at sea.'

9

'Why at sea?'

'He left instructions.' Wirrel came round the desk and handed Fisher a sheet of paper, a photocopy:

> I, Gerald Arthur Mather, wish to be cremated
> and my ashes are to be committed to the sea.

It bore Gerald's signature, cramped, small, mean, and beneath it there were two lines in Arabic script, which, Wirrel explained, were the signatures of the witnesses. 'The top one is a Mr Fawzi's – he's evidently Mr Mather's superior in the Ministry of Oil; the second is, I believe, a female secretary.'

'He left no other note?'

'No.'

Fisher said, 'Odd thing for him to do.'

'It's quite usual for people to want their remains disposed of in a particular way,' Wirrel responded, as though his word had been questioned.

'I meant odd for Gerald,' but Fisher couldn't explain why: it was an instinct, knowing what others would or would not do, never oneself. Suicide – that was always possible, Fisher thought: death was death to Gerald. But a burial at sea hinted of sentimentality and Gerald was never sentimental, not about death: not about anything.

'I'm really awfully sorry,' Wirrel said. 'This must be a terrible shock to you.'

'Yes.'

'Would you like a drink?'

'Is one allowed? I thought the place was dry.'

'In the Embassy's all right. Foreign territory. What'll it be, scotch, brandy?'

'A small brandy. Thank you.'

Wirrel lifted the telephone and asked for the drink. While they waited, he said, 'The foreigners brew their own illegal stuff. *Flash*, they call it. Pretty fierce.'

The tall thin girl brought the brandy and departed. Fisher sipped it slowly. He asked, 'Did you know Gerald?' He wanted, somehow, to make a connection in the present, however tenuous or remote, with the past.

'I met him once. At the Residence. On a Sunday. That's our open day. But he lived a somewhat solitary life. Didn't mix much. My wife knew him a little. They attended classes together.'

'Classes? For what?' What did Gerald have to learn?

Wirrel flattened his lips as though he'd sucked on a lemon and liked it. 'Meditation. Non-attachment. Mysteries of the East – that sort of thing.'

'Gerald was interested in the Mysteries of the East?' Fisher was unable to prevent a comic note from entering his voice.

'My wife could tell you more. Matter of fact, she's to represent their fellow-students at the funeral. She'll say a poem. I hope you won't mind.'

'No, of course not.'

'I'm off duty tomorrow so I've agreed to conduct some form of service. Unless you –'

'No –'

'Understood. There won't be many present. This Mr Fawzi's attending. Perhaps another from the Ministry. Oh, and Mr Nash, of course.'

'Who's he?'

'Calls himself a Consultant. Been here years. Rough diamond but soft-hearted. Insurance, investments, that sort of thing. He's taking care of the arrangements.'

'It's a long way to come for a burial at sea,' Fisher said sadly, and drank the last of the brandy. 'What was Gerald in the Oil Ministry?' he asked.

'Something administrative,' Wirrel said. He sounded evasive. 'Have the other half?' He took the empty glass from Fisher's hand.

Fisher declined and then, suddenly remembering, asked, 'Did Gerald have any money?' with a note of panic, knowing the question sounded callous.

'I beg your pardon?'

Fisher took time lighting a cigarette. He said, 'I'm sorry about this, but I'm in a bit of a spot.' He explained that his fare was to be refunded by Gerald on arrival. 'I'm just a bit short at the moment. I was hoping to be staying with Gerald, you see. I suppose there's no chance of getting his flat?'

Wirrel stiffened: he did not conceal his disapproval easily – a handicap, Fisher thought, for a diplomat. 'I'll see what can be done,' he said, and, without another word, left the room. But

11

Fisher had long ago ceased to be embarrassed by the need for money: he knew, from experience, how to wheedle, to beg and to borrow, and how to leave small loans un-repaid. And he remembered the last time he and Gerald had faced each other, at their mother's funeral, standing either side of the grave. He could not bring to mind clearly Gerald's face, but he had an overwhelming sense of his presence, austere, intense, disapproving. He recalled the journey back from the cemetery, seated in the rear of a spacious hired limousine, the chauffeur whistling under his breath, *Hold my hand, I'm a stranger in paradise*. Gerald said, 'Good of you to weep. You always do the right thing. Now you can tip the driver.'

'But, Gerald, I haven't any money.'

The tall girl re-appeared. 'Mr Wirrel's asked me to tell you he may be a little time. Can I get you a coffee?'

'And something to eat, if that's possible?'

She wasn't certain, she said, but she'd do her best. More than an hour passed before she came back with a plate of sandwiches, an empty cup, a tin of Nescafé and jug of water. 'I'm awfully sorry,' she said, 'but we've had to send out for this. Could you pay?'

He handed over some coins and she departed. Alone, he tucked into the sandwiches and tried to mix the Nescafé but the water was tepid. Presently, Wirrel, with a grudging apology, returned. 'It's not the best time to ask favours of them,' he said, resuming his position behind the desk. He watched, with a kind of fascination, the visitor stuff a sandwich into his mouth and sip tepid lumps of Nescafé. Fisher was a noisy, messy eater.

'How d'you mean?' Fisher asked. 'Not the best time?'

'You came by the ferry, didn't you?'

'Yes.'

'You know the airspace is closed.'

'Yes.'

'It's a protest. Against us, I'm afraid. We're holding two of their nationals for waving loaded revolvers about on a VC-10. So you see, they're not well disposed to do us favours.'

'I see.'

'But the Ministry's quite helpful. Evidently, there's a bit of a flap on. Mr Mather had taken home some official papers the night he – and now they can't be found. So, they've sealed his place and are having to search it. They think the papers are in his briefcase which is missing. It's possible you could have the flat by tomorrow.'

'What about tonight?' Fisher asked.

'I'm coming to that,' Wirrel said a little sharply. 'It appears that on official Government forms, Mather put you down as his next-of-kin. Are you his nearest relative?'

'I believe so.'

'He had no wife?'

'No.'

'We're telexing London for confirmation,' he announced as if he didn't believe Fisher. 'We have to find out if he made a Will. I won't bore you with the legal niceties but if you are the sole surviving member of the family, there is a little money in a bank account – I'm not certain how much. Nash could probably tell you more. It's bad luck about the policy.'

'Policy?'

'Life Insurance. Null and void. Disqualifying clause. Suicide.' Each phrase was an effort. 'As for tonight, we've booked you in at the Palace Hotel. It's rather pricey, but it's the best we can do at short notice. The town's horribly under-hotelled. Well, I think that takes care of everything.' He crossed to the door.

Fisher said, 'What about the funeral tomorrow?'

Wirrel considered for a moment. 'I'll get Mr Nash to pick you up at the hotel.'

In the hall, Wirrel asked the porter to summon a taxi, and he gave Fisher a card with the Embassy telephone number. While they waited Fisher felt the younger man's eyes on him, impossible to tell what he was thinking behind those shuttered eyes. He said, 'Was Mr Mather baptised?'

'Baptised? I doubt it. No, I'm sure not.'

'No, I thought not, too,' he said. 'Your taxi won't be long. I'll see you tomorrow.'

3

The darkness took Fisher by surprise: another day had passed; time had played its usual tricks, like a candle flame, still one moment, guttering the next. The taxi dropped him at the Palace Hotel. The desk clerk had no record of the booking. But the British Embassy made the reservation, Fisher complained.

'I'm sorry, sir, but we are full,' the clerk said, polite but intractable. Another hotel was recommended barely a hundred yards down the street: it, too, was full. 'May I suggest Hotel Afreka? Quite okay and always empty. A short walk, sir, first left, second right, first left.' Fisher trudged once more out into the chill evening air and quickly lost himself.

He rested once more astride his suitcase on a ragged square of waste ground, littered with tin cans, crumpled paper, rubble, a broken bedstead and a zinc bath. There was no one about, no lighted windows, no sign of life. He wished he knew where the morgue was. Again he had a yearning to see Gerald's remains, to be close to him, as though proximity would comfort them both and heal the wounds. The night grew cold.

He cried, not tears but silent whimpering. Alone, he could show his grief; in company, from habit, he concealed feeling. What, Fisher wondered, made the poor sod kill himself? What had driven him to such despair? Perhaps self-destruction was not a decision suddenly forced on a man, but a result of his every word, thought, emotion, act, an intricate, inevitable climax. Poor sod. Fisher regretted that they had not been reunited: he would have welcomed Gerald's forgiveness.

A stone struck the zinc bath like a bullet ricocheting. Fisher rose, terrified, looking this way and that, but he could see nothing, not even shadows: he heard scuffling steps and another stone landed near him. Unaccountably, the idea that he would die here, now, suddenly, in this dumping ground, this casual refuse-tip, seemed inevitable and he was rooted to the spot, paralysed by the certainty that death was about to strike. The night call from the mosques blasted out on loudspeakers to mock him. He lifted his suitcase and set off once more in search of the hotel. Immediately, he was dogged by the curious rhythm of a halting step, a persistent grating sound, as though someone was scraping fingernails down a blackboard.

He saw no one, but heard running footsteps and a man's voice call out. Then, another sound, somebody hurrying away. A second shout, then silence. Fisher was again overwhelmed by an intimate sense of loss, the loss of something precious. He

14

hurried on and, presently, the scraping sound returned to stalk him. He wanted to cry out, but his courage failed him. He wanted a place to sleep; he wanted inexplicably to see Gerald.

4

A passer-by showed him to the hotel. Even before he entered he heard a familiar, nervous, high-pitched laugh. A drain was blocked and had overflowed into the street; the sour smell of excrement filtered into the hotel lobby. The receptionist, a boy of sixteen in a waiter's white jacket, said, 'I have no single room. You must share.' In the lobby, which apparently served as the residents' lounge, sat the Japanese youths he had seen on the quay; the one who laughed paged through a battered copy of *Paris Match*; the others brooded and drank Pepsis.

'You will share?' asked the receptionist.

'If I have to.'

'How long you stay?'

'Just one night. I hope.'

'Two pounds.'

'All right.'

'Come. I show you.'

The room, on the first floor, was large and pentagonal with a high ceiling so that it felt like being in a tall funnel. It contained four camp beds and, beside each, stood a small table with a lamp, and a tin ashtray advertising Martini. The walls were pale hospital green, and against the fifth stood a shiny, laminated wardrobe inset with a Moorish design in white plastic. A three-pillared chandelier gave off a glow-worm light; there was a wash-hand basin in the corner that looked as if the plumbers hadn't finished their work, the cement roughly rendered round the pipes and over tiny, square ceramic tiles.

A small, sad man with the nose of an ant-eater sat bowed on one of the beds. He wore a black beret and a windcheater and did not acknowledge Fisher's arrival: he remained quite still, studying his hands which were folded on his lap as though time hung heavy for him. Fisher mumbled a greeting; without looking up, the man said, 'I am Jorda. Basque,' and that was all. He gave the impression of being cocooned in a protective bubble which kept out intruders. Fisher chose a bed and tested the mattress which was surprisingly soft.

The heat was stifling. 'Do you mind if I open the window?' Fisher asked. The Basque rose and slipped out of the room. Fisher pulled aside the heavy curtains which were also green but didn't quite match the walls, and undid the shutters. The smell of excrement floated up from the street; he refastened the shutters and resigned himself to the heat. He lay down and kicked off his shoes; even the backs of his hands were sweating. At intervals, footsteps pounded along the corridor outside; somewhere near, a baby cried. Presently, Fisher was aware of a slow and steady throbbing from some near-by machine, a generator perhaps, but out of rhythm with his own pulse, and with no warning at all it produced in him acute panic. The turmoil of the day, the heat in the room, the insistent throbbing aggravated a feeling of alarm. At one moment, he imagined himself wholly detached from his surroundings, observing from a point above a frightened, sweaty man, his long fair hair wet and dank, his slim body crumpled like soiled clothing, writhing on a narrow bed; at another, he was one with the man, fighting to regain control. A single goal insisted itself: to breathe in time with the throbbing: the more he tried, the more laboured his breathing became so that he thought his chest would burst. Into his mind sprang a confusion of images to do with Gerald's committal to the sea: a wrapped parcel, bound with string in neat segments, unmistakably a shroud, floating at an angle through the water. Fisher had, he knew, to scream –

'*Nummer fünfzehn?*'

Fisher sat up, gasping. The door was opened just enough to admit the face of a man, a large, enquiring face with a high, domed forehead. '*Sprechen Sie Deutsch?*' the face asked.

'No, I'm English.'

The face disappeared briefly and then the door was thrown open to reveal the rest of the body, short and powerful. 'I am German,' he said. 'Winzer is the name. Helmuth Winzer. This is my brother, Günther.' Fisher hadn't noticed the second man, a shade taller than his brother, but the facial resemblance was obvious because the foreheads matched. He wore dark glasses and carried a short white stick the length of a conductor's baton. Helmuth ushered him into the centre of the room and then reached out into the corridor to pull in two suitcases, one of which he heaved on to the bed the Basque had occupied.

'That's taken,' said Fisher.

'There is nothing to indicate so,' Helmuth replied firmly and without a hint of apology. 'Where is the WC?' he asked, opening one of the suitcases and removing a sponge-bag and towel.

'In the corridor, I suppose.'

With a curt nod, he disappeared. His blind brother, Günther, smiling sweetly, stood where he had been placed in the centre of the room. He said, 'May I feel your face?'

Fisher rose and guided Günther's hand. The touch was delicate although the fingers were sweaty, stubby and strong. Günther said, 'You are thirty-five, thirty-six and handsome, I think.'

'Would you like to sit down?' Fisher asked.

'No, but thank you. I wait for my brother. He looks after my needs.'

Fisher went to his bed and Günther waited for Helmuth, his head slightly to one side, wearing the cherubic smile. Several minutes passed before Helmuth returned, towel over his shoulder, smelling of cologne. He exchanged a few sentences in German with his brother, helped him off with his jacket and guided him to a bed. Helmuth said, 'This is a disgusting country. The hotels don't keep bookings and my brother is an important man.' Günther denied the claim with a gesture of feminine modesty.

'Did you come by the ferry?' Fisher asked.

'No, by taxi,' replied Günther.

'Imagine,' said Helmuth, 'a taxi from Tunis. But that's how they travel in this Goddamn place. You pile in the taxi with God knows who and then share the fare. Imagine!'

Fisher dozed in fits and starts. The presence of the brothers comforted him and ushered in a notion of security. It had been the same when he and Gerald shared a room, the reassurance of another's existence tempered the fear of darkness. If only death could be a shared experience. He thought of death often, daily and with greater frequency in recent months. And he remembered when he and Gerald had lain in bunk-beds, Gerald above, his feet sticking over the edge of the bunk, Fisher below, shortly after the destruction of the tree-house: Fisher could remember Gerald torturing him with his answers to night-questions, child-terrors:

'Gerald, what if there is a life after death?'

'There isn't.'

'But there may be a place, which we can't imagine, where we go after death.'

'There isn't.'

'But if there's a God?'

'There isn't.'

'How can you be so certain?'

'We spin in space. We're an accident. We're too many. We'll starve. We'll cool. There'll be nothing for ever and ever and ever and ever.'

'Is that all there is?'

'Yes. You and me. Here and now.'

'I'm frightened, Gerald.'

'That's because you know what I say is true.'

Difficult to think of Gerald dead, difficult to imagine such certainty brought to nothing, a cipher, ash, mere speculation.

'Gerald, just suppose you're wrong.'

'I'm not.'

'But, just suppose.'

God, what comfort there was in just suppose and what if, perhaps, you never know, could be. Far preferable to Gerald's certainty, it is, it is not. It gave Fisher smug satisfaction to think of Gerald as ash, resting in some morgue while he was here in movement, doing, breathing, thinking, cowering, but a censored memory, deeply buried, rose like a spectre: a court-room, a Bible, his mother's screams, Gerald, in the dock, smiling with thin lips. 'God!' he cried aloud. 'Something terrible is going to happen —'

'Stop making so much noise,' Helmuth barked. 'You are twisting and turning and talking out loud. Stop it. We are trying to get some sleep.'

The blind man said, 'You are having bad dreams, yes?'

Fisher stumbled out into the corridor, found the bathroom and washed his face. The cold water refreshed him but did not altogether dispel his misgivings. He wanted a drink, even a

18

Pepsi would do, and was halfway down the stairs when he heard from the lobby a voice say quite clearly the name 'Mather'. Instinctively, he leaned into the shadows and descended with caution until he had a view of the entrance. Some of the lights had been extinguished. The young manager was nowhere to be seen but the Japanese were there, and Jorda, the Basque: they were gathered round a lanky man with a boyish face, wearing a black T-shirt and jeans. He was American, and was saying, 'We have to wait, you understand? All of us.' One of the Japanese acted as interpreter; the Basque strained forward with a deep frown of concentration. 'It's too important to rush,' the American continued, pausing for the translation. 'We have to wait for Mather's man.' To the Basque, he said, '*Esperar.*'

The Basque understood. '*Esperar.*'

'They're looking for Mather's briefcase,' the American said. 'As soon as they find it, everything goes ahead as planned. We've got to play along with them. We're here for the money so we have to do things their way.' He addressed the Japanese. 'They have a certain formality when doing these things. You guys understand that.' The translation was answered by the whinnying laugh. 'So. Okay. As soon as Mather's guy turns up, it's all systems go.' He rose and turned so that Fisher could see more of his face: he was remarkably handsome, blond, blue eyes, fresh, deodorised. The Japanese bowed to him, and Jorda took his hand and kissed it.

Fisher darted back into the bedroom and shortly afterwards the door opened to re-admit the Basque. The man saw that his bed was occupied by Helmuth and, without complaint, lay on another.

'Who is that?' Günther asked in the dark.

'I am Jorda. Basque.'

'May I feel your face?'

'*No entiendo.*'

Fisher manoeuvred himself on hands and knees to the end of the bed so that his face was close to Jorda's. 'Excuse me,' Fisher whispered, 'but who was the American you were talking to?'

'I sleep,' said the Basque.

'He seemed to know my half-brother, Mather.'

'Please!' Helmuth cried. 'We are trying to get some rest!'

The Basque closed his eyes and turned away from Fisher who crawled back to his pillow and lay down. The generator still pounded but not so emphatically. Fisher slept, then was disturbed by another noise, an unidentifiable padding sound, like a small animal scurrying in fright to and fro. He switched on his light and saw the blind man, Günther, seated on his bed, across his knees a silent keyboard and he was practising at speed arpeggios, octaves, chords. He said, 'Do I make disturbance?'

'No.'

'The last sonata of Beethoven.'

Fisher switched off the light. Jorda grunted in his sleep; Helmuth lay quietly and the silent sonata continued. Doors opened and closed. Near by, in the next room perhaps, a man coughed often; from elsewhere farther off the sound of a group singing. And Fisher said to himself, before sleep, something terrible is about to happen.

5

Breakfast at the Hotel Afreka was served by the same youth who had acted as receptionist the previous evening. A long trestle table was laid out with neat parcels of cutlery wrapped in white paper napkins. The youth brought burnt toast, butter and sickly sweet jam; the water for the Nescafé was tepid. Fisher ate alone. He had hoped to question Jorda again but the Basque was not about. When Fisher had woken that morning, Jorda had already gone, leaving his bed neatly made. The brothers Winzer snored in close harmony, Günther with one blind eye open.

Fisher was lighting his first cigarette of the day when the youth showed a man to his table. He was flabby, slightly hunched, in his late fifties with sandy hair and bright blue eyes that missed nothing. There was something ungainly about him, not fat exactly but bulky, a little like a toad. 'Mr Fisher?' he said. 'My name's Nash. Harvey Nash. Gerald was my client.' He was jovial, and a touch too friendly. 'This must have been a terrible shock for you. I'm very sorry, I really am,' but his flat Midland accent prevented him from sounding genuinely sympathetic. 'Here, have my card, you never know when it'll come

20

in handy.' He presented his visiting card – HARVEY NASH, *Consultant* – and a small printed sketch-map of streets with an arrow pointing to: *Block of Flats and BMW showroom*. 'All directions are given in landmarks, you know,' he said. 'There are no signs in English. Order of the Colonel. Everything's in their damned spaghetti writing and even they can't understand that.' And then he went on nodding, intoning 'Yeah, yeah,' softly to himself as though he couldn't believe what he'd just said.

'How did you find me?' Fisher asked, tucking away the card into his breast pocket. 'I was just about to go back to the Palace in case you were waiting there.'

'How did I find you? All roads from the Palace lead here. When they said you weren't registered, I came straight over. I knew where you'd be. The inefficiency in this place works because it's repetitive. You know the form it's going to take so you can't go wrong. Well, I've come to collect you. I believe we're going for a boat ride.' He chuckled, a simpering, sucking sound.

When they were seated side by side in his car, a silvery BMW, he said, 'Welcome to our little town, the ass-hole of the Mediterranean,' and after he had manoeuvred into the incessant morning traffic, added, 'Now you're in for a treat. London has its Bond Street, Paris the Champs-Elysées, New York Fifth Avenue, Rome the Via Condotti. May I present this town's anal passage, the Avenue of the Bloodless Revolution.' Fisher laughed. 'Oh, you've got a sense of humour. That *is* a relief. Not like Gerald at all.'

They drove at speed between traffic lights. Nash drew his passenger's attention to the condition of the buildings which were run-down and in need of paint. 'A public urinal would be better kept,' he said, 'but who's complaining when there's money to be made?'

The Avenue, which was lined either side with palm trees and arched porticos, carried them westward, and for long stretches Fisher was reminded of the Corso, all bluff and grandiloquence. Nothing was quite in the proper perspective as though a turn-of-the-century architect had decided to copy official Rome after viewing it through a distorting lens. But there the Italian influence ceased and the ways of the Bazaar took precedence.

The larger shops were full of goods, the windows crammed haphazard with clothes, watches, shoes, jewellery, carpets. Kiosks selling magazines, cigarettes and postcards, mushroomed at irregular intervals, and the world's newspapers – 'always a month out of date,' Nash said – were displayed on pavement tables. But much of the apparent vitality of the place sprang from the fury of the motorists, of which Nash seemed to be a champion, driving at suicidal speeds, horns blasting and revving impatiently at traffic lights.

The pedestrians wisely took things more easily : men, often hand in hand or arm in arm, strolled in the shade, their women, covered from head to foot with only a single eye visible, following respectfully behind. Small boys crouched watchfully in doorways, not talking to each other and paying no attention to the hordes of cats, stray cats, which roamed the concourse; and everywhere, on lamp standards, in windows, on billboards, idealised, highly coloured photographs of the Colonel abounded, looking out with starting eyes. And each time they stopped, a sickly sweet scent floated into the car as though all the men used the same brilliantine.

'What's the smell?' Fisher asked.

'What smell?' replied Nash, and a little later said again, with some pleasure, 'No, you're not like Gerald at all.'

'Different fathers, you see.'

'I liked him. There was no bullshit about Gerald. He talked straight. I liked that. I didn't hold with all his views, but we got on. You know, I once poulticed a boil on his ass and you can't do that without developing a certain affection for a fellow.'

'You knew him well, then,' Fisher said lightly.

Nash held up a hand and assumed a wary expression. 'I never know anybody well. Trick of the trade. Insurance is a delicate matter. I only ask the questions on the form.' He put his head out of the window and yelled an obscenity in Arabic at an elderly pedestrian. 'They've no bloody sense at all these people. Potential suicides, the lot of 'em. Oh dear. I am sorry. That was tactless. What were we saying? Ah yes, Gerald. Funny way to go. Perhaps he was unhappy at work.'

Fisher began to have the uneasy feeling that he was being played with or tested for some reason, when Nash leaned across him and pointed to a villa set back from the road and guarded by soldiers. 'Here, here,' Nash said keenly, 'you mustn't miss this. See that place? That's where they treat the sewage.' He chuckled too long and too loudly.

'What do you mean?'

'Oh, didn't you know? A lot of the world's excreta is financed out of here, oh yes, rather. 'Course, it's only chat. In a place like this you can never know anything for certain. Here's something I wrote: "Tell me where is fancy bred and I'll answer in an Arab's head." Not bad, eh? And if you live here, you don't talk about it. In that way you don't have to take sides. Mind you, I'll say this, don't underestimate yonder Colonel. He's nobody's fool. And he's done some good. Better housing, better education, better health. Religious fanatic, you know. Prays five times a day. Can you see our PM doing that? Don't get me wrong. I've supported Labour all my life. Fought Hitler. I did. Here, in the bloody desert. Voted Attlee in '45, and never looked back. Never been back either.' The sucking sound and 'yeah, yeah.'

'So you've been here a long time.'

'Close on thirty years. My two sons were born here, my wife died here. I'm a proper little Arab, all right. And I'll tell you this: there's still money to be made, I tell you, there's still money to be made,' and he looked heavenwards at the thought of it.

They turned off the Avenue and began the ascent of a steep hill. Half-way up, Nash took another turning and entered through a gateway into a garden of palms and eucalyptus, and formal geranium beds; he did not lower his speed.

Fisher became apprehensive knowing that he would soon be close to Gerald. He remembered seeing his mother's coffin and the pounding of his heart. He asked, 'When did you last see Gerald?'

'The day he died. He wanted a briefcase added to his All Risks. Imitation crocodile. Made in England. Brand new. Never known anyone so keen to insure his possessions. Just the sort of customer I like.'

'How did he seem?'

'Same as usual.'

'Not under any strain?'

23

'He was always under strain. Worked too hard. When did *you* last see him?'

'Oh, not for years. Fifteen years. I have a feeling he must have changed.'

'Why?'

'I don't know. Just a feeling.'

'I'll tell you something, Martin, may I call you Martin? In my experience people don't change except if they go mad or die. Bang on cue. This is the morgue.'

6

The morgue was concealed by palm trees in the grounds of the City Hospital. Nash told Fisher that formerly it had been a Christian chapel, but the Colonel himself had ordered the place put to its present use. A rusted iron gate guarded the entrance to a compact, domed structure built of pink stone; a short gravel path led to the main door where two old men sat in the sunshine on small gilt chairs with worn upholstery, like convalescents.

'You wait here,' Nash said. 'I'll do the necessary.'

He was gone about five minutes; when he reappeared he was carrying a parcel the size of a brick wrapped in brown paper and tied with string. He marched solemnly down the path towards the car, the crunch of gravel underfoot a signal to Fisher that, like a muffled drum-beat, the funeral procession had begun. Nash opened the driver's door, balancing the brown paper parcel on the tips of the fingers of one hand. He said, 'Do you want to hold it? Or shall I put it on the back seat?'

'The back seat,' said Fisher.

They took the coastal road that marked the careless division of desert and shore, and they travelled in silence. Occasionally, Fisher glanced at the parcel. He tried not to think about what it contained; the words, 'My Dear Gerald', ran senselessly through his head as though he were composing a letter, but could think of nothing more to say. Nash pushed the car to its limits, anxious to reach their destination, and soon they came upon an isolated stretch of sand, a cove, embraced by an out-crop of rock. On the fine crescent of beach stood four people, two men, two women; one, Fisher recognised as Wirrel; the others he did not know. A small boat had been dragged from the water, and now rested in a shallow furrow of wet sand. A fisherman, wearing only khaki shorts, was bent over the outboard motor but straightened when he heard Nash's car. Nash parked between a bright blue Volkswagen and an official-looking car, a black Cadillac, flying a pennant of the national flag. A chauffeur, young, stout and unshaven, cleaned the windscreen.

Fisher said, 'I'll take the parcel now.'

Wirrel, who was dressed in a dark suit and black tie, came forward, his highly polished shoes sinking deep into the sand which made the going slow. He carried a Prayer Book, and stuck out his right hand to greet them but when he saw what Fisher was carrying instantly withdrew as though he might catch a contagious disease. He said, 'Allow me to make the introductions.'

He presented his wife first: much of her face was concealed by an enormous pair of sunglasses, like a domino; even so, Fisher saw that she was older than her husband by perhaps five or six years. Tall, stately, she was dressed in an exquisite black silk suit that looked too expensive for a diplomat's wife. Her hair, deep auburn and not entirely natural, loosely caressed her shoulders; her mouth was wide and, Fisher thought, tense.

'And this is Mr Fawzi from the Ministry of Oil.'

A stocky, bald man gazed at Fisher with bulging, unblinking eyes, as though he'd seen a vision that could never be erased from his mind. 'I'm so sorry, sir, so very, very sorry, sir.' His voice was hoarse and he reeked of insecticide; he had the manner of an anxious courtier, fawning and obsequious. He was badly in need of a shave and his podgy hands were speckled with ink and nicotine, the fingernails bitten-down and black. The cuffs of his brown suit were frayed, and beneath the jacket he wore a long-sleeved maroon cardigan covered in stains and holes. Apologetically, he ushered forward the second woman. 'This is Julnar,' he said, 'Mr Mather's secretary.' A frightened, sallow girl raised her eyes to acknowledge Fisher and lowered them at once. She too, wore black, but, lacking Mrs Wirrel's elegance and taste, looked as though she'd been prematurely widowed.

25

Wirrel drew Fisher aside, 'I can't remember. Did you say your half-brother was baptised?' he asked.

'No.'

Nash said, 'Well, don't let's mess about. We might as well get it over with,' and then he addressed the fisherman, whose name was Ali, in Arabic. Ali responded, pointing out to sea, shifting uncomfortably from one foot to the other. Nash nodded and together they pushed the boat down the furrow into the water watched by the others while Fisher held the parcel, a wooden box by the feel of it, and a part of him recognised the absurdity of standing on the sands in the bright sun with this package in his hands.

'Ladies first,' said Nash and offered his hand to Mrs Wirrel but her husband led her past him and helped her into the boat himself. Fisher wondered if a snub had been intended. No one helped Julnar; she surprised Fisher by springing into the boat with the agility of an athlete. Fawzi clambered aboard next, pushed by Nash and Ali and pulled by the girl: the boat tipped a little with his weight. Fisher and Nash followed, and last, Ali.

After two or three false starts, the outboard motor took life. Rocking dangerously, the boat began to move. The wind stung their faces and Fisher, nursing the parcel in his arms, noticed that, behind the dark glasses, Mrs Wirrel was weeping.

7

The shore was soon a distant, uncertain ribbon of white. Fisher was conscious all the time of Fawzi's bulging eyes studying him, scanning his face. At one point, the Arab leaned forward and asked, 'What does it mean, half-brother?'

'Same mother. Different father.'

'Yes, I thought that was what it meant.' And later: 'What is your work, Mr Fisher?'

'I teach.'

'What?'

'Foreigners to speak English.'

'I see.' He seemed disappointed or troubled and translated for Julnar who shrugged helplessly.

Then, at some moment imprecisely marked, Fisher became

aware that there were tensions, strains, subtle adjustments of attitudes, from his fellow mourners. The conviction grew on Fisher that he was a playgoer who had arrived late at the theatre, missed the exposition in Act One and was, as a result, at a loss to know why the characters behaved as they did. Nash offered the first pointer: he began to show off like an adolescent determined to impress. He said, 'I'm sure Mr Fawzi won't mind, but I've brought this.' Out of a pocket he produced a silver hip-flask. 'I think we'll be needing it.' He unscrewed the top and handed the flask to Fisher. 'This is the home-made variety. *Flash*. 190 proof. So take care. Three swigs and you won't need the boat for the return journey. You'll walk it.'

Fisher drank: the liquid burned his throat. Almost at once his head began to swim. He thought: it can't be the drink, it must be the boat. He offered the flask to Mrs Wirrel who refused it; so did the others; but Nash himself took a gulp and winked heavily.

Fawzi said, 'This is far enough.' His servility vanished and he displayed, instead, a gruff authority.

'Certainly,' said Nash who had taken out his pipe and was filling it. He held up a hand and Ali cut the motor. The boat bobbed and rolled and drifted on the choppy sea. No one spoke or made a move; each sat gazing either at the water or the horizon, except Fisher: he was intrigued by Mrs Wirrel and by leaning back against the side, he could see behind her glasses: her eyes were closed but the tears had stained her cheeks; from time to time she bit her bottom lip as though to prevent her misery from escaping; her hands, which held a black handbag and gloves, were never still.

Julnar vomited, and Fawzi held her forehead while she retched, whispered into her ear, petted and soothed her. Wirrel turned his head away and looked back at the shore, as if he found the whole proceedings distasteful, and wished he had never come.

Fawzi said, 'Shall we make a start, please?'

Fisher held up the parcel, a gift to be offered to the congregation, but there were no takers. He said, 'I think I'd better open this, don't you?' He slurred his words a little.

'Better have another before you do,' said Nash.

'No thanks.'

'Go on.' He tossed the flask; involuntarily, Fisher caught it with one hand. 'Well held,' said Nash.

Once more, Fisher drank, wiped his lips, and laughed foolishly to himself. Summoning all the concentration he could muster, he untied the string and tore off the thick brown paper to reveal a container with a sliding lid and an indentation for the thumb, like a pencil-box he had owned as a child. Cautiously, he opened it: inside the box was a transparent polythene envelope containing ash; stapled to the neck of the envelope was a label on which was written in untidy letters G. A. MATHER and beneath in Arabic script, Fisher guessed, a transliteration of the name. He did not touch the envelope, but was fascinated by it. He thought: this was once Gerald. Unrecognisable fragments. Soulless matter. He shut the lid quickly, frightened by the sight and the accompanying thought. He glanced up apprehensively at the others, but no one was looking at him.

'Mr Wirrel has agreed to hold a short service,' said Fawzi, issuing an official communiqué.

'As long as there's no hymn-singing,' said Nash. 'Unless of course it's "For those in peril on the sea"!' He set to the task of lighting his pipe, crouching low in the boat to prevent the wind from blowing out the match; he had little success.

Wirrel said, 'Since the deceased wasn't baptised, I thought I would just read a few words suggested by the Book of Common Prayer.' His voice and pronunciation made clear he had missed his vocation: he used a sing-song which suggested that, like all Church of England ministers, he was tone deaf.

' "I am the resurrection and the life, saith the Lord: he that believeth in me, though he were dead, yet shall he live: and whosoever liveth and believeth in me shall never die." ' He turned to another page and began, ' "Forasmuch as it hath pleased Almighty God..." '

Terrible indecision gripped Fisher: should he open the envelope and commit only the ashes to the sea? Or the ashes in the envelope? Or the ashes in the envelope inside the box?

' "We therefore commit his body to the deep, to be turned into corruption..." '

What would be proper? What correct? He remembered

Gerald's words, 'You always do the right thing', but what, in the circumstances, was right?

'"... who at his coming shall change our vile body, that it may be like his glorious body ..."'

Then, Fisher discovered that, try as he may, he could not bring himself to touch the envelope in the box, as though there existed round it a powerful force, a magnetic field which his hand had not the strength to penetrate. He eased the lid of the box shut.

'"... whereby he is able to subdue all things to himself."'

'Amen,' said Nash jovially.

Fisher was about to let the box slip from his hand when Nash said, 'No, not like that!' Rudely, he snatched the container, extracted the polythene envelope, tore the neck open with his teeth, and poured Gerald's ashes into the choppy sea: like a cloud they billowed and sank: in the water, clear as glass, they plummeted unwillingly, drifting into a darker, azure gloom. And then, there was no more to be seen.

'It is customary,' Wirrel said, 'to say a few words in memory of the departed,' though it was obvious he wished no one would.

Silence. All, except Mrs Wirrel who was rummaging in her handbag, turned to look at Fisher.

All Fisher could think of was, 'My Dear Gerald', but that wouldn't do: 'I've nothing I want to say,' he murmured.

Julnar began to moan softly, but whether from grief or sea-sickness, Fisher didn't know. Fawzi, who was patting the girl's hand, said, 'I want to say something, if you'll permit it.' No one objected. 'Gerald Mather was my friend and my colleague. He was loyal in both capacities. He served our Revolution in this country and was, in his own way, a soldier in the battle for freedom of all men who are oppressed. Thank you. That's all.'

'Home, everybody?' Nash asked, comically falsetto.

'No. I've something to say, too.'

Mrs Wirrel had spoken for the first time. Her accent was foreign, but Fisher couldn't place it exactly. In her hand she now held a book – *The Perennial Philosophy*, Fisher read on the cover – and a torn piece of paper marked the place to which she turned. 'Mr Scott-Burrows and Gerald's fellow-students asked me to say these lines at an appropriate moment.' Fisher marvelled at her control, for the tears he had seen were in no way betrayed in her voice which had an unusual calm to it, as though she were not present herself, but had sent a recording. Her husband nodded encouragingly and she said, 'This is by Jalal-uddin Rumi:

> "I died a mineral and became a plant.
> I died a plant and rose an animal.
> I died an animal and I was man.
> Why should I fear? When was I less by dying?
> Yet once more I shall die as man, to soar
> With the blessed angels; but even from angelhood
> I must pass on. All except God perishes.
> When I have sacrificed my angel soul,
> I shall become that which no mind ever conceived.
> O, let me not exist! For Non-Existence proclaims,
> 'To Him we shall return.'"

That's all.'

'Anyone else got anything to say?' asked Nash, looking from one to the other. 'No? Right then, I proclaim Gerald Arthur Mather well and truly buried.'

8

By the time they reached the shore, Fisher had drained what was left of the *Flash*, but continued to swig from the empty flask; he giggled stupidly. The others paid him little attention, and remained locked in their own thoughts, witnesses not to a shared experience but to some individual and inward response. Wirrel, however, by the merest pursing of his lips, let Fisher know that he disapproved strongly of drunkenness. And so they sat, Fawzi with a paternal arm round Julnar, his eyes fixed on some distant point, she shivering and subdued; Mrs Wirrel like a statue, reading her book; her husband upright with silent disapproval; Nash, asleep or pretending to sleep; Fisher, tipsy, lolling against the side, one hand trailing in the water: they could have been survivors from a shipwreck.

When they landed, Fawzi drew Nash aside and said, 'Give

please Mr Fisher this key. To Mr Mather's flat. We've finished our search. Without success, I fear. He's at liberty to use it.'

'I'm perfectly capable, you can give it to me,' Fisher said rather too loudly, but his knees buckled under him and Ali, who had previously remained impassive and detached, came to his assistance. Fawzi shook his head sadly at the sight of Fisher propped up against the boat, and, in turning, directed his contempt at the others, as though all of them contaminated the air. He marched off with Julnar across the sands to the Cadillac. Mrs Wirrel was impatient to follow, but her husband said, 'I'd better give Nash a hand with Fisher.' He knew his duty.

Nash thanked Ali and paid him. '*Assalaam aleikum*,' he said.

'*Wa-aleikum assalaam*,' replied the fisherman.

Wirrel said, 'I'll take one side, you take the other,' and tightly gripping Fisher's elbows they steered him towards the road, Mrs Wirrel slowly bringing up the rear. Half-way, Fisher stopped and tried to struggle free, looking back at the woman who kept her eyes downcast as though she might find something valuable in the sand.

Nash said, 'Keep going, we're nearly there.'

'You shouldn't have brought the damned stuff,' Wirrel complained, tight-lipped.

'We're not all diplomats, you know,' Nash replied lamely.

Meanwhile, Fawzi had reached the Cadillac. The young, stout chauffeur banged the doors to and climbed into the driver's seat. With a roar the car pulled away, rear wheels spraying sand.

Fisher mumbled, 'I'd like to get out of here. Quick. But I haven't any money.'

'Who has?' said Nash.

'Will you hurry things up?' Fisher asked, lolling towards Wirrel. 'Can you get me some money? I want to get out.'

'We're doing all we can,' Wirrel said primly.

'I want to meet that American,' Fisher said.

' 'Course you do,' said Nash to humour him.

'He knew Gerald.'

'We all did, me old son.'

'He was talking to the Japs.'

'There's no accounting for taste.'

'And the Basque was there, too.'

'Sounds like the United Nations.'

'They're after the money, too.'

'Who isn't?'

'I am. If I don't get the money, I don't get out.'

'That's the same the world over.'

The two men eased Fisher into Nash's car. He rested his head against the back seat and closed his eyes. He heard the three exchanging farewells, formal and distant, a slamming of car doors, and then Nash was beside him and, at speed, they headed back towards the city, leaving the bright blue Volkswagen a long way behind.

The wind had risen, blowing snakes of sand across the road, and invading the palm trees to make the leaves patter like distant machine-guns. The afternoon sky had turned a rich, deep blue but there was as yet no hint of sunset. The two men were, to begin with, silent. The effects of the alcohol, though receding, still clung obstinately, giving Fisher a blinding headache: the glare hurt his eyes. He said, 'Did I make an exhibition of myself?'

'Yes, you did.' Yeah, yeah.

'I'm sorry.'

'Don't apologise to me. I'm not easily offended.'

'My head hurts.'

'I did warn you about *Flash*.' His fingers drummed a self-satisfied tattoo on the steering wheel.

Fisher said, 'Tell me about the woman.'

'Which one?'

'Mrs Wirrel.'

'Paola.'

'Is that her name? She's not English.'

'No. Yugoslav or Italian or Hungarian or all three. I've never known for certain. Not really interested.'

'Why was she crying for Gerald?'

'Was she?'

'She was crying for something, somebody.'

'I wouldn't know.'

'Was she in love with Gerald?'

'I've no idea. Anyway, you mustn't ask me about love. It's a bad insurance risk.'

'She was crying.'

Nash exploded suddenly and vehemently. 'She's a high-class whore, Fisher. And sometimes not so high-class. Nothing would surprise me. God, I'm too old for these bloody charades! I am the resurrection and the life! When I die, me old son, I shall leave strict instructions that my ashes are to be flushed down the nearest bog!'

'I shall leave no instructions at all,' Fisher said, and meant it, although when he thought of his own death he imagined a grave and spadefuls of earth.

With relish Nash said, 'Isn't life disgusting!' and spat out of the window. 'Hateful! Disease and sores. Pissing and shitting, fucking and farting. I hate it all!'

'At that level –' Fisher began tamely, thinking, how like Gerald, but Nash interrupted. 'At that level! What other level is there?'

Fisher inhaled deeply. 'It requires a certain courage to answer that question,' he said, like a sigh.

'Oh my God! Do I detect in you a noble belief in mankind?'

'Noble isn't a word I'd use.'

'You ought to meditate more, me old son. You should attend classes like Gerald did. You should visit Mr Scott-Burrows, our resident nancy, aged ninety, who preaches non-attachment and right-livelihood and gets buggered twice a day by his half-wit servant. The whole bloody hypocrisy makes me sick. Why don't we face *facts*!'

The city had, without their noticing, enveloped them: it had woken from the afternoon sleep with renewed energy and the air was suddenly oppressive with bustle and heat and noise. Nash's savagery subsided: he said, 'I think I also must have had too much *Flash*. I don't usually sound off like that. But the whole bloody nonsense on the boat revolted me. What about you?' Fisher didn't reply. 'I liked you for getting pissed and disgracing yourself, Fisher. You made my day. You're the kind of cheerful, harmless sod I admire. You don't get in anybody's way. You want a quiet life, don't you?'

'Something like that,' Fisher said.

'You want me to collect your bags and take you to Gerald's flat?'

Fisher, after a moment's hesitation, said, 'I want you to do me a favour.'

'Ask.'

'Show me where Gerald died.'

'Nothing to see.'

'I'd like to.'

Nash squinted sideways at him, and smiled grimly, and then headed for The Square – not really a square but a triangle where, at the apex, the three main boulevards converged, bordered on one side by buildings, on the second by the Spanish castle and on the third by the sea; in the centre stood an island of palm trees where the shoe-shine boys waited for custom. Just beyond the ruined castle lay the Old Quay, which had once served the Spaniards as their port; now, it was used by the fishermen, their boats close-packed, a forest of masts. Nash found a parking place at the water's edge. 'Over there,' he said, 'where they're repairing the rails.' Fisher climbed out of the car but Nash remained behind the wheel. 'Don't be too long,' he said, filling his pipe. 'It'll be dark soon.'

It was an open place: standing with his back to the Castle, he faced the harbour and, in the fading light, Fisher could make out at the farthest quay, perhaps two miles away, the silhouette of the ferry which had brought him from Genoa. He turned to look at the Castle: the superstructure, with its arches and stairways and crumbling battlements, had been made into a museum; at street level, there was a police station. Next to the Castle stood the mosque with a tall minaret; to the rear, the antique brickwork of what once was the outer wall of the city. Fisher could not see what lay beyond the wall.

Slowly, he wandered over to where the workmen with blow-torches were cutting free the tangled metal railings that guarded the quay. Some thirty feet below a rusting landing-stage listed heavily in the water, and while Fisher was gazing down, he became aware of Nash standing behind him. 'They've a saying here,' Nash muttered, drawing impatiently on his pipe. ' "To be near where a man dies, is to be near the man." Is that why you wanted to see the place?' He was amused by the idea, and Fisher was surprised by his insight.

'Perhaps. Do you know what happened?'

'Apparently, he made straight for the sea.'

'How do they know it was suicide? Couldn't it have been an accident?'

'The police have a witness.'

'Who?'

'The scarecrow.'

'Who's that?'

'The girl on the boat. The girl who vomited. Julnar, is she called?'

'Is she the witness?'

'Rather. They'd been working late, she and Gerald. Three, four a.m. Very conscientious. He was taking her home. She lives near here, evidently. Well, he dropped her off. And then, she said, she turned and waved. Gerald saluted, she said, and then he drove at the railings.' Yeah, yeah.

'I wish I'd spoken to her.'

'No you don't. Her breath smells. Seen all you want to see?'

They began to make their way back towards the car. He had no feeling of Gerald. I've buried him, Fisher reflected, and I've seen where he died and I don't feel him.

The evening call went forth from the mosques all over the city, summoning the faithful to prayer at the precise moment when the dusk dissolves. The sun had dipped out of sight behind the cranes, the tankers and the freighters leaving a collar above the horizon of deep orange. Fisher glanced upward and saw atop the minaret that towered over the Castle and the Quay, an old man – was he not called the *muezzin*? – clutching the balustrade, swaying to and fro as he intoned the sacred, atonal chant. Nash, following Fisher's gaze, said, 'Do you know what he's saying?'

'No.'

'"God is most great," that's how he begins. Four times.'

'"God is most great,"' Fisher repeated quietly.

'I expect he believes it,' Nash said. 'Well, he should do. He trots up and down those stairs five times a day and they tell me he's got the blood-pressure of a twenty-year-old. "God is most great." Not the same for intelligent people like us.'

Who was he mocking, Fisher wondered, God or me? Nash blew smoke-rings at the windscreen, eyeing Fisher's reflection in the glass and somehow Fisher knew that the man was summing him up, wondering whether or not he could be relied on, confided in.

Nash said, 'I've taken a fancy to you, Martin. I'd like to help you.'

'Help me? How?'

'On the beach, after the funeral, when you were pissed, you said you needed money. Was that true or just *Flash*?'

'True. I don't have my return fare. Though Wirrel muttered something about Gerald having a few pounds in the bank. He thought perhaps I could get my hands on it. Takes time, of course.' He'd been deliberately forthcoming about his finances. It was an old trick: to be frank about penury was always disarming.

Nash said, 'In this place it could take a year. Did you know he had a Life Insurance with me?'

'Yes. Wirrel told me.'

'Ten thousand pounds sterling. Not bad. But, alack and alas, we don't pay out on suicide.'

'So I've been told.'

'On the other hand, if we could prove it wasn't suicide, there'd be ten grand, now, wouldn't there?'

'Go on.'

'Difficult for me. I live here. But you could ask a few questions.'

'Such as?'

'Such as — how could a man drive a car into the water when he couldn't drive a car?'

Fisher turned to him. 'Couldn't he? Couldn't Gerald drive?'

'No, he couldn't. He always had a Ministry car and a chauffeur. Mind you, it's difficult to prove after a man's dead that he couldn't drive. Still, it's worth a try. Ten grand's a lot of bread. Think of what you could do with ten grand. Or better, think of what you could do with five.'

Fisher turned away and closed his eyes. Nash had echoed something his mother had once said and Fisher heard her voice, as if she were beside him, tempting: Think of what you can do with a hundred pounds, Marty. Such a small favour. A hundred pounds is a lot of money, Marty. Do it. For my sake. For Gerald's. Fisher said, 'I wish you hadn't told me that he couldn't drive.'

'Why?' Nash asked, offended more than surprised. 'Now, why should you say a thing like that?'

36

Fisher chose not to answer. He couldn't tell Nash it was a pattern he'd known before: Gerald had a way of creating whirlpools and sucking you in. Even in death. 'Why should they want to make it look like suicide when it wasn't?'

'Who can say?' Nash asked blandly.

'It doesn't make sense.'

'Not much does.'

'What are you suggesting? That there's something to hide? That they're covering —?'

'No, no, no, no. Heaven forfend. All I know is that if you tell me a man drives his car into the sea and I know he can't drive, then there's something fishy. I'm in Insurance. My mind works in wondrous ways its wonders to perform. I can smell a fart as well as the next man. Just ask about. Somebody must've seen something.'

Four or five young Arab men chattering noisily and gesticulating, passed the car; one, handsome and insinuating, looked in and made kissing noises at Nash who responded good-humouredly with a wave of his pipe. Then the man saw Fisher and licked his lips suggestively. 'Café Damascu, Café Damascu,' he sang.

Nash barked rudely at him. The man pulled away and, laughing, chased after his companions.

'Bloody queers. Town's full of them. If you go anywhere near the Café Damascu wear your jock-strap back to front and don't bend down to pick up the soap in the showers.' He started the car. 'Well, think about what I've said.'

But Fisher didn't want to. In a distracted, preoccupied way, he murmured, 'I wish I could identify the scent they use.'

Nash replied, 'If you shovel shit, you must expect to smell,' and he pointed his pipe at the old man atop the minaret, swaying to and fro in the vanishing light.

PART TWO

The telephone stopped ringing as Fisher entered Gerald's flat and the silence that followed again made him wary and ill-at-ease: he had the sensation that someone was hiding there, lying in wait for him. And the place stank of stale insecticide.

The flat comprised one room with an alcove framed by a Moorish arch where the bed stood and, beside it, a table and the telephone. A small bathroom and even smaller kitchen led off the main area which was almost without ornament but for a large white plaster bust of the Colonel that rested on a bare dining-table made of polished teak. Two armchairs, upholstered in garish green exotic flowers, faced the glass doors that opened on to a small balcony but which now were shaded by a multi-coloured venetian blind. To Fisher, the room looked as though it was deliberately intended to reflect a disregard for comfort, warmth or homeliness, like a seaside flat furnished to let by the week. He noted wrily that the bust of the Colonel had a broken nose, and also that there was nowhere for anyone to hide.

Although he expected the bareness and the severity, he was surprised by the unnatural tidiness and by the absence of books: he remembered Gerald's room at home cluttered by discarded clothes, shoes, magazines, newspapers, and by books strewn all over the place, even, he recalled, in the washbasin. Here there was nothing, and he speculated that, when the place had been searched, for some reason all the books had been taken away.

Fisher opened a cupboard in the alcove and found suits and trousers and jackets neatly hung; on the bedside table lay a paperback edition of *The Perennial Philosophy*. On the flyleaf Gerald had scribbled in pencil: *Every man, wherever he goes, is encompassed by a cloud of comforting convictions, which move with him like flies on a summer day*, but Fisher could not identify the author.

He raised the venetian blind, opened the doors to let the air in and stepped out on to the narrow balcony which faced another apartment block and, beyond, a modern minaret, smoothly painted olive green and coral red, crowned by a star nestling in the crescent moon, palely lit by a circle of electric light-bulbs. The evening was cool and when he turned, he saw the scaffolding poking over the balustrade. He felt vulnerable out there on the veranda, vulnerable in the flat: retreating into the room, he locked the balcony doors and lowered the blind to shut out his uneasiness. He needed activity, and began to pack away Gerald's things into an old suitcase and found, at the bottom of the wardrobe, a record-player and a small pile of records, Chopin, Rachmaninoff, Schumann – unlikely composers, he thought, for Gerald.

The telephone rang again, bleak and unnerving. He did not move at first, but stared at it as though the insistent jangling sound inhibited action and thought. Who could it be? And then, when he realised that Nash or Wirrel could be at the other end of the line, his fright subsided and he chided himself for wondering who would telephone the dead.

'Yes?'

There was a click, and then a hollow crackling sound. Slowly, he replaced the receiver, aware that he was panting; and he had the absurd notion that Gerald's flat was a cell, and that the light would never go out, and that somewhere near a gaoler lurked. He tried to shake free of the terror, but his senses, unwittingly, were tuned to detect danger – and there was nothing to hear, only the night traffic, and nothing to taste or smell or feel except his own fear, and all he could see was the barren room where Gerald had lived.

He said to himself: this fear is irrational, to do with me not the place; Gerald is dead; and I am alive and therefore frightened. He breathed deeply but there was no relief. He cursed Nash: the man had lifted a stone and allowed the worms to escape to gnaw at a wound Fisher thought had long ago healed. (And he remembered Gerald standing in their front room, between the two policemen, and mother's unspoken plea.) We were to be reconciled, Fisher repeatedly affirmed, we were to

42

be reconciled – that is my only reason for being here. But nothing would assuage his anxiety.

And then a hail of gravel rattled the glass doors. Fisher held his breath, frightened into stillness, as though his own immobility would stop time from passing. Again the sound came like heavy rain. Fisher grabbed the key from the table and hurried out, avoiding the lift, and running down the stairs into the street. And when he found himself crossing a patch of waste ground – it may have been the same waste ground where he rested the previous night – he heard a voice call, 'Hey, you – over here – over here.'

2

The faster Fisher ran, the closer he seemed pursued. The streets were empty and only occasionally a car or motor-cyclist roared by. At each and every corner he stopped, turned round, but did not see even a shadow moving. Yet, once he started to walk again, or trot, or run, the sensation of being followed returned, closer and closer, now behind him, now to the side, now in front, as though an invisible web was being spun and he knew that soon he would come face to face with whoever was stalking him. Fisher remembered that for long periods as a child he believed every action he performed was closely scrutinised, every thought known, every deed recorded by some invisible agency empowered to assess him. Gerald had said it was a symptom of self-importance, the myth of a personal god. And then, turning a corner, Fisher collided with a human form, reeled backwards and almost screamed. Helmuth Winzer said, 'Where are you going to in such a hurry? We have been trying to catch you up. You have found the whore-house, perhaps?'

The blind Günther said, 'There is no whore-house in this town.'

Fisher leaned up against a wall, and lit a cigarette. When he exhaled the smoke, it felt as though it was the first breath he had ever taken.

'We are doing our constitutional,' Helmuth said. 'You accompany?'

'Yes,' Fisher said. 'I'd like that.' With Günther between

43

them, they set off. Fisher thought: only those who never knew Gerald are immune from danger.

Günther tapped Fisher's arm with his short, white stick and asked hopefully, 'You think there is a whore-house in this town?'

'I don't know,' said Fisher.

'You must forgive my brother,' chuckled Helmuth. 'But, as the Albanians say, even the blind have balls.'

'You and Basque have left us,' Günther said. 'You have found another hotel?'

'No. I have the use of someone's flat.'

'So. You are lucky,' said Helmuth. 'We have been looking for a better place but there is nothing. This flat of yours, it has no extra room? We could pay something.'

'I'm afraid not.'

Günther said, 'I wish to make apology to our sleeping companion. I think he leaves our room because I disturb him in the night with my practising.'

'Not at all,' Fisher said, remembering the silent sonata as an accompaniment to a dream.

'We must soon be getting back. Günther must practise again now.'

Fisher wanted to stay with them as long as possible. In their company, he knew, he was safe – but from what? – and he said, 'What's the reason for your visit?'

'We have a difficult life,' Helmuth confessed cheerfully. 'Günther is concert pianist of some considerableness. That's why he must practise. Better in silence than with a grand piano in the room, ja?'

'Are you here to give a recital?'

'I am his business manager,' Helmuth said. 'I make a deal with our Foreign Ministry for Günther to give concerts at our Embassies. Even diplomats need culture, no? It's a good scheme, you agree?' From his inside pocket he removed an envelope bulging with press-cuttings and handed it to Fisher. 'This is only the tip of the iceberg. From everywhere we have raving criticism. Ireland, Malta, Cyprus, even in Majorca they are raving. In Majorca Günther plays Chopin.'

Günther said, 'And you? I have the impression you are something secretive.'

'I'm a teacher.'

'In what discipline?' Helmuth asked.

'English.'

'You are here to teach the Arabs?'

'No.'

'You are here for what purpose then?'

'A family matter.'

'Yes,' said Günther, 'secretive.'

'My brother has extraordinary perceptions, no?'

'Extraordinary.'

They had reached the Afreka, and stood at the entrance. Through the glass door, Fisher could see some of the Japanese being served Pepsis. 'You know why he has these perceptions?' Helmuth asked.

'No.'

'Because he was born blind. As a matter of fact, I confide in you something. We are looking for a rich patron. That's the *Realpolitik*, so to say, of why we are here. The Arabs have much money. All the time they are looking for new outlets.'

Günther said, 'My brother is not secretive.'

'We are chained together,' Helmuth said. 'We are Polydeuces and Castor.' Ceremoniously he linked arms with Günther. 'So, if you meet a wealthy patron you'll remember us.' He grinned and his large face disintegrated into an intricate map of lines and creases. '*Auf Wiedersehen.*'

Fisher wanted to delay them, would have reached out to hold them had he not found some line of attack. 'When is the concert?' he asked. 'I should like very much to attend.'

'Easy. We will arrange tickets.'

'Thank you. I'd like that.'

'Give me your new address. I come round personally with the tickets,' Helmuth suggested, quick to seize an advantage.

'I don't remember it off-hand. I know where it is. But not the name of the street.'

'As you please,' said Helmuth, who was also quick to understand a rebuff.

'When is it?' Fisher asked again.

'In four, five days,' Günther said. 'We have to arrange with Ambassador. Also the piano needs tuning.'

'Perhaps you could leave the tickets for me here at the desk of the Afreka?'

And from Helmuth, 'It's possible. *Auf Wiedersehen.*'

As they turned, Günther waved his stick in farewell and they walked into the hotel. Fisher watched them summon the youth, obtain their key and still arm in arm slowly mount the stairs until they were lost to sight. Fisher was alone in the street, envying them their companionship.

He turned and saw, as inexplicably he knew he would, a figure beneath a yellow streetlight at the end of a gently curving alley. Fisher's instinct was to run, but the figure started towards him and, because of the spills of light from the lamps, was brightly illuminated one moment, invisible the next. A few feet distant, the figure stopped in shadow. 'Hey, you! Why you run away?'

Fisher asked, 'What do you want?' his heart thumping.

'I am friend. Friend of Mather.'

'What do you want?' Fisher asked again more urgently.

From the shadow stepped a boy, not more than twenty, shirt open to the waist, a cheap imitation bronze medallion hanging on his hairless chest. He had questioning eyes that examined Fisher a little defiantly and were, like his hair, jet black. After the first brief show of wariness, he smiled, wide and friendly, and was instantly handsome.

'You frightened?' he asked like a teasing child. The smile vanished and he was once more serious, intent, beetle-browed. 'Come,' he said. 'We not talk here.'

'What do you want to talk about?'

'No. Not here. We go drink. I take you nice place.' He spoke quickly, in short bursts.

Fisher hesitated.

'Come,' the boy said, 'I am friend. My name Kamal. Come.'

'Where are we going?'

'Nice place. Café Damascu. Very nice.'

3

The café stood in an enclosed circular piazza just off the Avenue. Kamal led Fisher through one of the two curved colonnades into a cool, empty inner room out on to the terrace

46

which, by day, would be open to the sky, but was now covered in plastic deckchair awning of green, white and red stripes, and round the wooden pillars and struts which supported the roof frame clung blighted vines like limp, faded streamers. Half the tables were occupied, the conversation subdued to harmonise with the drone of insects. Fisher had the impression of stragglers at a party that had long since ended.

The customers were mostly middle-aged men, sombrely dressed and in manner restrained. But a familiar laugh drew Fisher's attention to a long table immediately to his left as he entered, and partially hidden. There sat two of the Japanese party showing cameras to some of the young men whom Fisher had seen on the Quay; the impudent one who had poked his head into the car caught Fisher's eye and a look of recognition was exchanged.

Kamal said, 'You sit. I talk to my friends. I come soon,' and he joined the others to examine the cameras. The Japanese with the laugh ran his hand up Kamal's leg.

Fisher took a table where they could not see him. A tired waiter approached and said in a sing-song, 'Peach nectar, pear nectar, Pepsi, Coke, coffee, orange juice, tea.'

'Tea,' Fisher said.

An elderly Arab, immaculately dressed in European style, was table-hopping, pausing to talk, to laugh, to scribble something on a card, welcomed with respect by each table he honoured with a call. His progress was stately. Sensual lips, beaked nose and dark purplish patches beneath the eyes – the look of a tired vulture; he wore a dove-grey suit, the jacket edged in silk of lighter grey, a broad-brimmed hat and he carried an ivory-handled cane – the dress of an ageing Edwardian dandy. And when Kamal joined Fisher, the stylish bird of prey tipped his hat to them. Kamal made the introductions, but reluctantly : he sprawled in his chair, glowering, as though he was trying to hide.

The elderly man's name was Dr al Mahdi Swediq. He said in impeccable English, 'Do me the honour of taking my card. Any service, large or small, will be my honour to perform. Medical or otherwise. If you wish to learn our impossible language, I can arrange lessons.' He showed Fisher a Teach Yourself Arabic cassette. 'I know England well. I had digs in Bayswater before

47

the war. When I read Part Two of my FRCS. I was assistant-registrar at Bart's. So nice to have made your acquaintance. Do let's meet again.' He extended his hand: on the little finger he wore a gold ring inset with a large solitaire. 'Cheery-bye,' he said and passed on to the next table. How quickly, Fisher thought, one collects visiting cards abroad.

Kamal warned. 'Be careful that one. He knows more than me.' He smiled. He had, apparently, only two expressions: the frown of concentration which made him look a little stupid and the smile which was irresistible. He was insolent and knowing and pleased with himself; his vitality Fisher found attractive.

'You like my sandals?' he asked. They were made of translucent yellow plastic.

'Very dashing,' said Fisher who thought they were hideous.

'From Cairo,' he said proudly.

'Was it you who tried to telephone me?' Fisher asked.

'Me, phone? No.'

'Did you throw the stones at my window?'

'Sure. Mather not want me coming to flat. We meet here. I throw stone. He come.' From his trouser pocket he took a pack of small patience cards which he shuffled expertly, mostly with one hand.

'What is it you want?' Fisher asked.

'You name Martin, yeah?'

'How do you know that?'

'Mather your brother.'

'You're well informed.'

'Me, I know everything. Hear everything.' He laughed but with little enjoyment as if he hadn't understood a joke.

The waiter brought Fisher's tea and, without being asked, for Kamal a coffee *à la Turque*, oil-black and sickly sweet. From a glass Kamal spooned in water to cool and dilute it. He said, 'Mather owe me money. Twenty pound.' He did not look at Fisher.

'For what?'

Kamal took to shuffling the cards again. 'How old you are?' he asked sharply.

'Old enough,' Fisher replied.

'Me, I'm nineteen.'

48

'That's old enough, too.'

'I speak good English?' he asked threateningly.

'Very.'

'I learn in school. I know everything.' He laughed again in his humourless way. 'Where you get that jacket?' he demanded, leaning forward to study the flowers embroidered over Fisher's breast-pocket and on the shoulder.

'In Rome.'

'Much cost?'

'Do you like it?'

'The jacket nice for me, I think.'

'Come back to the flat and try it on.'

The boy smiled. 'You like card-tricks?' he asked.

'Why?'

He held up to Fisher the back of one of the small playing cards: instead of the usual abstract design there was a photograph of two naked men entwined. Kamal riffled the pack a few inches from Fisher's eyes: each card appeared to be backed by a different sexual act, some of men, some of women, some of both, varied, yet repetitive. Fisher watched the display and affected to be amused. Behind the cards Kamal hummed as though he'd found Fisher out.

'You give me jacket?'

'If you like.'

When they rose to leave the café, Kamal took Fisher's hand tightly so that he couldn't pull free: the boys at the long table whistled and made kissing noises. But the moment they were out of sight, Kamal let go and was silent; he followed Fisher to Gerald's flat walking a step or two behind.

4

He was shy, nervous and inexperienced. Afterwards, lying in the bed beside him, Fisher asked, 'Is this what Gerald owes you money for?'

'You crazy? Mather? You crazy?'

'What then?'

'Cards.'

'Cards?'

'Cards, like mine. Games.'

49

'What games?'

'Games for Mather. Boys and boys, girls and girls. Anything. He looks. He likes to look. He pays.'

'Only looked.'

'Sure. Also movies. I arrange. You like movies?'

'Some.'

'Me, too. Not Mather kind. Ugly like pigs. All wearing socks. Me, I like movie with song and dance. Cliff Richard. He is dreamboat. I like dance. You twist?'

'I used to,' Fisher said gently.

'I am best twister in town.'

'Tell me about Mather.'

'He owe me twenty pounds. You pay.'

'I haven't got twenty pounds.'

'You get. From Nash you get.'

Fisher glanced sharply at him. 'You know Nash?'

'Sure. Stinking European rubbish.'

Fisher lit a cigarette. 'Why should I get money from Nash?'

'Sure, sure, I know about it.'

'What do you know?'

Kamal sprang from the bed and tried on Fisher's jacket, admiring himself before the wardrobe mirror. He emptied the pockets of visiting cards and tickets and book matches as one who has taken possession; then, he caught Fisher smiling.

'Why you laugh?'

'Because you look funny with just a jacket on.'

'Not nice jacket,' he said crossly, and flung it on the floor. He climbed back into the bed but was careful not to touch Fisher. 'You want me to help you get money?' he asked.

'How?'

'I find out things for you.'

'Did Nash send you?'

'Nash? He not like me.'

'Why?'

'His son. He friend of mine. From *Wool*-ver-hampn,' he said with effort.

Patiently, Fisher asked, 'How do you know about Nash and the money?'

'I know everything,' he cried irritably, and turned his back on Fisher. He said, 'I am hairdresser. Palace Hotel. Very smart.

50

Very shick. Very expensive. All ask for me. American, English, German bitches. All ask for me. I know everything.'

'But someone must have told you about me. Who was it?'

'What you talk? Mather owe me money. Twenty pound. You give me twenty pound. I go.'

'All right. Go.'

Kamal fell silent, but Fisher guessed he was frowning, trying to decide on another line of attack.

'Why you not like me? I give you nice time. Why you not like me?'

'Because you won't answer my questions. I want you to tell me how you learned I could get money from Mr Nash. And why you offered to find out things for me. What things?'

'Small town,' he said. 'Everybody knows everything.'

'Fuck off.'

Kamal climbed out of the bed and began to dress, scowling and pouting. Fisher tucked his hands under his head and gazed at the ceiling. This is Gerald's pattern, he thought: the whirlpool and secret eddies.

Kamal sat on the bed to put on his yellow plastic sandals and shot testing glances at Fisher, but seeing no response said, 'Martin, look. I nice to you. You be nice to me. I help you. Police say Mather he drive into sea with white Mercedes. Who knows? I find out. Nash give you plenty money.'

'But how do you *know* about it?'

'Martin, I am Bedouin, from the desert, like the Colonel. We hear on the wind. I help you.'

'I don't want you to help me.'

Kamal narrowed his eyes. 'You stinking European rubbish.'

'That's right.'

The boy's tone changed again, wheedling, soft, affectionate. 'We be friends. We make money. Then I go *Wool*-ver-hampn.' He smiled.

'Yes, you go.'

Venomous, now: 'Okay, sure, I go. I don't need you. I'm all right,' he said, rising to comb his hair. 'I got big flat in Old City, bigger than this. I got jackets better than you. Also Vespa scooter. I am pretty. English bitch once paint picture me because she love with me. I'm okay.'

'Yes, you're okay.'

Kamal hesitated by the door. He said, 'Here, we be friends,' and he threw Fisher the pack of cards. He smiled. 'I take jacket, okay?' and he was gone.

5

Fisher removed from Gerald's letter Anne's photograph and, propping it up against the bust of the Colonel with the broken nose, wrote to her in Accra:

Dear Anne,

I hope you received my last letter, written from Rome, telling you I'd had an invitation from my half-brother Gerald to visit him – after fifteen years of not hearing a word from him. Well, it's been an unhappy and melancholy journey because when I arrived I learned that Gerald was dead; he'd killed himself; today, we committed his ashes to the sea.

It's difficult to mourn someone who disappeared from one's life such ages ago, but I am filled with regret rather than grief because I would so much have liked to have seen him again. He always mattered to me. Years ago, when I was in adolescence, I was made to feel I'd done him a great wrong but – well, even now I'm not able to face what happened. I still have nightmares because of it. It would have been good to have seen him again face to face, to shake hands, to forgive each other. I believe deep down that that is why he asked me to come and see him. Life is too short to bear a grudge.

Now, I am more or less stuck here for longer than I want to be. I laid out a lot of money for the fare on Gerald's promise to return what I'd spent when I arrived. I am told that to sort out his affairs may take time, and it simply isn't possible for me to go back to Rome, where I owe last month's rent and one or two other small bills, without being refunded in full. As I told you, I have been giving lessons to one or two Italians, but not really enough work to keep me going. It is the old story.

Dear Anne, I suspect that before you opened this letter, you guessed its real purpose. Let me come back. Please send

52

me a cable telling me to return. There is still a life for us together. There is no reason why we shouldn't marry and have children.

I love you. You must believe that. You accused me of dishonesty. Yet, I told you voluntarily what I'd done without being asked or being caught out and, as a result, brought down Armageddon. If I hadn't we'd still be together. So I'm paying the penalty not for telling lies and deceiving you – quite the reverse.

If it isn't too embarrassing perhaps you could give some of the children in my class my regards. Tell them to learn:

'O happy living things! no tongue
Their beauty might declare:
A spring of love gush'd from my heart,
And I bless'd them unaware:
Sure my kind saint took pity on me,
And I bless'd them unaware.'

Please, dearest Anne, accept me even if you cannot forgive.

Martin.

Fisher struggled for sleep that night. He beat his head into the pillow, Gerald's pillow, and tried a thousand tricks insomniacs acquire from a lifetime of nights such as these: imagining a race of inordinate distance and, upon entering a packed arena to cheering crowds, breasting the tape to collapse unconscious in loving arms; to guard some costly treasure and, after a night-long vigil, to be relieved by the next sentry, and then, one's duty done, to fall senseless; to concentrate on a single, unblemished colour; to be safe and warm in a storm; to sleep. But it was not to be; for hours he twisted and turned until a sudden insight came, like a stab of pain: I feel, he realised, affinity only for the dead and the absent.

And when sleep finally surrendered to him, he dreamed of a stone staircase leading down into what he understood to be a dungeon. As he descended, he saw on each step a diamond-shaped flagstone inset, and on it written a word. There were several such words and the strange thing was that, during the course of the dream, he understood each clearly, as though he were the recipient of a magical revelation, and, as he proceeded down the steps, along a vaulted corridor which was empty and echoey but not in the least frightening, the frequency of the words increased, making phrases, and finally a complete sentence of astonishing wisdom, which he repeated over and over and over again, saying to himself, within the dream, I must remember this when I wake, but when he woke the sentence receded instantly and, whereas in the dream he had experienced great excitement and wonder, in waking he was left desolate with the familiar sense of loss.

6

The telephone rang. A voice said, 'Mr Fisher?'

'Yes, who's that?'

'Paola Wirrel. I must see you. It's important. Can we meet this morning?' He tried to clear his mind of troubled sleep. 'It would suit me if we could meet as soon as possible. In an hour say.'

'All right.'

'Do you know the Suk?'

'I know nowhere.'

'Walk through the main arch of the Spanish Castle. You will come into the Suk, the bazaar. Take the second left. You'll see all the silversmiths. About three doors along there's a café. It's the only café in the street. I'll be there. Have you got that?'

'I think so.' He repeated her instructions.

'In an hour then,' she said, and replaced the receiver.

The call intrigued and excited him: he could not discover in himself the reasons why, but it occurred to him that Nash's estimate of her – 'a high-class whore', he'd called her, 'and sometimes not so high-class' – must have played a part in arousing his interest. Fisher had always been stimulated by what he liked to believe was an objective assessment of another's sexual appetite. And this mood of expectation was immediately answered, when he passed through the arch of the Spanish Castle and entered unknowingly the Suk, the streets of the Old City which were one continuous market. The shifting scenes, the noise, the patchwork of faces, goods, costume and colour, an ambience quite new and foreign to him, so took him by surprise, as though he was astonished to discover life in the city at all, that for a while he wandered through the maze of alleys, and quickly and deliberately lost himself.

In holes in the walls, tailors sat cross-legged at their sewing-machines, Singer, Mercedes, Butterfly; cobblers cut and nailed leather, and spice merchants displayed their wares in bulging sacks. In shops like hundreds of caves side by side, in halls, in rooms, in cubicles, out in the streets, along the pavements and in private courtyards, bargains were noisily entered into and concluded. Clothes, shoes, transistors, toiletries, basketware, hats, calculators, jewellery, handbags, rose stone from Tunisia, cloth from Samarkand, cotton from Alexandria, umbrella stands by the dozen, and the most popular commodity of all, suitcases, row upon row, pile upon pile of suitcases. There were barber shops and toolmakers, and art dealers selling artificially coloured portraits of Nasser, Arafat and, of course, the Colonel in full-dress uniform hung with golden chains, medals, stars, buttons, decorations, and wearing a silly smile as though he'd only dressed up for a joke. Fierce, bearded merchants waited belligerently for custom; others, less ambitious, slept sitting, kneeling, leaning. Old men wearing their *taghira*, the white cap, or turbans, or the Bedouin head-dress of red gingham with a tassled fringe, read aloud the Koran. Boys in black and white checked caps stood at stalls eating sponge cake and milk, and rich, honey-soaked pastries. The women, always in twos and threes, covered but for a single greedy eye, tested the quality of fruit and vegetables, and bought yards and yards of cloth that would in time hide their faces and their bodies from the men. And everywhere, from record-players and radios, came the monotonous, chanted music of the market-place.

In the honeycomb of commerce, the aristocrats of the Suk conduct their affairs in the streets exclusive to their trades: the goldsmiths, the silversmiths, the brass-workers cluster to their own in quieter, tidier alleys, some of which are roofed over like tunnels, and sparkle and glow with trays and bowls and lamps; one such passage is rich only in copper hues so that to walk its length is to see the world in a perpetual burnished dawn. There is a street for dyers, for tailors, for engravers, and for the public scribes who read and write for the illiterate. And in vast and silent halls, the carpet-sellers brush and smooth the silken threads from Anatolia, Izmir, Kazakhstan and Shirvan. In one emporium a fat, self-important dealer informed Fisher in faultless English that here they sold carpets made solely by the Turkmen tribes, and he recited their names as though intoning a verse from the Holy Book: the Teeke, Yomud, Afghan, Saruk, Ersar, Beshir and Baluchi. Fisher began to understand that, in this place, the exchange of goods for money was not simply the means to satisfy a man's needs or his atavism, but an activity to be enjoyed and savoured for its own sake, for the contact it made between men, for the pleasure it gave both buyer and seller. To haggle over a price, to agree, to wrap an object, to count notes and coin, to shake hands – these were both sensual and mysterious expressions of more profound transactions. And Fisher, who never needed much encouragement to open an inward eye, reflected that, by comparison, his own attitude to money was harsh and pagan, without dimension, without value, as if money was the only reality: in censuring himself, his expectations foundered, and turning into the street of silversmiths he saw the boyish handsome American, whom he had heard speak Gerald's name, gazing intently into a window, but, as Fisher approached, the man moved on. And Fisher was puzzled to find that the window which had absorbed the American's interest was filled with a display of Christian altar ornaments and sacred vessels, candlesticks, chalices, glass cruets with silver stoppers and patens. And in the window, dimly reflected, he saw opposite the café where he was to meet Paola Wirrel.

She waited in the corner farthest from the low doorway, seated in an alcove like a stall. The place was shadowy and quiet, warm and seductive with the perfume of spiced coffee. As soon as he had joined her, she tugged at a length of string and a badly stained, coffee-coloured satin curtain enclosed them: like a confessional, thought Fisher.

'Thank you for coming,' she said.

She was nervous, frightened – that was Fisher's first impression of her. Beautiful in a dramatic sort of way, she was dressed very simply in a cream linen dress with an open collar, and round her neck hung a small gold cross suspended from a slender chain. A scarf, tied in an original and striking style, kept her hair from her face. She used no make-up except to her eyes which were very dark brown and expressive of quickly changing thoughts and attitudes. Fisher was just a little disappointed: perhaps, he had hoped for a whore. He saw instead an overwrought, unhappy, anxious woman.

She said, 'I hope I haven't put you to any trouble. But I mustn't be seen.' Her accent was difficult to place, Italian possibly, or Greek.

'No trouble. I was hoping to meet you.'

'Of course,' she said and a shadow of a smile played round her wide mouth; she'd heard those words before, she seemed to say sadly.

An uneasy moment or two ensued. Fisher said, 'I've been wandering through the market.'

'Yes,' she said, 'but it isn't much of a market. Not if you've been to Marrakech or Casablanca,' and again the faint smile as though she were apologising for spoiling his fun.

'I haven't.'

A waiter, wearing a fez, poked his head over the curtain. She said, 'Will you try the local coffee?' Fisher nodded. To the waiter, she said, '*Ghah-wa.*'

They lit cigarettes and she talked of the climate: she warned him, with too much concern, that the changes of temperature were abrupt; sometimes the heat could be unrelenting; then it would suddenly cloud over and a cool sea breeze made one's eyes water. The sky was seldom the vivid blue of the northern Mediterranean, but duller, more dense, as though the sun went about veiled – like the women, she said. It all seemed so important to her, as if to warn him against the weather was the sole reason for asking him to meet. Fisher listened politely, nodding and raising his eyebrows at appropriate moments, but he observed her closely, marvelling at how regular and even her features were, at odds with her jittery, effusive chatter.

The coffee, almond-scented and heady, the texture of treacle, was brought in a copper jug. When he winced at the taste, she said, 'One gets used to it.' She took up a match and drew circular patterns in the ash. After a while, she said, 'I paint, you know.'

'In oil?'

'Oil, crayon, pen and ink. That's how I met Gerald. I had a

57

little exhibition here. He came. We met.' A flick of the hand told the rest of the story. 'I suppose Harvey Nash gave you the gossip.'

'No, he didn't.'

'That was good of him.' She sounded surprised. 'You don't know then about me and Gerald. That my husband doesn't know.' Confessions did not come easily to her.

She watched the smoke of her cigarette curl to the ceiling. 'In a way that's why I had to see you. It's about Nigs, you see, my husband. He mustn't ever know about Gerald and me.' Her hand went to the little gold cross round her neck, then to the chain which she raised to her mouth: like a delicate bridle, Fisher thought.

He said, 'I won't tell anyone if that's what you want.'

'Thank you, but I'm sure you wouldn't be indiscreet. If you're anything like Gerald – he was the most private, secretive really – no, it was something else.'

He wanted to find words to put her at her ease, but he couldn't: she was fidgety and nervous and ashamed of having to explain herself; he could do nothing to help.

'Are you married?' she said, frowning, as though she'd mis-heard a previous answer.

'No.'

'I've been married twice. My first husband was a diplomat, too. I left him for Nigs. He was a Turk, extremely honourable, a cultivated, civilised man in every respect. When I left him, he resigned. I ruined his career, really. I couldn't do that again, not to Nigs. It's not possible.' She shut her eyes, and although she did not shake her head, she gave that impression.

'Now that Gerald's dead, what danger is there?'

'No, no,' she said quickly, 'I would never leave Nigs, and I don't think he would leave me, or throw me out. You may not understand this, but a marriage of any worth can accom-modate passing fancies of husband or wife. No, it's nothing like that. You see, I've been a bloody little fool. I wrote Gerald letters. Really so very stupid, utterly stupid of me. And I must get them back.'

'I see.'

She started forward, her head to one side. 'You've got his flat, haven't you?' The question was in itself a desperate plea, and she regretted it instantly, withdrawing, playing with the burnt-out matches. 'I'm so sorry to be a nuisance.'

'You're not.'

She summoned her failing courage once more and looked at him imploringly. 'Could you search for the letters? They must be somewhere in the flat. Please.'

'I'll look, but I think I ought to tell you that the flat has already been searched.'

'Who by?' she asked in a whisper. 'The police?'

'No, by Gerald's Ministry, I think. That man Mr Fawzi perhaps. They were looking for some documents.'

Her entire body appeared crushed by Fisher's news: she retreated into the corner, visibly contracting like some strange creature withdrawing from the light. Defeat was written all over her. She said, 'Well, that's it then,' and smiled her hopeless smile.

The silence that followed was long and, for Fisher, agonising. Five or six minutes may have passed; beyond the satin curtains he heard the café-chatter, and the Suk-music which had no way of intruding on Paola's anguish: she sat absolutely still, oblivious to her surroundings. Fisher could not remember many women who drew from him such exacting concern. Her anxiety, the nervous playing with the necklet, the occasional moistening of her lips, and now this faraway look, this perfect stillness, told of her vulnerability. Was that the quality, he wondered, which touched Gerald? The more he tried the less he could imagine their relationship. He had never known Gerald touched by anyone, except comrades. He tried to imagine her in Gerald's arms but for some irrational reason was convinced that they'd never really been lovers. His intuition said that they sat, like this, for minutes, hours, without speaking. They may have held hands, he supposed, or embraced; she may have rested her head on his shoulder, and he may have caressed her breasts, but no more than that, he was certain. Looking at her, he could believe only in her intensity not in her passion.

Yet, her grief, he realised, was probably never far beneath the surface: at any moment, he thought, she was liable to break down. He pictured her having to hide her sorrow from her husband: to cry would be to confess, and Fisher could not begin to know how she had managed to conceal her pain. He would have liked to tell her now that tears would not embarrass him: he could soak up another's misery like blotting-paper. And so, when he felt besieged by her withdrawal, Fisher said, 'I realised yesterday at the funeral that you were in mourning for Gerald. I can't really imagine what you must be going through.'

She glanced up and regarded him coldly, as though she'd been accosted by a stranger. In a quiet, toneless voice, she said, 'I'm not good at hiding my feelings. I'm not English. I'm a mongrel. Some Italian. Some Slav. A bad mixture. I was born in Trieste. Apt.'

'I'm a mongrel, too,' he said.

And seeing the sympathy in Fisher's eyes, she unexpectedly pulled a face as though she'd tasted something sour, and made him smile. 'What am I going to do?' she asked wearily, smiling herself but not with pleasure or amusement.

'How many letters are there?'

'About a dozen.'

'Stupid of Gerald to keep them,' he said with some edge.

'You don't understand,' she said with that flick of her hand which was dismissive and final.

Fisher, afraid of another impasse, hurried to the first thought in his mind. 'Tell me about these classes you and Gerald attended,' he said more brusquely than he intended. 'The poem was –' but he couldn't find the words.

'Gerald was very fascinated,' she answered at once, some of her jitteriness returning. 'Of course, he used to scoff in the beginning. We used to argue terribly.'

'Why did he go in the first place?'

'For my sake,' she said as if it was the most obvious reason in the world. 'Spiritual matters are very important to me. So, he went for my sake.' The words tumbled out as though she couldn't keep up with her thoughts. 'We used to sit in the Roman Ruins, they're right next to Aubrey Scott-Burrows' house, and we used to have a picnic. Talk. Argue. I gave Gerald books to read, records to play, romantic music, not too austere, anything to try to soften his attitude. To begin with he always had an answer. Or someone else's answer. He was so clever. He used to quote Bertrand Russell at me. Stupid old man. He said something about man's beliefs being comforting like flies on a summer day. I said to Gerald, have *you* ever been pursued by flies on a summer day? There's nothing less comforting in the whole world. When I think of the fights we had! But I was beginning to win him round. He was beginning to see my point of view, no, no, I don't mean *my* point of view, I mean *another* point of view, not so – so earthbound.' She gazed at Fisher, biting her bottom lip as he had seen her do at Gerald's funeral. Then the necklet went into her mouth again, and her fingers played with the little gold cross. 'He was the only man who ever saw something *in* me, I mean, something –' Her voice faded and again her manner abruptly altered. She put a hand on his and said with urgent sympathy, 'Oh, forgive me. I prattle on and on and forget that you are in mourning, too. Forgive me.'

Fisher said without looking at her, 'Tell me, did Gerald ever mention me?' and he could sense rather than see her shaking her head. 'Why – why did he kill himself?' A shrug. 'Haven't you any idea?'

'No.'

'Did he seem nervous, altered, under strain?'

She thought for a moment. 'I couldn't detect anything. Perhaps if I'd been more sympathetic. I talk too much about myself. We're all very selfish. We run in our own little circles. People enter, and we may pause, and then we go on running again, round and round, our own lives, our own concerns. He may have cried out, "I'm dying!" and I would have said, "Excuse me, I have other things to do." That's the way of the world, isn't it? You understand?'

Fisher nodded; he understood, or thought he understood. How many times in the past had he not hoped or dared to know someone intimately, imagined them readily available, only to find them in love or heartbroken or trapped in their own eternal circle? That was what Gerald cursed most in life: his concerns were not the world's concerns and should have been.

She said, 'You see, I was away for almost two weeks. I have to go to London from time to time, I –' she waved the explanation aside. 'I got back the day he died. And then I only saw him briefly. It was difficult for us to meet, you understand, very difficult. My husband's position and so on. Anyway, we met at Aubrey's. I had some things for him from London. Silly things. He'd been in a sentimental mood the last time we'd spoken –'

'How d'you mean, sentimental?' Fisher asked, always caught by the unexpected in Gerald.

'Oh, silly things,' she said, not wanting to explain. 'I had photographs to give him. And a present, of course. A brief-case. He seemed moved by the photographs and indifferent to my present. And we promised to meet again soon, when-ever it was possible, we kissed –' She buried her face in her hands. 'Oh my God, why did he keep those letters? Why? Why?'

'He may not have kept them. How can you be so certain?'

'Because I know he did. He put them in the briefcase I'd given him. He'd been keeping them in his pocket, you see, and he transferred them to the briefcase. He was so funny with presents. I had his initials put on. It was only imitation crocodile – you know how Gerald disapproved of all those things like real animal skin, and fur, and all that sort of thing – but it looked very good, I assure you. I like giving presents, but Gerald was so funny, he was embarrassed always to receive things. He never knew how to say thank you. It was very endearing.'

'I'll certainly have another look through the flat. If I find the letters –'

'Yes, please, do look.'

'How do I get in touch with you?'

She gave him a telephone number Gerald had used, the number of her hairdresser. 'Leave a message. I go twice a week. And if it's really urgent, they know how to reach me. They're open until eight. Just say the dress is ready or something. I'll come.' She opened her handbag and took out her dark glasses, slipping them on to her nose, the domino hiding her face. 'I'm sorry about these,' she said, 'but I mustn't be seen.' She put some coins on the table, drew back the curtain and reacted physically at being exposed. Fisher, too, was suddenly made to feel defenceless although there was only the waiter in the café, reading a newspaper, and he took no notice of them. And a little later, when Fisher stood in the Suk watching her hurry away, her intensity remained with him, a heavy, glowering cloud.

<h1 style="text-align:center">7</h1>

'You know that bitch?'

Kamal appeared from nowhere, wearing Fisher's denim jacket. Fisher walked away, turning into an emporium walled with suitcases, rich in leather smells. Kamal came after him, like a mosquito at his ear. 'That bitch, I took letters from her to Mather. She paints my picture. I told you. She's crazy. Sometime laugh all day. Sometime never speak. Crazy. What you talk with her?'

'Go away,' Fisher said.

'Martin, Martin, I got news for you. Important news.'

Fisher walked more quickly, out into an alley where old, disfigured women sat beside bulging sacks of sesame seed, pine nuts and dried olives, into the lane where the public scribes conducted other men's business.

'Martin, I find Mercedes,' Kamal sung temptingly. 'White Mercedes.'

Fisher stopped. 'What d'you mean you've found the Mercedes?'

Kamal smiled but didn't answer directly. He preened. 'Jacket look pretty me?' he asked.

'What did you mean about the car?'

'Oh,' he said and gave his vacuous laugh. 'You listen to me now? Oh yes? Mercedes from the sea. Many stories to tell. Very beautiful car. You come Vespa?'

Riding pillion, Fisher put his arms round Kamal's waist and felt the boy's body warm to his. Through narrow streets they sped impervious to traffic, Kamal now hunched over the handlebars, now laughing at the near misses, looking back at Fisher to see how he reacted. Fisher laughed, too, exhilarated by the speed and by the boy's daring. They made first towards the south, then westwards, but never leaving the environs of the city and when, at last, they were in sight of the modern Sports Centre, Kamal swerved into a road where on either side houses were being built. At the farthest end, in the centre of a large expanse of open ground, stood a mound of motor car chassis, rusted hulks piled like a sculpture against the clear blue sky. Before they weaved between two wooden posts that marked the entrance, Fisher saw the battered remains of the Mercedes, streaked slime-green and black from the sea.

A lone man wearing a tattered, shabby overcoat was perched half-way up the mound, sorting, it seemed, bits of metal one from the other. Seeing Kamal, he waved and nimbly hopped down to the ground in time to meet him. They shook hands, tapped hearts, talked busily and secretly as though afraid that Fisher would understand what was being said; they tried to hide the pack of small patience cards which Kamal slipped to the man who smiled shyly. Then, they turned their attention to Fisher.

'This my cousin, Sulamein,' Kamal said.

Sulamein removed a woollen cap from his head and looked everywhere but at Fisher.

'Come,' said Kamal, 'he show us car. Many stories to tell. He no speak English. Bloody fool.'

The Mercedes lay on its roof like a dead animal. Sulamein prised open a rear door and crawled in; he pulled and tugged at the upholstery and slid out backwards dragging with him the bench seat. He pointed to two large dull marks and explained briefly to Kamal. With a pen-knife he cut the stained portion free.

Kamal said, 'This for you, Martin. Police come dump car. My cousin Sulamein know everything about cars, accident, smash. He see this.' Kamal took the jagged piece of fabric and held it to Fisher as though he were recommending his best sample. 'Funny this,' said Kamal. 'They say Mather he drive into sea, yes?'

'Yes,' said Fisher.

'Why he got blood on back seat?'

'Is that blood?'

Kamal asked Sulamein for confirmation; Sulamein nodded reassuringly. Kamal said, 'You tell me how man drive into sea bleeding in back seat? How? He got long arms? How?'

'It may not be blood,' Fisher said.

'If Sulamein say blood, is blood.'

But Fisher resisted the currents of the whirlpool, and instantly a memory of Gerald occurred. Fisher recalled an eight

64

millimetre home-made film, for instruction purposes, slowed down to demonstrate detail, frames isolated and stilled to emphasise a point: Gerald showing how to mix dragon's blood with glycerine to give the effect of human blood, and applying it to his forehead. And later, in a newsreel, he saw a comrade – was his name Peter? – being led from a London square through a gauntlet of policemen, blood streaming from a gash under his eye and yelling something at the camera – an obscenity? an accusation? Later, Fisher remembered, a policeman was convicted of assault.

Fisher said, 'But if Gerald's head was cut the blood could have dripped on to the back seat.'

'In the water? In the sea? No. Wash away.' He checked his reasoning with Sulamein who appeared to agree with him. 'Yes,' Kamal said, 'wash away.'

Fisher took the piece of fabric; he felt, as he did when he tried to lift the polythene bag of ash, repelled. 'It would have to be properly examined,' he said.

'Sure. You talk Nash. He know everything. Smash, car, insurance. You get money. You give me twenty pound.' He smiled, but not for long: he saw and sensed Fisher's reluctance. 'What matter with you? You go now Nash.'

'I don't think this is enough,' Fisher said. 'They could be old stains. Who's to know?'

Kamal's eyes hardened. He snatched the material out of Fisher's hands. 'Stinking European rubbish,' he said and marched towards the Vespa. Fisher followed but Kamal said, 'You give Sulamein one pound. He's good man. Sulamein, *assalaam aleikum.*'

'*Wa-aleikum assalaam,*' Sulamein replied, and when Fisher turned to pay him Kamal hopped on to the Vespa, started up the engine, and drove off alone.

Sulamein accepted Fisher's money with both hands, bowed and then retired behind the mound, slipping from his pocket the pack of small patience cards. Alone, Fisher found his way back into the city and to Gerald's flat. His right foot was blistered. Exhausted from the heat, his legs leaden, he fell on to the bed and was soon deeply asleep, to be awakened when it was already dark by a tattoo of stones against the window. Somehow, he knew that Kamal had more to tell him.

Fisher could not come quickly enough to his senses to rise from the bed. He thought: why can't I sleep like this at night? – and when the second shower of stones struck: I will get up in my own time. He lay, for a half-hour or more, smoking in the dark. In the slow process of waking, thoughts insisted themselves: if there is money at the end of this journey I will not share in it, was one; another was, I have to earn Gerald's forgiveness; and a third: resist, resist, resist.

The Café Damascu was peopled with much the same clientele as on the previous evening. At the long table near the door, the boys and their Japanese friends made kissing noises as he entered; Dr Swediq, in a white suit and crimson shirt with ruffled front, was doing his rounds. Kamal wasn't there.

The doctor spotted Fisher. 'May I join you?' he said and sat before Fisher had time to reply. With a flourish he removed his hat, but sat with difficulty, easing himself into the chair. 'Waiting for our young friend, I presume? Allow me to buy you a drink.'

The tired waiter brought two glasses containing the juice of blood oranges.

'Cheers,' Swediq said.

'Cheers.'

'I'm awful sorry about Gerald,' he said.

'Did you know him?'

'Not well. We met at Aubrey's. Out at the Roman Ruins.'

'Aubrey's?'

'Scott-Burrows. Awful nice type. A mystic. Good for the soul.'

'Did Gerald come here?'

'Oh no. Much too austere was Gerald. Your brother, I believe?'

'Half-brother. How did you know?'

'One hears. Such a small town. Not like London. Have the other half.' Swediq re-ordered. 'In this town everyone knows everyone else's business. Everyone of consequence, that is. You meet the same people over and over again. Awful suburban, don't you find it so?'

'I haven't been here long enough.'

'But you've done so much –' Swediq paused as though he'd committed a *faux pas*, waved his hand elegantly to dismiss it, and continued, 'Some people have a way with cities. I expect you find the absence of alcohol annoying. Our government is awful puritanical. Revolutionaries are always prudes. If ever you feel in dire need do call on me. You'll find, after a short while, in a dry city, even a moderate drinker craves like an alcoholic. Do tell me, how is dear old England? Not quite the place it once was, I believe.'

'I've been away some time myself.'

'I'm going to London next week,' Swediq said. 'To shop. For girls and boys. I hope to bring back two or three. My cousin in Damascus told me all about the business arrangements. Two-year contracts with board and lodging. At the end of the period you put ten thousand Swiss francs in a numbered account and give them a car of their own choice. He says they're queueing up in London for these opportunities. Is it true, d'you think, or is my cousin lying? He says that in the West, in America even, they lick our feet and will do nothing to offend us. Well, we have to spend our money somehow. The fun for me, I expect, will be interviewing my prospective employees.'

A man entered whom Fisher remembered seeing before: the stout unshaven youth who had driven Mr Fawzi's Cadillac. He didn't stay long. He looked around, perhaps he nodded to Swediq, and then left.

Swediq said, 'I've been having a little trouble getting my visa. Relations are a little strained just at the moment. Two of our naughtiest boys were caught waving guns in mid-air. Our dear Colonel is rather put out. Three of a kind, I always say. Now I *am* being indiscreet. You'll forget what I've said. But your Embassy's most helpful. It is still a pleasure to deal with gentlemen. Chap by the name of Wirrel. You know him?'

'Slightly.'

'Awful good sort. Charming wife. A little dotty, though. Do you know her?'

'We've met.'

Swediq saw someone over Fisher's shoulder, and his face clouded. 'Will you excuse me? Two awful boring Germans are headed this way. See you anon, perhaps.' Having to rise quickly made him wince with pain. He gathered his hat and stick. 'Cheery-bye,' he said, leaving Fisher to pay the bill.

'So! It is our friend from the first night,' Helmuth said in a fog-horn voice. 'How goes things?' He guided Günther into a chair and then sat himself. 'You are comfortable in your flat?' he asked with a trace of envy.

'Thank you.'

'We are still in Calcutta-hole. Each day we go round looking for hotel rooms more pleasant but there are none to be had. Our Embassy is not also helpful.'

Günther tugged at his brother's sleeve and prompted him in German; an argument ensued which Helmuth stopped by saying with an apologetic shrug, 'Günther is anxious you should know we have found the whore-house.'

'It is very clean,' said Günther eagerly. 'My girl she is called Zubaydah. We are having such a good time together. She is like a cello her shape. And beautiful! I have felt her face and she has very fine, strong features. Helmuth agrees she is glorious.'

Helmuth, nudging Fisher, said, 'I hope Günther has also felt other things besides her face.'

Günther beamed with sweet good nature. 'Oh ja, she is very comely, like Watutsi. She is coming here to meet me, you will see. After maybe we take you to the house, yes? There are plenty girls. Helmuth has one called Satina. He says all are lovely but I myself have not felt all the faces.' When he laughed he blinked repeatedly.

'I'm sure this gentleman has better things to do, Günther,' and while Helmuth addressed his brother he shook his head at Fisher as if to imply his was the wiser advice.

'What better things?' Günther asked. 'There is a doctor, a real gentleman, I think, who looks after them. The girls are clean. You can smell the antiseptic. Better than the Hotel Afreka, I'm telling you. You can even get perhaps a drink of *Flash*.'

'I'm sure this gentleman has made his own arrangements.'

Günther said, 'You must tell me honestly, sir, what you think of Zubaydah. A second opinion, ja, Helmuth? Helmuth says she is glorious.'

Helmuth took a coin from his pocket and deliberately

dropped it on the floor. 'I have dropppd some money, Günther!' he cried in mock alarm. 'Perhaps you would give me a
hand to look,' he said to Fisher with imploring glances. Helmuth slipped on to his hands and knees, pulling Fisher down
with him: they met under the table. Helmuth whispered at
speed, 'I have to ask you a favour. Please, make no comment
when you see this girl Zubaydah. To a blind man cunt is cunt.'

Günther said, 'Have you found it?'

'We are looking, we are looking,' Helmuth said and with a
conspiratorial finger to his lips for Fisher's benefit, cried, 'I
have found it!' and rose to sit once more at the table. He said,
'You must have tickets for Günther's concert. Such an inter-
esting programme.' He took a book of green cloakroom tickets
from his pocket. 'Admission free. The Embassy pay. How
many you want? Two, three, four?'

'Zubaydah is coming to the concert,' Günther said.

Fisher said, 'I'm not certain if I'll be here for much longer.'

'Ah, that's so? Your flat it will be empty?'

'No. It's a government flat, I'm afraid.'

The brothers tensed. Günther said, 'You are in the government?'

'No.'

'That's the truth?'

'Yes.'

'Thank God,' he said. 'Zubaydah she is illegal, you understand. And we are recommended to this whore-house by our
Commercial Attaché. He must not get into trouble.'

'I don't work for the government.'

Helmuth said, 'Okay, okay, take a ticket for the concert.
Take two. Here.' He tore off the tickets and gave them to
Fisher. 'You will enjoy, I'm sure.'

Günther said, 'The Beethoven is better when you hear the
notes.'

Helmuth roared with laughter but stopped abruptly. 'Zubaydah is here,' he said and winked at Fisher.

'Zubaydah?' Günther cooed excitedly, his head turning this
way and that uncertain from which direction she would come.
He stood.

To hoots and cat-calls from the boys at the long table,
Zubaydah made her way towards Günther. She had a grotesque

squint, one eye jammed hard into the corner nearest the nose. She took Günther's hand and Fisher glanced at Helmuth who replied by wearily raising his hands as one who'd been caught out and admitted blame.

'Beautiful, huh?' Günther said, slightly inclining his head towards Fisher.

The girl was short and lumpy with a moon face, reminding Fisher more of a tuba than a cello. 'Beautiful,' he said. The girl smiled, impossible to tell in whose direction.

'We go now?' Günther said.

'The young lady has drink first, Günther,' Helmuth chided.

Nervously, Günther began to snap his fingers for the waiter when, outside, came the sound of a harsh, metallic clash. For a moment, all those in the café were silent. Then, two or three of the boys ran out to see what had happened.

Helmuth said, 'The drivers here are worse than in Hamburg even,' and while Günther continued to snap his fingers and Zubaydah to squeeze his hand, a boy charged into the café and beckoned to Fisher urgently.

'Me?' said Fisher.

'Yes, you. You come. Kamal. Yes, you come.'

9

From nowhere, it seemed, people appeared in alleyways, at windows, out of the shadows. Some laughed and talked as they hurried in the direction of the accident, and Fisher followed, caught up in what was a festive atmosphere, like following a circus procession. Presently, they came upon the scene, a tight knot of noisy spectators crowded round a lamp-post and spilling into the road.

From some yards away, he saw the yellow plastic sandals, and his own flower-embroidered jacket; when he drew closer he saw Kamal groaning on the pavement, blood trickling from his nose and ears spilling on to the tarmac and catching the phosphorescent light. Fisher pushed his way through the small crowd to the injured man's side; his presence quietened the onlookers: they stood back respectfully, as though he were a doctor, chattering now in whispers.

'What happened?' Fisher asked of the nearest man, but he

shrugged helplessly. Another said, 'A car hit him. Not stop!'
And one of the café boys, 'Is dead?' and burst into tears.

'Kamal?' Fisher said. 'Kamal?' The boy groaned. 'No,'
Fisher said. 'He's not dead.' He took a handkerchief and
mopped Kamal's brow; the handkerchief was quickly soaked in
blood.

The police and an ambulance arrived almost simultaneously.
And when the attendant lifted Kamal on to a stretcher, he
screamed in pain, opened his eyes and looked directly at
Fisher. 'Martin,' he whimpered. 'Martin! Here, please, here –'
Fisher walked beside as they carried him towards the waiting
ambulance. 'In my pocket,' Kamal hissed. 'My pocket. Look in
the pocket.'

From the pocket Fisher managed to extract a piece of
paper, just as the attendants tipped Kamal at an angle, and
began to slide the stretcher into the ambulance. 'Go there,'
Kamal said hoarsely, 'go there. I know everything, Martin.'
Then he cried out again, a short, truncated noise; his head
lolled and he turned an awful ashen grey. They closed the
doors and drove him away at speed, and Fisher realised he had,
for the first time, witnessed the passing of a life.

10

The crowd dispersed. The street was once more deserted.
Fisher stood in the doorway of a souvenir shop against a back-
ground of dolls and leatherwork and beads; a faulty light in
the window flickered intermittently; a half-starved cat
emerged from a pile of discarded cardboard boxes behind him.
Fisher thought: a man died with my name on his lips. He
walked forward and stood beneath the streetlamp where
Kamal had lain, and carefully opened the piece of paper he had
taken from the boy's pocket: on it, written in pencil, were the
words *Moathen Harba*, which meant nothing to him. Was it a
village? a person? a street? what? *Go there, go there*. And as
Fisher slowly folded the piece of paper, saying to himself the
words *Moathen Harba*, he happened to glance down at the
pavement and saw that he was standing in the dead man's
blood; and at that moment, from the mosques, the final call to
prayer went out over the city, and along the coast and deep

into the desert, *'God is most great'*, an acknowledgement, thought Fisher, of helplessness.

He did not return to the café, or to Gerald's flat, but walked the streets for an hour or more. Kamal's words held him in a vice: *Go there, go there* – but where? or who? or what was Moathen Harba? and who would tell him? And when he did go back to the café seeking anyone who could explain, the doors were locked and the lights extinguished. There was no one about.

Did death, he wondered, always signal regret? If only. Were final partings always poisoned by remorse? The more he argued with himself that the death of Kamal was an accident, as far removed from him as the death of any creature here or on the other side of the Earth, the more clearly came the answer that Kamal was not anonymous, had died speaking Fisher's name, in his presence, in this street, and Fisher dreaded the possibility that the verdict would be death by drowning in a whirlpool.

The boy's face was vividly etched in his mind. He could not recall Gerald's face as clearly; or Anne's. And he cursed himself for feeling anything at all. He hadn't liked Kamal, hadn't trusted him and yet here he was haunted by him. Who was he? Where had he come from? Why had he pursued Fisher? And why did Fisher feel reluctantly bound to him? He remembered him in bed, awkward, rough, clumsy, and Fisher also remembered words he himself had once spoken to Anne in self-defence which made him now uneasy: the physical act is a physical act, he had said, no more, signifying nothing. And yet, Fisher concluded, without that brief, unsatisfactory collision would he be so caught by the memory of a smile, a physical presence, the balm to an hour's solitude?

A chill wind had risen and Fisher was shivering. He craved a drink but all he found was a stall in the Avenue selling *brik* and warm Pepsis. The street, perhaps the city, was empty.

Fisher's instinct told him to do nothing, to keep perfectly still without and within, but even as he acknowledged the wisdom of his inner voice, his hands searched in his pockets for the card with the arrow pointing to the BMW showroom.

Fisher turned into a quiet, residential street. On either side were modest bungalows standing in small, manageable gardens. Further along, on a triangular site, protected by palm and eucalyptus, stood a block of mansion flats, four storeys high, the brickwork a deep terracotta and each floor delineated by an elaborate cream-coloured cornice, all scrolls and curlicues. On the ground floor, facing him as he approached, Fisher saw a large plate-glass window, and on it was emblazoned the letters BMW. He entered by a tall doorway and in the vestibule read Mr Nash's name on a residents' list, gold leaf on a wooden plaque. It was a minute or two after one.

The building was a solid, self-satisfied affair, erected at the turn of the century by over-confident Italian colonisers. There was no lift but a wide, rather grand central staircase dotted with fake alabaster and marble statues, decapitated Roman generals and limbless women. In the darkness Fisher had the feeling of being caught in a museum after closing time. He came to the door on the first floor and hesitantly rattled the heavy door-knocker.

A sleepy-eyed servant opened the door to him.

'I want to see Mr Nash,' Fisher said.

'You friend or customer?'

'Tell him Mr Fisher wants to see him.'

'You wait here.'

The servant disappeared down a long, wide passage, leaving Fisher in the hall, tastefully and prosperously furnished with fine rugs and rich hangings, by an exquisite octagonal rose-wood table covered in well-thumbed periodicals at least five years out of date. *Punch*, the *Gramophone*, *Woman's Own*, the *Daily Telegraph Magazine*, something called the *Wine-makers' World*, *Autocar* and piles of Arabic newspapers all of which appeared to carry the photograph of the same luscious, round-faced girl with sensual lips and a beauty-spot on her left cheek. One wall was hung with prints of vintage cars, Hispano-Suiza, Bugatti and Daimler, Bentley, Rolls-Royce and Mercedes-Benz. There was a smell of wax polish and that look of un-natural tidiness which comes from having servants.

Nash appeared in a doorway at the farthest end of the

corridor. 'Who wants me?' he shouted, and came staggering towards Fisher, the servant in attendance behind him. When Nash reached the hall he stopped and planted his feet firmly apart to keep his balance, staring at Fisher with a glazed, unsteady look. 'Who are you?' he demanded. He was profoundly drunk.

'Fisher. Gerald Mather's half-brother. You remember.'

'Never heard of you. Never seen you before.'

'On the boat. The burial at sea.'

Nash narrowed his eyes and leaned forward at an improbable angle, giving no sign of recognition. 'Burial?'

'Mather –'

'What are you doing here? Do you know – do you know what time it is?'

'I've come to see you, but it's obviously inconvenient –'

'Wait a moment, wait a moment, wait a moment, don't try and fob me off. What did you say your name was?'

'Fisher.'

'Fisher!' he roared as though remembering someone from his childhood, and stumbled forward to grab hold of Fisher's arm and to pull him the length of the corridor into a room filled with tubes and flasks and pipettes, bubbling liquid and sediments like a mad scientist's laboratory; there was the faint stench of yeast. 'Fisher, you bugger, we must meet more often. Now, what'll it be? Claret? White Burgundy? Hock? Or some of the hard stuff?'

'Not the hard stuff.'

'Try this. Château Nash, seventy-two.' Into a cut-glass goblet he poured a liquid that looked like blackberry juice. 'Bottoms up.'

'Cheers.'

'What do you think of it?'

'Fine.'

Château Nash, seventy-two. Not *Flash*. Nash. Get it?' He gave his attention to an air bubble in a tube which he tapped furiously. 'Fisher, Fisher, when did we last meet?'

'A day or two ago.'

'Too long, you old sod, too long. We should meet hourly, morning, afternoon and night. I could keep my eye on you then, could stop you making a fool of yourself. Mind you,

you're a fast worker, I'll say that for you. You've put the town's tart in turmoil. What did you do to her?'

'Who?'

'Who? The town's tart, you old fart. Mrs Wirrel.' The name caused Nash difficulty, he repeated it several times but only managed the growl of a tetchy dog. 'Paola. Hear she's taken to her bed. In a helluva state. What did you do to her? Well, you know what she needs, don't you?' He made the repeated motion of a piston with his fist and chuckling, refilled their glasses.

'I didn't do anything to her,' Fisher said.

'You upset her, you rotten shit.'

'I couldn't have. We've only met once –'

'I know, in the Suk. But what went on behind the *bardayeh*, that's the question? What did you do? Take it out and show it to her? Waggle it about? What did you do?' He shook his head sadly. 'She's frail, you see, she's very frail.'

Fisher drained the wine and refilled his glass. He said, 'Is there nothing one can do here without the whole town knowing?'

'Nothing.'

'Did you know Kamal was killed in an accident this evening?'

'Kamal? Who's Kamal?'

'Didn't you send him to me?'

'I? Kamal? Who is he?' Nash asked trying to heave himself up on to a bar stool.

'He knew your son.'

Nash floundered, almost fell. He turned slowly. 'Oh, yes,' he said softly. 'That little queer. Yes, I know him. Porn-merchant. I know him.'

'You sent him to me, didn't you?'

'Me? Piss off! I don't touch turds. Dirty, filthy little sod.' He managed to mount the stool.

'He's dead.'

'Good riddance.'

'I think he was on to something.'

'Some*body*, more like, some*body*. Leech. Bloodsucker. Cocksucker. Vermin.' Yeah, yeah.

75

Fisher told him about the Mercedes, about Sulamein and the bloodstains on the upholstery.

'Where's the stuff now?' Nash asked.

'Kamal had it.'

'Pity. Pity. I know Sulamein. Eye like a hawk. Can look at a wreck and tell you what speed the car was doing, where it was hit, tell you the length of the driver's cock. Well, well, well, blood on the back seat. Yes, there's money to be made. Any other witnesses?'

'I don't know,' Fisher said, carefully setting his glass down on a work-top. He took out Kamal's piece of paper. 'Do you know what the words *Moathen Harba* mean?'

' 'Course,' said Nash. 'So do you.'

'What?'

'You've met him.'

'Have I?'

'Seen him, then, not actually met him. Amazing blood-pressure.'

'Who?'

'The moathen, you ass-hole, the moathen.'

'Who is he?'

'You've got a terrible memory. The little bugger who goes up the minaret. The moathen.'

'Isn't he called the *muezzin*?'

'The moathen, local dialect. The moathen by the harbour. Famous character. Won't have loudspeakers, you see.'

'The harbour, I see.'

' "God is most great" and all that garbage.'

'I understand.'

'In person.'

'Yes.'

'What do you want him for? Will you drink up or do I have to pour it down you?'

They drank; they finished one bottle of Château Nash, 1972, and opened another.

'What do you want the moathen for?'

'I don't know.'

'You're more pissed than I am.'

'I want to talk to him.'

'Well, you can't.'

76

'Why not?'

'He's asleep.'

'When's he awake?'

'At dawn.'

'What time's that?'

'When the sun rises.'

'Not before?'

'Five times a day. Sunrise, noon, afternoon, evening, night. Is that five?'

'Five.'

'"God is most great. Prayer is better than sleep." Five times a day.'

'From the minaret?'

'The *mathana*, yes.'

'At dawn?'

'Absolutely.'

'By the harbour?'

'The very one.' Yeah, yeah.

Slowly and deliberately, Fisher said, 'Let me get this straight. This old man –'

'Right.'

'Climbs up there –'

'C'rect.'

'Five times a day –'

'Bravo.'

'Beginning at dawn.'

'Ten outa ten.'

'What time did Gerald die?'

'Three, four, five in the morning.'

'What time's dawn?'

'Three, four, five in the morning.'

Fisher frowned with concentration. 'Wait a moment, wait a moment,' he said, having the glimmer of an idea.

And Nash, too, said, 'Wait a moment.'

'Are you thinking what I'm thinking?' Fisher asked.

'Are you thinking what I'm thinking?'

'Up there, at dawn –'

'Looking down –'

'He'd see the Quay –'

'He'd see –' began Nash, but broke off, beginning to laugh,

silently at first, his gut shaking. He staggered senselessly around the room. 'A witness – a witness–' he cried, and, 'there's money to be made!'

Fisher joined in the laughter, not knowing or caring why, but infected by Nash's enjoyment and enthused by the strong home-made wine. They laughed long and helplessly; Fisher sank to the floor, holding his stomach and rolling over and over until, on his back, in the feeble aftermath, when tears were running down his cheeks, he stammered, 'Moathen *harbour* not harba.'

'What's the difference?'

'You tell me.'

'Have another drink.'

'Thanks, I will.'

'And lay off Paola Wirrel.'

'Anything you say.'

'Queen of tarts.'

'Cheers.'

'Ass-holes.'

Shortly after two o'clock, Nash fell asleep in a chair; Fisher slept, too, a dreamless, untroubled sleep as though something secret had been resolved. He woke with a start; it was still dark; the sun had not yet risen.

12

He made for the Old Quay where Gerald had died, crossing the Square empty of traffic. Two or three taxis waited near the Castle and a policeman strolled lazily along the waterfront. As on the previous morning in the Suk he heard again a strain of music, ugly to his ear, but haunting nevertheless, growing louder when he neared the Quay, then suddenly ceasing, only to come again farther off like an echo, an apt accompaniment to the cold shadows, seductive, as though the cadence was meant to charm the sun over the horizon.

Slicks of oil, purplish green, floated on the water and caught the dying rays of the moon. The fishing boats, bobbing gently, made a continuous hollow clatter like the noise of a distant battle being fought far out at sea. Near the spot where Gerald's car had plunged through the rails, Fisher waited, gazing upwards at the tall white minaret, at the circle of naked electric light-bulbs that illuminated the star and crescent which adorned the apex of the tower.

The mosque was hemmed in by houses abutting to right and left and, at the rear, an enclosed passageway at ground level led to the adjoining building which looked like part of the Spanish Castle. The streets were empty, although from some of the houses Fisher could hear the sounds of people stirring, the opening of windows, the cry of a baby, coughing; and again the haunting musical strain. He was dimly aware of distant traffic; quite close, beyond the sea wall, a ship's siren sounded. If he concentrated he could hear, too, the lapping of water and, as the minutes ticked by, lights came on in the houses of the Old City, there was chatter and some laughter and the singing once more drifted into the darkness.

The sky turned from black to red; out of the calm sea the first rays of the sun flared in the east, like the plumage of some exotic bird on the horizon.

'God is most great,' came the cry and, looking up, Fisher saw the figure of the moathen clutching the balustrade atop the minaret, swaying to and fro, bowing to the rising sun.

Like a sleepwalker Fisher found himself stepping out into the open, almost against his will, experiencing an unexpected excitement: it was as though the moathen's summons was for him and him alone. He crossed the Quay, over the cobbled stones to the door at the base of the tower.

He turned the brass doorknob: it opened easily and silently; Fisher stepped quickly inside and closed the door behind him. He found himself in a dark, oppressive space smelling of salt and damp. To one side, an open door led to a small room with a bed, the moathen's, he supposed, and an oil lamp aglow. Facing him were stone steps worn in the middle with use. They spiralled upwards and he began the ascent, the way becoming darker and darker as he lost the light from the room; he felt his way with his hand on the roughcast wall that was cold to his touch. The going was hard. Up and up he went, the voice of the moathen from above as distant as ever. Fisher's chest ached and he could barely catch his breath. Quite suddenly, the voice was close, caught in a dying fall, the notes descending in a lilting, final phrase. Fisher climbed faster, until he could go no farther: he had come to a narrow open arch through which he passed and found himself out on the balcony.

The wind almost knocked him backwards; he clutched the flimsy, wooden balustrade and eased his way round the circular platform until he came face to face with the moathen: he was ancient and small, of child-like proportions: tiny hands and feet, and a miniature face rimmed by a grizzled beard and dominated by two enormous eyes. He wore a striped brown jacket that once belonged to a suit, grey trousers and, on his head, a cap, the white *taghira*. When he saw Fisher, the eyes, which were already huge, grew, and he opened his mouth to scream but a choked cry was all that issued forth. He began to wave his arms senselessly as though to ward off poisonous insects.

Fisher, clinging to the rail, tried to work round towards him, but with each step he took, the moathen edged farther away. And then, Fisher looked down and saw the Old Quay, the Harbour, the streets, the lights, the palm trees, and he caught his breath with wonder at the sight. When Fisher glanced back at the moathen, the man was trembling from head to foot.

'What did you see?' Fisher called, his voice carried on the wind.

'No see nothing!' the old man whined. 'I no see nothing. Go away! Go away!'

'The car. The white car. In the water.'

'I no tell, no tell, you go, you go.'

Fisher moved a step closer. 'I want you to tell me –'

'Trouble, trouble,' the old man chanted.

'You won't get into trouble. Please, please, tell me –' Fisher reached out and grabbed hold of the man's lapels, shaking him. 'Please!'

The moathen's terror and confusion mounted. He whimpered like a child afraid to be beaten. 'Push – push – car – push –' he said demonstrating wildly.

'The car was pushed?'

'Push car – in water – I see –' He pointed to the Quay below. 'I no tell –'

'Who pushed the car?'

He held up a forefinger. 'One man – he push –'

'But you must tell the police, the police, do you understand?'

'No, no, no, no tell –'

'You must!'

The moathen broke free and turned to face the harbour.
With all his strength he cried, 'Yousaad! Yousaad!'

'I won't harm you –'

'Yousaad!'

Running footsteps in the street below, and anxious voices,
slamming doors and a child howling.

'Yousaad!' called the old man.

Fighting against the wind, his eyes watering, Fisher struggled back towards the low arch and found his way once more
into the dark perpendicular tunnel, and began to descend as
fast as he dared, when he heard footsteps coming up from
below, strong, vigorous, male steps, bounding upwards towards
him. He stood dead still, listening, terrified. The moathen's
voice was no more than a distant sigh, but the footsteps came
each second closer. Fisher flattened himself against the cold
wall and waited: not daring to breathe, hoping, praying that
the man would pass him without seeing or sensing him.

The footsteps slowed as the climb grew steeper, then they
stopped altogether, perhaps a landing-and-a-half away. Was he
resting or listening? He took a step, another and another.
Silence.

'Yousaad!'

The moathen's voice resounded almost as though he were
standing next to Fisher. The old man was shouting down the
staircase, his voice spiralling in echoes towards his rescuer. The
shout so startled Fisher that he was propelled into movement,
stumbling, reaching out for something to keep his balance,
anything that came to hand in the pitch blackness, the wall, a
rail, anything.

And then he grabbed hold of the man. There were shouts,
cries from above and below, as they struggled, the man trying
desperately to get a grip of Fisher, and Fisher, just as desperately, trying to break free, scraping his nails against stubble on
the man's face, so that the man cried out. In that moment,
Fisher slipped, his feet sliding from beneath him and, in the
fall, he slithered out of the man's grasp, stumbled awkwardly

twisting his ankle, yet managing to hobble and hop down the stairs. Shouting, the man came after him but Fisher had the advantage now and reached the door at ground level, opening it on a crowd of petrified faces who, amazingly, stood back, parted their ranks to let him through. The moment he had darted past them, they realised who he was and what had happened, and chased after him, barking like pariah dogs.

Through the ill-lit streets he limped, now running, now walking, the pain shooting up his leg. He could hear the angry voices of his pursuers, sometimes close, sometimes as if they had taken the wrong direction, but each time they came again as though he had been spotted, and he looked up and saw the moathen atop the minaret pointing to him, directing the hunt from on high. Fisher ducked into the shadow of a doorway, edged along and shot down an alleyway so narrow not even the moathen on his perch could see him. He rested, his breathing harsh and terrifyingly loud. Footsteps passed at the head of the alley; men called to each other but the shadows were long enough to hide him. Then there was silence.

He heard the harbour water lapping the Quay; slowly, painfully, he made his way down the alley and emerged on to a ramp that led gently to the water's edge. He paused, wondering whether or not he dared risk the open space of the Old Quay. He removed his denim jacket and tied the arms round his head like a clumsy turban : from above, he reckoned, he would not be recognised.

Trying desperately not to limp, he walked stiffly along the Quay, and from under his makeshift headgear looked back towards the mosque. The moathen and another man, a stout, younger figure, were on the perch gazing down : they must have seen him, but they let him pass.

13

Limping, Fisher returned to Gerald's flat and shivered as though with fever. He fell on the rumpled bed, emitting the harsh, painful cries of an exhausted animal. When he was able to prevent himself from rehearsing the terror he'd experienced in the perpendicular tunnel, he searched for the card Wirrel had given him and telephoned the Embassy.

Wirrel was brusque and non-committal. To Fisher's explanation – 'I've found out something about Gerald's death – a witness – it wasn't suicide–' Wirrel said, 'I see, I see, I see,' as though he were dealing with daily routine business. 'I'll inform the police,' he said and hung up.

Tilting the slats of the venetian blinds to blot out daylight, Fisher slumped into an armchair, twisted and rubbed his ankle to ease the pain. He sat, dozed, woke startled, dreamed unremembered dreams and then entered that demi-world, somewhere between sleep and wakefulness where censored thought and feeling break loose. In this unbordered territory he was once more atop the minaret, standing again on the high balcony and he saw below the empty quay where Gerald's car had plunged into the water. And as if expecting the scene to be peopled, so was he filled with a sense of anticipation, like a man awaiting a visitor who is late.

Wirrel arrived shortly before eleven with a uniformed Police Inspector, a man with an unremarkable face which betrayed neither emotion nor thought. He spoke little, and when he did he addressed only Wirrel, and then in Arabic; occasionally he scribbled in a small brown ring-back notebook with the word 'Renown' on the cover.

The story took time to relate because Fisher had to pause while Wirrel translated in halting Arabic for the Inspector. He told of Kamal and of the man's dying words; he reported what the moathen had said; he described the struggle with his unknown pursuer in the minaret. When he was done the Inspector commented and Wirrel translated, 'He says you should not have entered a mosque.' A terse exchange took place. The Inspector rose and made for the door. Wirrel rose, too. 'You'll have to accompany us,' he said. 'He wants to question the moathen.'

At the harbour mosque, the Inspector knocked on the door at the base of the minaret. Wirrel and Fisher stood some yards back from him, and Fisher remembered from the boat Wirrel's talent for exuding silent disapproval.

A man not the moathen opened the door: stout, young, unshaven rather than bearded, wearing what looked like a fixed sneer but which was, Fisher saw, a look of pain or discomfort from a deep, newly made scratch down his left cheek which he dabbed from time to time with a blood-spotted hand-kerchief. He was Mr Fawzi's chauffeur.

'That's the man I fought with,' said Fisher. 'Fawzi's chauffeur. D'you remember him?'

'Are you certain?' asked Wirrel.

'Certain.'

The Inspector questioned him and then addressed Wirrel over his shoulder. Wirrel said, 'Evidently the moathen has gone away. He's sick.' The Inspector pointed to the sky. Fisher glanced up. Two workmen were wiring loudspeakers to the balustrade. Fisher said, alarm growing, 'Find out how he got that scratch.'

Through Wirrel the question was asked and through Wirrel the reply given. 'He cut it shaving he says.'

The door was closed. The Inspector turned to them and shut his notebook as though he'd made up his mind no more need be done. He and Wirrel chatted, amiably it seemed to Fisher; the Inspector saluted half-heartedly and wandered off, hands behind back, breathing deeply the fresh air.

Wirrel said, 'He's promised to try and talk to the moathen. If he ever finds him.'

'Thank you for your help,' Fisher said.

They walked along the sea front in the shade of the palms that lined the pavement; Wirrel made no allowance for Fisher's limp.

Wirrel said, 'Do you mind if I'm severe on you? I'm not best pleased. You've behaved foolishly, if I may say so. Why didn't you report all this to us first? Why did you go it alone?'

'No reason. It was the way it happened.'

'Well, it shouldn't have happened that way. Things are tricky enough without people like you crashing about. You don't understand how things are done here. You've no understanding at all of the national character. You believe every word you're told. To lie is part of the social fabric. I knew that pimp who was killed. Kamal, was he called? A back-street pornographer. A male prostitute.' He was angry.

'The moathen saw someone push Gerald's car into the sea,' Fisher said wearily.

'How do you know he wasn't lying? How can you be sure you understood him correctly? Do you **speak the language?**

No, you don't. Hyperbole is to the Arab what understatement is to us. You'd do well to remember that.' He removed his glasses to wipe them with a spotless handkerchief; without them he looked as blind as Günther Winzer.

Suddenly, thinking it for the first time, Fisher said, 'I just want to get out of here.'

'And what will you use for money?' Wirrel asked. 'Or are you hoping to be deported again, all expenses paid, as you were from Accra?'

Fisher paused, leaned back against the railings and lit a cigarette. He felt as though he were in the act of falling and that should he land he would fragment into a hundred million pieces. He smiled. He wouldn't show Wirrel what he was feeling.

Wirrel said quietly, 'And by the way, I can't imagine what possible excuse you have for seeing my wife, but leave her alone, will you? She's not a well woman. In future, just leave her alone,' and with a curt nod he slipped the glasses back on to his nose, turned and walked away.

Nash's BMW nosed into the curb. Puffing and blowing, Nash eased himself out of the car and joined Fisher. He looked out to sea, Fisher at the city.

Nash said full of expectation, 'Well? What's occurred? What's the curate been saying to you?'

'The curate?'

'Wirrel. He's impotent, you know. Can't get it up. The only thing he can raise is an eyebrow. What's he been saying to you?'

'He told me not to interfere.'

'Would do. Would do. I've some news for you. I went and saw our friend Sulamein. Wanted a look at the Mercedes. It's been removed. Squashed into the size of a matchbox. Sulamein's been given a black eye. Said he didn't know anything about bloodstains. That means we're on to something.' Yeah, yeah. 'Any luck with the moathen?'

Fisher repeated the story. Nash listened attentively as though every word contained a clue. He said, 'You see? There's money to be made. Now, let's have a think.'

'About what?'

'Obvious. You'd need someone pretty strong to push a

Mercedes into the sea all on his own. The Quay's flat. There's no hill.'

'I don't know if we should –'

'Of course we should. We're talking about ten grand. Five for you, five for me. All we want is one sworn statement. Don't mind about Wirrel. He's got his job to do.'

'It's probably impossible to push a car that size through the railings and into the water,' Fisher said. 'Wirrel's most likely right. I got it wrong.'

'No, you haven't,' Nash said, his eyes twinkling.

'Haven't I?'

'I wonder.'

'What?'

'Well. There's only one man I know with that kind of strength.' Yeah, yeah.

'Who?'

Nash smiled encouragingly. 'Interested in the Mysteries of the East?'

PART THREE

About seventy kilometres to the west of the city on the sea lie
the Roman Ruins, but they are concealed from the main
coastal road by woodland. From the bus stop, Fisher took a
taxi which made towards a cypress grove but, when it drew
near, entered unexpectedly an avenue of tall trees, cool and
aloof. Through gaps, at a distance, Fisher glimpsed the Ruins, a
fallen pillar, a crumbling wall, an imperfect arch. He saw the
sea beyond and, briefly, a majestic colonnade of fluted and
broken stone. The road forked and, by taking the right-hand
prong, Fisher was surprised to find the sea now ahead of them;
but before the land spattered into an outcrop of rock, a village
barred the way. The surface of the road changed from dust to
irregular scabs of asphalt. Either side stood shabby, square
houses and shops; there was a filling station with brand new,
streamlined petrol pumps, an old run-down mosque, its minaret no taller than the telegraph poles which formed a kind of
guard of honour along the road. Beyond the mosque, on a steep
rise overlooking the sea, stood an isolated bungalow with green
roof tiles and coral walls. It could have been a modest seaside
bungalow anywhere. There was nothing distinctively Arabic or
Moorish in the architecture: the walls were stucco, and
wrought-iron grilles guarded the windows and window-boxes
bright with geraniums. It was at once apparent that much
effort had been made to maintain the place: the paint had not
been allowed to peel, the tiled roof was uniform and intact,
and three neatly made flower-beds, a square, a circle, a
crescent, were arranged to make a short, winding path to the
front door. Five or six motor-cars were parked outside, but to
the left, and separate from the house stood a makeshift
carport: four poles supporting a corrugated asbestos roof
sheltering a black windowless van. The bodywork gleamed, the
chrome gleamed, the glass of the windows and headlamps

gleamed: the van looked as if it had never been used, but was even so always kept in readiness.

The door to the house was open; hanging from the lintel were eight or nine postcards stuck one under the other to a length of adhesive tape which spun and spiralled slowly like fly-paper. On the top card the word ENTER was written in a clumsy, child-like hand; the other cards bore the words in French, Italian, German, Spanish, Swedish, Greek and Arabic – to the last a transliteration had been appended: YAD-KUHL.

A short corridor led to a curtained arch. Fisher drew aside the curtain, which was of several thicknesses of muslin, and entered a sparsely furnished room. In a semi-circle, seated cross-legged on cushions, half a dozen or more people surrounded a figure wearing a white burnous ensconced on an elaborately carved heavy oak chair, like a throne. The curtains were drawn, but several candles were placed at strategic points on the floor casting huge, ungainly shadows. There was no sound, except the breathing of those present, deep, rhythmic, relaxed like the rush of the sea. No one stirred or paid any attention to Fisher who made his way quietly to the back of the semi-circle, and so could not see the faces of the listeners. But the central figure on the throne drew what light there was: from the wide sleeves of his robe his hands and forearms were visible, bony, sinewy and arid. His face, because of the hood, was in deep shadow but it was a long, angular face and once, when he turned slightly, Fisher caught sight of eyes deep set in craters, lips inverted, flesh around mouth and cheeks sagging with extreme age; his forehead, however, looked to be quite unlined, smooth as a skull.

Presently, there came the sound of the noon summons from the village mosque and this everyone appeared to take as a signal that the concentration in the house could be relaxed, but in a frail, piping voice the old man asked the gathering to pause, and to address their innermost thoughts to a list of three or four names, one of which was Gerald's. 'Let them be eternally present. Let there be an awakening into an awareness of eternity so that we may discover the eternal in them within ourselves. As has been written: Good men spiritualise their bodies; bad men incarnate their souls.' Perhaps a minute passed before the curtains were opened by an Arab servant and daylight flooded the room. There was a murmur from the small audience, a closing of books, general movement. Two or three gathered round the old man; some lit cigarettes and talked among themselves.

When Fisher looked about, he recognised two people: Dr Swediq, in fawn, and the handsome young American who had spoken Gerald's name in the Afreka. He met Fisher's steady gaze with a look that was frank, appraising and blatantly sexual. 'Fascinating stuff,' he said. 'Our values in the West are in need of an overhaul.' He lost confidence almost at once and assumed a serious expression which accentuated his ingenuousness.

'I'm afraid I arrived late,' Fisher said.

'Aren't you a Disciple?'

'No.'

'Joseph Brogan's the name,' the American said, extending a hand. 'You're new to all this, too!' His grip, Fisher thought, was too firm, too affectionate.

'Yes. Are you?'

'My first time.'

'My name's Martin Fisher. You knew my half-brother, I think.'

Brogan answered with a lopsided grin. 'Your half-brother?'

'Yes. Gerald Mather.'

'Mather, Mather,' he repeated. 'No, not that I recall. What makes you think I did?'

'I'm sorry. I must be mistaken.'

'Guess so,' Brogan said earnestly, without hint of suspicion or anxiety, an attitude so convincing, Fisher doubted for a moment his recollection of the scene in the lobby of the hotel.

A woman with a contour map for a face joined them. 'May I introduce Mrs Carson?' Brogan said. 'Mr Fisher.' She would be in her late fifties, Fisher guessed, petite, inquisitive, worldly. She wore a green turban with a garish jewel at her forehead, a sleeveless silk shirt, revealing ugly and flabby upper arms, and silk trousers gaily patterned. She was sunburned to a deep walnut. 'Are you one of these meditation buffs?' she asked; she too was American; her voice was deep as a man's.

Brogan answered for Fisher. 'He's making his first visit, too, Ella.'

'Kindness and love, that's all that matters,' she growled, lighting a cigarette and puffing deeply. Her fingernails were crimson claws.

'Mrs Carson's husband, Stanley, is a Member of the American Diplomatic Mission here,' Brogan explained.

'And you?' Fisher asked.

'I write,' said Brogan.

'About what?'

'Archaeology. I'm here for the ruins.'

'That's why he's with me,' said Mrs Carson drily. The men laughed politely.

'What are you doing here?' asked Brogan.

'Family business.'

'How long are you staying?'

'I'm not certain.'

Mrs Carson said, 'We have quite a life here, Mr Fisher. People ask me if I get bored, but there's so much going on: antiquity, and bridge, and a poetry circle, and music. By the way, do you play tennis?'

'A little,' Fisher replied.

She turned to Brogan. 'When a Britisher says "a little" it means he's Wimbledon champion.'

'I'm not very good,' Fisher said. 'I've hurt my ankle.'

'We play Thursdays and Sundays and swim afterwards. Will your ankle be better by next Thursday?' She produced a diary from a chain-mail handbag. 'No. Sorry. Thursday's out. We're invited to the Germans, and we get to meet Günther Winzer.' She dropped the name as though it were a household word. 'Afterwards he's giving a recital. Beethoven. Imagine! You see? People say we're a backwater but we get to hear Winzer! However, if you're still about next Sunday –'

'I'd like that,' Fisher said.

'And will you be coming to classes again?'

'I doubt it.'

'I've been coming for months. I don't understand a word the old gentleman says, but he comforts me. Kindness and love, that's all that matters.'

'And you, Mr Brogan?' Fisher asked. 'Will you come again?'

'I guess not. I prefer regular church.'

The Arab servant entered bearing a tray of iced drinks.

Fisher had previously caught only a glimpse of him opening the curtains but, now, close to, was brought face to face with a bizarre, grotesque figure, whose age it was impossible to guess. He was under five foot, but his head was disproportionately large and triangular, crowned with hair dyed pale gold and frizzed in tight screws. He had huge shoulder muscles which merged with those of his neck. His body was the body of a muscle-bound acrobat, his face the face of a malevolent clown whose make-up had faded in the sun. And yet, his expression and demeanour were gentle, polite, servile, and slightly feminine – the way he tossed his head, or pursed his lips, or used his hands like an ageing ballerina. 'You are new, monsieur,' he said in a nasal voice, fluttering his eyelids like a comic vamp.

'Yes, I have come to see Mr Scott-Burrows,' Fisher replied, taking a glass of orange-juice.

'*Qui vous a recommandé?*'

'Paola Wirrel,' he said on Nash's advice.

The smile vanished, and the gaze hardened. He said, 'I don't know if *le maître* will see you,' and passed on to another group. When he was out of earshot, Mrs Carson said, 'That's Abdulsalaam. Isn't he heavenly? They say he's over sixty. He looks after the old man like a baby.' And then mischievously asked. 'So you know Paola Wirrel, do you?'

'Slightly.'

'She's not entirely welcome here.'

'Yes, I gathered that. Why?'

'I don't know,' Mrs Carson said a little too sweetly. 'But she's going through a hell of a time at the moment, poor girl.'

Brogan asked, 'What's wrong with her?' affecting a keen interest as one who had long practice of pleasing older women.

'I mustn't gossip,' said Mrs Carson, 'not in front of her friend, but if you want to know –' and then stopped, and asked Fisher, 'You're not a friend of the husband, are you?'

'No,' Fisher said.

'Oh-oh,' Brogan crooned. 'I detect infidelity in the use of the definite article, Ella. No one ever says "the husband" or "the wife" unless one of 'em's cheating.'

'Oh well, okay, if we've gone this far. You're right, of course, Joe. Paola Wirrel has been having the most passionate dalliance with a very unlovely guy. The guy kills himself in an automobile. You ready for this? The husband doesn't know she's been cheating, just like you said, Joe. So she has to hide her grief from him. You ever heard anything like that? Too awful, imagine having to hide your grief.'

'Ah, c'mon, Ella, that's an old story,' Brogan said tartly. 'Women's magazines thrive on garbage like that.'

'You kidding, Joe? That's pure Flaubert.'

'Why was the guy unlovely?' Fisher asked carefully, watching Brogan now, but the American waited interestedly for the reply, not giving any hint that he knew who was being discussed.

'Why was he unlovely?' repeated Mrs Carson, glancing this way and that, as though first having mentally to rehearse what she was about to say. 'He was rude, condescending and superior. Those were his likeable qualities. I was always frightened of him. The few times we met, I was always convinced he was going to do damage to somebody or something. Probably me. He gave me the feeling that he was physically dangerous.'

'Perhaps that's what she liked,' Brogan said smugly.

'Perhaps. Not me. Kindness and love, that's all that matters to me. And Mr Mather was neither kind nor loving.'

'Mather?' said Brogan. 'Oh dear.' Fisher could not tell whether his alarm was assumed or genuine.

'What is it?' asked Mrs Carson.

'I think Mr Mather was this gentleman's brother.'

Her head shot round to Fisher and she narrowed her eyes. 'And my husband, aged sixty-two, wonders why he never got to be Ambassador,' she said, and smiled. 'I hope my indiscretions won't stop you coming to play tennis with us.' To Brogan she said, 'I'm going now,' and to Fisher, over her shoulder, as she went, 'You should've stopped me, you know.'

With fussy courtesy, Brogan escorted her to the door, and Fisher saw Abdulsalaam chase after them. He held a wooden bowl and said, 'Pardonnez-moi. Pour le maître.' They each dropped a note into the bowl and as they were going Brogan called, 'See you around, Mr Fisher.'

The others, too, began to take their leave, placing their offerings into Abdulsalaam's bowl. On his way out Dr Swediq paused by Fisher and said, 'Ah, to give before being asked,' and shook his head admiringly as if such altruism was beyond his power; he dropped coins in the bowl and departed, which Abdulsalaam took as his cue to remove the strip of adhesive tape with the postcards, and to shut the front door.

Fisher stood facing the old man now: his eyes were closed; he may have been asleep: there was no doubt that he exuded an air of calm and quietude which Abdulsalaam interrupted asking him, as one might a baby, 'You want the sun now, *chéri?*' Inside the cowl, the old man nodded; in a single movement the servant lifted him in his solid oaken chair, carried him out of doors on to a wide terrace and gently lowered him to the ground. It was an astonishing display of strength. Then, the servant whispered to him and received a reply. Abdulsalaam put his head into the room and said to Fisher, 'He will not see a friend of Madame Wirrel. *Je suis désolé. Au revoir. Le bol est sur la table. Au revoir, monsieur,'* he sang like a Parisian concierge.

'Tell him,' said Fisher, 'I'm Gerald Mather's half-brother.'

'Monsieur Mather!' cried the servant, clapping his hands with delight, and then his face instantly assumed a look of sorrow. '*Il est mort.'* Another change of mood came with a gesture of reassurance. 'Wait. I'll tell *le maître.'*

Gerald's name dissolved the barrier. Fisher was invited out on to the terrace and formally introduced; the old man's hand was cold and brittle to the touch. He said, peering at Fisher, 'You are very beautiful. You must call me Aubrey.'

The sun, which had been obscured by a light morning haze, now emerged and beat down on them. The sea solemnly and rhythmically fell against the rocks below. The house was spectacularly set, the centre-point of a narrow inlet. On the adjacent headland, to the east, Fisher could just make out the vague shape of a ruined temple, truncated pillars and a jumble of reddish stones warmed by the sun; to the west, a flat cliff top. Aubrey said, 'Abdulsalaam, fill me a pipe, if you please.'

'What pipe?' asked the servant, fussing round the old man, arranging the folds of his robe and the set of the hood.

'You know what pipe.'

'I dunno what pipe.' His eyes flicked towards Fisher now, seeking approval for the teasing.

'I mean my pipe in the house,' the old man said, patting Abdulsalaam's forearm to placate him.

'Ooooh! Dat pipe! I t'ought the pipe *entre vos cuisses*!' And he cackled like a chicken, quack-quack-quack-quack.

'Go and do it.' The old man was flustered and impatient.

With an exaggerated marching step, Abdulsalaam stomped into the house, found the pipe and filled it with stuff from a ceramic jar. For himself he rolled a cigarette in bright yellow paper and, while he did so, called to Fisher, 'Does monsieur smoke?'

'I have my own, thanks,' Fisher replied.

'But dese are special. Shit. Hash. Thai-sticks. You want?' he asked like a child eager to share.

Fisher declined and watched the servant carefully lick the paper and seal it, and then he returned to the terrace bringing Aubrey his pipe and holding a taper to it; he watched the old man inhale weakly. Satisfied, he sat cross-legged at his master's feet, and they gazed out to sea; Fisher's presence was ignored.

Aubrey said, 'Is that young man still here?'

'*Quel jeune homme?*' the servant demanded. '*Il n'est pas jeune.* He is old, very old, and ugly like a pig!'

'Be still,' the old man said, trailing a bony forefinger down Abdulsalaam's thick neck, and feebly stroking the over-developed muscles of his upper arm.

Fisher said, 'Yes, I'm still here.'

'So, you are Gerald's brother.'

'Half-brother.'

'An unnecessary distinction. I liked him.'

'Did you?'

'Oh yes, we liked him, didn't we, Abdulsalaam?'

'He gave me money. He very nice,' the servant said, inhaling deeply.

'I don't wish to hear about money,' Aubrey said feebly, and, to Fisher, by way of an apology, 'Abdulsalaam's a Catholic. A sect not quite as universal as they would like one to believe. All my fault. All my fault. When I adopted him, I had him baptised by a bishop. My cousin Guy Scott-Burrows. Also Catholic, I fear. Still, they have their uses. When I die Abdulsalaam is going to live with the fathers in Florence, aren't you, Abdulsalaam?'

'When you die, yes, *chéri*,' the servant said lovingly.

'You've seen the hearse?' Aubrey asked.

'The hearse?' queried Fisher.

'Outside. In black. Abdulsalaam is going to drive me to Florence. I wish to be buried near a friend. Perhaps you knew him: P. F. Springer. He translated Srimad Bhagavatam. We were up together. Then Abdulsalaam will live with the fathers. "Learn to look with an equal eye upon all beings, seeing the one Self in all."'

Fisher allowed a respectful pause before asking, tentatively, 'You – you liked Gerald, did you?'

'Gerald, Gerald –?'

'Mather.'

Aubrey exhaled the smoke, then pulled it back up his nose, causing it to trickle through his nostrils like incense. He said, 'Not to begin with. Inner chaos always alarms me. But later, I was struck by his honesty. She, I liked at once. But not now.'

'Quack-quack-quack-quack,' went Abdulsalaam softly, deep in his throat.

'Why don't you like her?' Fisher asked.

'Because of what Gerald told me.'

'What was that?'

'A private matter. On the day he died, I seem to think.'

'He saw you the day he died, did he?'

'Did he? I cannot be certain. My memory of the recent past is so very suspect.' His voice gave the impression of an ever receding presence, growing fainter and fainter. Fisher said, 'Yes, he did see you,' and turning to the servant, added, 'And you saw him too, didn't you, Abdulsalaam?'

'Quack-quack-quack-quack.'

'He talked of the woman,' Aubrey said with distaste.

'*Il vous a posé des questions au sujet de la mer,*' Abdulsalaam said, turning mischievous eyes on Fisher.

'Yes, so he did.'

'What did he want to know?' Fisher asked.

'I'm asked so many questions.'

'But not about the sea, are you?'

'Was it the sea's mystery he was concerned with? The mystical significance, was that it?' Aubrey asked.

'Was it?'

'I told him that the sea unites. He seemed pleased. I told him it is a symbol of unity. He appeared satisfied. I told him it was the element which separates and yet brings together. He was convinced.'

'Why was he interested in the sea?'

'Quack-quack-quack-quack.'

Aubrey smiled and his dentures slipped a little. He patted Abdulsalaam's head. 'A little less noise, if you please, young man. There'll be tears before bedtime.' And to Fisher, 'Too much Gide, I fear. All my fault. Too much Gide. *L'Immoraliste est un livre formidable.*' And he closed his eyes; the pipe hung limply from his lips.

Fisher knelt beside Abdulsalaam and talked softly to him. 'You know all about it, don't you?' He smiled his friendliest smile.

'Me? I know nothing.'

'Of course you do. You were the last to see him, weren't you?'

'Quack-quack-quack-quack.'

'A lot of people saw him on the day he died, Abdulsalaam,' Fisher said as though to a child. 'But you were the last,' as if to flatter.

'A lot? Who?'

'Aubrey, for one. Mrs Wirrel. She gave him a present. A briefcase.'

The servant's eyes lit up. 'You know about the briefcase? You are the only one. All the others ask for papers, but you are the one who knows about the briefcase.' He clapped his hands delightedly.

'What others?'

'The ugly girl. Julnar. Swediq,' and he put his tongue out.

'Have you got the briefcase?'

'*Mais oui*, I took it from the car,' he replied cockily.

'Where is it?'

'Quack-quack-quack-quack.'

'What were you doing with the car, Abdulsalaam?'

Suddenly, Aubrey woke with a start. He looked about as though he expected to see demons and then took hold of Fisher's hand so that Fisher was obliged to lean forward and face the old man in his cowl: there was a musky scent of decay, the sweet smell of corruption. Aubrey said, 'You mustn't lie to me, you know. You must learn to distinguish.

98

There is right and there is wrong. What is it you don't want to face?' The pipe slipped from the old man's mouth on to his lap; he was again asleep. When Fisher straightened up, Abdulsalaam stood also, putting a finger to his lips. '*Le mur byzantin*,' he said, crossing his hands on his chest like a tragedienne. 'Go now, I will come to you there.'

'Will you bring the case?'

'Quack-quack-quack-quack.'

2

The Byzantine Wall bisects the ruined city like a fallen pillar, smooth stones not quite conjoined, reaching out to the northernmost limits where the ancient conurbation meets the sea. To east and west of the wall, in hemispheres, the Romans built their city. To enter the Ruins, Fisher had passed a small white lodge where two men sat in the shade of a eucalyptus tree playing draughts. They were, for a while, the last reminders of the modern world; leaving them behind, he saw no official guides, no tourists, no forbidding notices; it was as if he had been the first man to stumble upon the place and found it empty. He walked the length of the wall until he reached a spattering of smooth rocks, stepping-stones, leading mysteriously nowhere but to the calm depths of the sea.

Having no guide or book, Fisher was able to identify only the Theatre which had been carefully restored; for the rest, the temples and baths, the basilicas and houses were to him a jumble of stone; here the remnants of an arch, there the echo of a dome, an obelisk, a doorway worn by wind and spray and time. Turning his back on the sea to survey the compact city, small, comprehensible, built for humans not for gods, he regretted that his mood did not invite enjoyment or appreciation : he was too watchful to allow the historical force to work on his imagination, too alert to the present to be seduced by the past; waiting for Abdulsalaam Fisher was robbed of susceptibility to his surroundings.

Others entered the environs of the old city : the party of Japanese boys, one earnestly reading from a guidebook, the rest busy with cameras, light meters and lenses, wandered along the ancient pavements. And a little later, the sound of footsteps against shattered stone caused him to look round. At the white lodge he saw Brogan strolling along, hands thrust deep into his pockets, head bent. He gave no sign of having seen Fisher or the Japanese, but continued on towards the Theatre. He disappeared through the arcades at ground level, then reappeared on the uppermost platform. He sat dangling his legs over the edge and waved to Fisher, who did not respond, and to the Japanese, who did. Outflanked, Brogan to his left, the Japanese to his right, Fisher waited for Abdulsalaam with a vague, familiar feeling of alarm.

Abdulsalaam appeared at the lodge, instantly saw Fisher and sprang with ease on to the wall; nimble as a tightrope-walker, he darted along, jumping the gaps where necessary, never once losing his foothold or his balance. Arms outstretched he flew at speed towards Fisher; in his left hand he held a black brief-case.

At once, Fisher was aware of a reaction from the other visitors to the ruined city : the Japanese no longer took photographs; their guide fell silent, they formed themselves into a line, watchful, their arms folded, the one with the laugh whinnied. On the upper tier of the Theatre, Brogan rose, black against the bright sky, a crow waiting to swoop.

'*Bonjour, mon ami*,' Abdulsalaam said. 'See? I have brought the case, *la serviette*.'

Fisher put out his hand to take it, but the servant held it close to his chest, turning away a little like a woman covering her breasts. 'What's the matter?' said Fisher. 'Aren't you going to give it to me?'

'*Il faut me payer d'avance*,' the servant said.

'Why should I pay you? It was my brother's. Now, it's mine.' He spoke again as to a child, simply but without condescension, though the lilt of his voice made him feel like an actor in a play, repeating well-rehearsed lines. Aware that he was watched from either side, it occurred to Fisher he did not want for an audience.

'Monsieur Mather always he pay me.'

'For what?'

'Quack-quack-quack-quack.'

'*Dis-moi*, Abdulsalaam,' Fisher said gently.

Abdulsalaam considered for a moment, pouting his lips, clutching the briefcase more closely. 'Because I see dem,' he said. 'I see dem *près du mur.*'

'See who?'

'Monsieur Mather and La Wirrel. Many times I see dem. There.' He cocked a thumb, indicating some point behind him along the wall. 'He give me money not to say nothing to *le maître.* Plenty money.'

'What did you see?'

The servant grinned wickedly. '*Ils étaient nus tous les deux,*' he said, cupping his hand to shield his mouth, like an impish schoolboy.

'Were they making love?' Fisher asked.

A worried look crossed Abdulsalaam's face. 'You not tell *le maître?*'

'I won't tell anyone.'

The servant whistled with relief and flicked his fingers. 'If *le maître* know, he cross with me. *En colère, vous comprenez?* He's not speaking to me for days.'

'I won't tell *le maître.* What did you see, Abdulsalaam?'

He sniggered. 'I saw dem, you know, no clothes. *Elle a de gros seins!*' He made an open gesture with his right hand. 'But no love, no. *Ils ne baisaient pas.*' Suggestively, he thrust his hips back and forth. 'No. He cries.'

'Cries?' Fisher repeated. '*Il pleurait?*'

'Oh yes,' Abdulsalaam said, suddenly sitting cross-legged at Fisher's feet. 'He is sad like a baby. Dey sit. He put his head on her shoulder. She make so wid his hair' – he patted his own tight curls – 'and he cries, oh, he cries,' and he heaved his massive shoulders up and down, an absurd Harlequin who wiped huge imaginary tears from his eyes.

'And they saw you?'

'Oh yes –' and at once he launched into an elaborate panto-mime, acting out Paola's embarrassment, her scream, her scramble for her clothes, and Gerald's alarm, his hands placed strategically to cover himself, his terrible awkwardness. Fisher would have laughed out loud had he not witnessed the scene unaccountably with Brogan's eyes, a distant observer watching an incomprehensible charade.

'And Gerald paid you to keep silent? Not to tell anyone?'

'No, not anyone. I not to tell *le maître*,' he replied pedantic-
ally.

Fisher asked, 'How much do you want for the case?'

'Much money.'

'How much?'

'*Trois livres*,' Abdulsalaam said, but he had no confidence in
the price.

'Too much. One.'

'*Deux cinquante.*'

'*Deux.*'

Fisher paid him and Abdulsalaam handed over the imitation
crocodile case, the initials G.A.M. embossed in gold. Too easy,
thought Fisher. 'How did you get the case?' he asked casually.

Abdulsalaam counted the two notes over and over again. He
said, 'From the car.'

'What were you doing with the car?'

'Pushing it into the sea,' he answered as if it was the most
natural thing he could think of.

'Why did you push the car into the sea?'

'She ask me.'

'Who? Julnar?'

'She is ugly.' To illustrate he sucked in his cheeks and held
his hands like claws. 'Monsieur Mather he introduce me. I do
t'ings for dem. Carry. Push. Load boat with cases, guns, I t'ink.
I am strong. And y'know, *je ne suis ni curieux ni indiscret.*
Dey pay me. Monsieur Mather he know if I get de money I not
tell dat I see him wid La Wirrel. *Comprenez-vous?* So, when
dey want de car in de sea, dey come to me. I tell no one. Dey
know dat.'

Fisher nodded. 'When you pushed the car into the sea was
Gerald inside?'

'Gerald?'

'Mr Mather.'

'*Mais oui.* He was dead.'

'In the back or the front?'

'First in back. Then we move him to front.'

'Who's we, Abdulsalaam?'

'No.'

'Was it Julnar?'

He shrugged and continued to play with the money.

'Go on. You said he was in the back.'

'Yes. Bleeding.'

'Alive?'

'No. Dead, I told you.'

'How did he die?'

Abdulsalaam made the noise of an explosion. 'That's what she tells me –' He put a hand to his lips, realising his indiscretion.

'Julnar told you?'

Again the shrug.

'Then what happened?' Fisher asked. 'Tell me in English.'

'We put him in the front. Strap him in. She goes. I push. And what happens? The boot opens. There is the briefcase. I take it. And then I push the car in the sea.'

Fisher was conscious of an uncomfortable reaction within himself: he took, without hesitation, the servant's tone, the same view of events, lending to the conversation an ordinary, everyday quality, as though he, too, like Abdulsalaam, was in some way morally deficient. We're talking about violent death, he said to himself, about a bleeding corpse, about deception and theft, and Fisher accepted it all because he knew his senses had been blunted. To say you have done wrong to Abdulsalaam would be to provoke a look of bewilderment. Gerald had sometimes had that effect on him, too: a perverse logic, an absence of morality, black is white, right wrong; and the louder your protest the greater your isolation until yours seemed to be the only voice of reason, like being in a madhouse. And he remembered once remaining silent when Gerald said that both the guilty and the innocent must die in the cause of freedom.

Fisher said, 'And then you were paid?'

'No.'

'Well, what happened?'

Falsetto, he imitated the moathen's call from the minaret and chuckled.

'The moathen?' Fisher said.

'*Oui.* He sees me. I run.'

'When were you paid?'

He grinned wickedly. 'Before. I was paid before.'

'And then they came and asked about the papers?'

'*Oui.*'

'Julnar and Dr Swediq?'

'*Oui.*'

'Together?'

'No. First Swediq. Then Julnar.'

'What did you tell them?'

'That I have no papers. It's the truth.'

'But you didn't tell them about the briefcase?'

'No.'

'Why not?'

'They did not ask.'

'Abdulsalaam, would you tell all this to someone else?'

'No.'

'Why not?'

'No.' He was adamant.

'Why are you telling me?'

'Because you know about the briefcase. Because you are his brother. Because you pay me.'

'I'll pay you even more.'

'For what, *chéri?*'

'If you tell the police.'

The servant caught his breath and sucked his bottom lip. In a whisper he said, 'You not tell the police.'

'No. I won't. But I want you to.'

A smile creased Abdulsalaam's face and he looked up at the sky. 'I am so happy, *si heureux!*' He rose. 'Quack-quack-quack-quack,' he cackled, and began to strut round Fisher imitating the movements of a chicken, elbows twitching, chin poked forward, bottom arched. 'Quack-quack-quack-quack.' Now the bird became sinewy, seductive, slower in its undulations, developing hands like butterflies that floated before Fisher's eyes; the muscular body twisted and coiled, hips again thrusting forward savagely and often, a grotesque belly-dance, a snake. 'Hisssssssss...' The snake, its eyes never leaving Fisher's face, excited, penetrating eyes, licked its lips, made a sudden lunge, at once retreated, and slithered away, keeping close to the wall – 'Hisssssssss...' until it was lost to sight.

Fisher, clutching the handle of the briefcase with both hands, watched Abdulsalaam depart, and even when the servant could no longer be seen, the sound of his hissing, by some trick of acoustic, persisted. Slowly, deliberately, Fisher began to walk after him, back towards the white lodge, understanding intuitively that he must look neither right nor left, for to do so was to provoke danger. His ankle hurt.

In the ruined city, a ritual was being enacted. The Japanese youths had fanned out in front of Fisher, dotted in pairs like sentinels. Brogan had relinquished his perch, had come down the steps of the auditorium, and appeared in the deserted street, a tiny figure framed between two severed columns. Fisher walked on, his heart beginning to pound, seeing only what was at the outer limits of his field of vision – the Japanese and Brogan. For each step Fisher took, time was stretched to breaking point.

Near the white lodge, Fisher halted. The Japanese had once more formed up in a solid phalanx; Brogan Fisher could no longer see or sense. Because of the sloping ground Fisher observed, behind the Japanese, the two lodge-keepers playing draughts, and smelled the scent of eucalyptus; will they, he asked himself, come to my aid? Why do they sit there as though all was well?

Neither Fisher nor the Japanese youths moved; nothing moved. But when Fisher made to go to the right, they shuffled sideways in the same direction, like soldiers ordering ranks.

Fisher, in a voice not his own, called 'Hello-o-o!' hoping to catch the attention of the lodge-keepers and one did briefly look up but immediately resumed his game. Fisher glanced backwards but Brogan was not to be seen. Fisher had taken his eyes off the Japanese for two, three seconds, no more, and when he turned and faced them again they had, to his surprise, already spread themselves into an arc. The laughing one gurgled as though he was clearing his throat, and Fisher knew that something must be done, that help could not be expected from any other quarter but his own. He walked at them. Everything happened slowly and calmly: one made a grab for the briefcase, but Fisher held on tight and so they all closed in on him and screamed into his ears, short, piercing, savage screams, like wild birds; shocked, he lost control of his legs and fell on his knees, cowering as one who expects a death blow.

The screaming stopped abruptly. Brogan stood among them outraged, furiously berating them. 'Cut it out! You crazy or something? Cut it out!' He pushed them back clearing a space round Fisher. 'Tell them to stop it,' Brogan ordered the man who acted as interpreter. 'Tell them to do as they're told, no more, no less, tell them!' While the translation was made, Brogan helped Fisher to his feet, dusted him off, hovered protectively. 'Are you all right, Mr Fisher? I can't tell you how sorry I am, these guys are crazy. I owe you an apology and an explanation. C'mon, I'll get you home. C'mon now.' And he led Fisher, who still clutched the briefcase, through the dispirited Japanese ranks – they bowed to him as he went – past the white lodge where the keepers played draughts.

In a clearing they came upon Brogan's car and set off towards the city. Passing in sight of the lodge, Fisher saw the Japanese interpreter counting out notes and paying the keepers.

'They're crazy, those guys,' said Brogan, 'really crazy.'

3

Brogan talked without stop, obsessively, repetitively, and a little hysterically, often contradicting himself, as though the incident in the Ruins had released a brake, and the vehicle was out of control. When it was discovered that Fisher's knee was cut and his jeans torn, Brogan fussed and fumed like an elderly spinster. Fisher was given no opportunity to interrupt with either question or comment. The young man's instability was at odds with his solid, handsome, laundered appearance.

'I only said, "Don't let him leave until I've talked to him," and they have to go and behave like that, like refugees from a Kung Fu movie, y'know what I mean? They're crazy, those guys, really crazy. Heavens, I didn't mean them to harm you, I hope you appreciate that. I simply wanted to talk to you about the attaché case. Heaven knows what you must have thought! Were you frightened? I guess you were frightened, were you? All that screaming. I would've been frightened. Does your knee hurt? Is it still bleeding? We're gonna replace those jeans, have no fear about that, my friend, I'm gonna see to it that we replace those jeans.

'I guess you're wondering what I have to do with your attaché case, your brother's attaché case, your half-brother's attaché case, well, I'm gonna tell you, I'm gonna level with you, because you have had a terrible experience, and I want to make amends, I want you to be able to say when I'm through, "I forgive you, Joseph," that's what I want to hear you say.

'I have to explain and I have to apologise. You asked me at Aubrey's if I knew Mather, and I answered "no" – remember? Well, it was a half-lie, a half-truth, and I deeply regret it. I never met Mather, never met him face to face, although we once talked long distance on the phone, me in Boston, Massachusetts, and he here. So, when I said I didn't *know* him, that was true, but I knew *who* he was – so, I guess you could call it a half-truth. And I apologise for that. And I want you to know that I deeply regret not meeting him, and I want to offer my sympathy sincerely, and I want you to know I'm going to remember him in my prayers.

'I'm not gonna make any secret of the fact that Mr Mather and I work for Mr Fawzi. So do those crazy Japs. Well, not actually work *for* him, but *with* him. The only thing I'm gonna conceal is the nature of the work. But you can be sure that your half-brother and I were comrades, I guess I don't have to tell you any more.

'Well, it's like this. We're all waiting, waiting, you see, for a document that Mather hid or lost or burned, but we have just simply got to find out what he actually did with it. And I happen to think that you may have it in that attaché case. I'm gonna tell you a little more, perhaps I oughtn't to, but I'm gonna take a chance. The document we're looking for is a report on a guy Mather's had staked out for some time, a guy we need for a special duty. I can't say more than that, believe me, I may have said too much already. But whoever Mather's man is we've got to find him, and find him quickly, because there's a lot at stake, the personal freedom of at least two people, and God knows how many lost souls.'

4

Like a limpet he fixed himself to Fisher. When they reached the apartment block, Brogan insisted on helping him out of the car, but at the door to Gerald's flat, in the shadowy passage, Fisher said, 'Thank you very much. I hope to see you again.'

'I have some *Flash* I'd like to share with you,' Brogan said and took a small leather-covered flask from his back trouser pocket and grinned crookedly, an adolescent with forbidden fruit.

'No, thanks.'

'Hey, wait a moment, what about the case? I levelled with you, Mr Fisher, why, the least you can do is let me see what's inside it.'

'But I don't have a key for it.'

'We can break the lock.'

'But it's not yours. It's mine.'

'Oh, c'mon. I've explained. There may be a highly confidential document in there.'

A door farther down the passage opened a crack and a pair of eyes investigated and then disappeared. Fisher said, 'I'd like to examine my half-brother's papers myself. If there's anything that belongs to you or Mr Fawzi, I can let you know.'

'But this is urgent, Mr Fisher. I thought I explained.' He leaned across the door frame, his arm a bar to Fisher's entry, but his attitude was in no way threatening, exasperated rather, impatient.

'One more day won't make any difference, will it?'

'Just let me come in and we'll talk,' Brogan said, a whining note intruding.

'No,' said Fisher firmly. 'Now, please, let me pass. I'd like to bathe my knee and wash.'

Immediately Brogan withdrew his arm. 'Look, I'm not trying to stop you, don't get me wrong. I just think you ought to reconsider. C'mon, let's have a drink, discuss this like adults.' Saying that he looked more boyish than ever.

'Isn't that what we're doing?'

'What's the matter with you, Mr Fisher? I'm not here to make trouble. You may have something we want. Just let's see if it's in there, and then I'll go.'

'I don't think you understand what I'm saying. I want to examine these things in private,' Fisher said, finding the key to the flat.

Brogan again stretched out his arm across the door, casually, as though it was the only position in which he was comfortable. 'I'm sorry about what happened out there at the

Ruins. Those guys are crazy, I thought I explained. I thought you understood –'

'Yes, I do –'

'Then I tell you what,' Brogan said, slipping in between Fisher and the door so that Fisher was forced to retreat a step, still holding the key as if searching for the lock in mid-air. 'I'll come in. You open the case. I won't peep. You have a look at the stuff. If what I want is there, give it to me and I'll go.'

Again the door down the passage opened, the eyes flashed, the door closed. Fisher said, 'We're making too much noise –'

'Let me come in then –'

'No.'

Brogan shook his head sadly. 'I had you figured wrong, Mr Fisher.'

'Please, may I get into my flat?'

Brogan did not move. 'You looked kinda friendly when we met at Aubrey's. I thought we were – we were kindred souls. I thought you took a liking to me. You're not married, are you?' He narrowed his eyes, repeating the frank, sensual look Fisher had seen before. 'Are you? Are you married?'

'Are you?'

'C'mon,' Brogan replied quietly as though he expected Fisher to have more sense than to ask. 'Now you invite me in, okay?' Fisher hesitated. 'I promise you,' Brogan said, lowering his voice to a whisper, 'I'm on the side of the angels. I'm on Mr Mather's side. And I'll tell you what I think. I think you're on Mr Mather's side, too. Matter of fact, I think you're the guy we're expecting.'

'Why do you think that?' He had a stricken trace of memory: Gerald between two policemen saying, "This is Martin, he's my alibi." '

'Something about you fits. Hey, what are we doing out here in the passage? We're wasting time, Mr Fisher,' he said and smiled.

Fisher could feel the sweat running down his back. Brogan unscrewed the top of the flask and toasted Fisher. 'Cheers,' he said, 'isn't that what you Britishers say?' He took a swig and offered Fisher the flask but when Fisher made to take it, Brogan held back. 'Not out here,' he said intimately. 'Let's go in.'

With some effort, Fisher said softly, 'Get out of my way. Now.'

Brogan's eyes turned to stone. He studied Fisher's face holding the other's gaze, but there was no invitation in the look now, only anger.

'I don't know what your game is, Mr Fisher, but I have to tell you we're gonna get what we want whether you like it or not.' He pushed past Fisher who immediately set about opening the door, but his hand was trembling and he had difficulty fitting the key into the lock.

'Mr Fisher,' Brogan called. Fisher looked over his shoulder: the American was standing by the lift, leaning on the button. He said, 'Here,' and threw the leather-covered flask which Fisher caught awkwardly in the crook of his arm but it dropped to the floor. 'Sorry,' said Brogan, 'but you'll need a drink, and I don't want you to think of me as uncharitable. I'm gonna remember you in my prayers.' The lift arrived and Brogan stepped in.

Fisher quickly gathered up the flask, managed to open the door and almost fell into the flat. Down the hall the inquisitive neighbour peered out into the shadow for the third time, but the passage was empty.

5

Fisher drank deep. Brogan had frightened him: why did the American think that Fisher was expected? And by whom? (And Fisher heard again the barbaric cries of the Japanese.) What snare had Gerald posthumously set? Fisher's head began to spin and the briefcase hung like a dead weight in his hand. Now he acknowledged that all previous hope he may have nursed of Gerald's forgiveness had turned to ice.

In the kitchen Fisher found a kebab-skewer and a meat-hammer. Placing the point of the skewer in the lock, he tapped gently with the hammer. The lock held. He assembled more tools: a tin opener, a steel, another skewer. He fiddled and strained for almost five minutes, pausing only to drink, until the lock suddenly gave. On his trousers he wiped his hands dry of sweat, and opened the case. He saw first his cable to Gerald – ARRIVING GENOA FERRY 15TH PLEASE MEET – and then a dozen or more large, unmarked manilla envelopes, some fat with papers, others looking to contain nothing at all. He sprawled on the bed and searched each envelope in turn.

First, Fisher found money, a wad of five pound notes. He laughed out loud. He counted the money: three hundred pounds, more than enough to pay his air fare and to settle his debts in Rome. Tomorrow, he rejoiced, I can get out of here, and he thought of it as escape. He drank in the spirit of celebration.

From another envelope he removed a sheaf of papers covered in technical drawings of some circular object like a yo-yo. In the third envelope he discovered typewritten pages stapled together and headed CONFIDENTIAL REPORT but in code – AJLZ PTRY VIZX JKQW it began – and Fisher murmured, 'That's broken my dream.' In the fourth he found photographs which surprised and baffled him: of his old school in South London taken from several angles. He squinted at the prints. At first he wasn't absolutely certain that it was his school, but the Victorian schoolhouse with its pitched roof was unmistakable; what confused him were the new buildings, erected since his time, long, low, flat, all glass and coloured wall panels, stifling in summer, he guessed, freezing in winter. But it was the old building, looking somehow disapproving of modernity, which stirred his memory and he smelled again the classroom, the wide, tiled corridors, the lavatories and changing-rooms, stale cheese sandwiches, urine and chalk.

Hadn't Paola Wirrel said she'd given Gerald photographs? Fisher couldn't remember. Why of the school? He cursed Gerald for being secret and unpredictable as though he were still alive.

The next envelope contained a packet of letters held by an elastic band, heavy dark-blue paper with scalloped edge, the first beginning, 'One'.

The thought that he should not read the letters from Paola Wirrel to Gerald never entered his head; even before he had time to make a scrupulous conscientious decision he was half-way through the first letter and he read, in all, twelve. To begin with, he was shocked by what they contained: towards the end, he was randy.

In a way, Fisher supposed, they could be thought of as love

letters, obscene love letters, filled with intimate, minute details of what sexual acts they would perform at their next meeting, held before the reader like an aphrodisiac. Her descriptions were explicit and immodest; the language ugly and artless, as though an added excitement and pleasure came from using words she would at other times censor. The limit of her sexual vocabulary, both verbal and imaginative, was quickly reached. From the fourth or fifth letter onwards, the writing was repetitive and there being so few words in English to suit her purpose she resorted to synonyms in Italian, in Arabic and Serbo-Croat, in turn comic, distasteful and exciting; by the time he came to the last letter, he felt as though he were reading a monstrous, prurient litany, a libidinous, hypnotic chant. And he was randy.

The afternoon had surrendered to dusk. The evening summons from the mosques issued forth over the city. Fisher lay amidst the contents of Gerald's case, the papers strewn across him, on the bed, spilling on to the floor. I shall be gone tomorrow, he thought. I shall buy a one-way ticket and go. He dozed fitfully, the flat suffused in the fluorescent light of streetlamps and the bright early evening moon. Later, he dialled the number of the hairdresser. To the woman who answered, he said, 'Please tell Mrs Wirrel that her dress is ready for collection.'

6

A note of self-congratulation entered Fisher's drowsy euphoria: luck had been on his side, he had found enough money to slip out of reach. He took Anne's photograph and, chuckling inanely, kissed it. Content, he reflected that to return Paola's letters was the least he could do: it seemed an honourable act. He counted the money again and remembered, as though he'd been stung, Harvey Nash. He reached for the telephone and dialled.

'No luck, I'm afraid with Abdulsalaam –' Fisher lied.

Nash interrupted. 'I can't talk just now. I've got somebody with me.' There was an unusual tension in his voice.

'I couldn't find out anything. He may have pushed the car into the harbour, on the other hand –'

'I can't talk now –'

'Well, I'm off tomorrow, so I'll say goodbye.'

'Just as well. Better to drop the whole thing anyway.' Yeah, yeah.

'Goodbye, then.'

'*Wa-aleikum assalaam.*'

He dropped the receiver on to its cradle as though it were infected. Easier than I'd imagined, he thought. He rose and showered vigorously as if he were washing off deeply embedded grime. He recited aloud:

'All, all of a piece throughout:
Thy chase had a beast in view;
Thy wars brought nothing about;
Thy lovers were all untrue.
'Tis well an old age is out,
And time to begin a new.'

He decided to mark this conviction that somehow he'd escaped a terrible danger and had been given the chance to make a fresh start by treating himself to an expensive meal.

He took two tenners from the wads of notes; the rest of the money, together with the other papers, he returned to the briefcase, which he slid under the bed; Paola's letters he replaced in their manilla envelope and stuffed it into his shoulder-bag.

He found a restaurant with an imitation crystal chandelier hanging from a peg-board ceiling and playing the Russian folk-song 'Kalinka' over and over again. The walls, the same hospital green as in the Hotel Afreka, were decorated with garish, chocolate-box paintings of Swiss lakes, snow-covered Alps and wooden chalets. Above the service hatch was a calendar with a colour photograph of men at work in a heavy machinery plant, and on the glass doors to the street transfers of Donald Duck and Bambi. The food was Italian; both the *spaghetti milanese* and the *osso bucco* were flavoured with pine nuts and spiced olive oil to render them indistinguishable; he was given to drink the juice of blood oranges; he was the only customer. Tomorrow, he thought, I shall buy my ticket and be quit of the place; but he hesitated for one moment: when he was at the desk paying his bill, he saw through an open door a girl in a cream overall, on her knees, scrubbing the tiled floor of the women's lavatory. Something about her was familiar and, as she turned, he recognised Julnar. She did not see him. His impulse was to question her but he stopped himself. Resist, he said. Escape. He paid and walked out into the street feeling light-headed.

Paola's blue Volkswagen was parked outside the apartment block. She must have seen him approaching: she waved. When he drew level she said, 'Where've you been? Get in quickly. I've been waiting nearly an hour. We mustn't be seen. Please keep low in the seat.'

She headed towards the harbour. 'You've got the letters?'

'Yes.'

'You haven't read them, have you?'

'No.'

'They're very private.'

'I can give them to you now,' Fisher said. 'There's no need –'

'No, no,' she answered quickly. 'I want some help.'

She stopped first at the corner kiosk and bought two tins of fruit juice, Hope's Peach Nectar, made in Japan. Then she took the perimeter road along the harbour – the road Fisher had walked on the day he arrived – and parked within the giant legs of a tall crane. She turned off the headlamps. Fisher tried to give her the letters but she refused them as if she was not yet ready. They both lit cigarettes, tore the metal strips off the tins and gazed out at the harbour, at the lights from the ships, small squares of yellow, uneven in perspective, at the silhouettes of other cranes, and at the blackness of the water. The smell of oil and fish mingled with Paola's heady scent.

'Yes, give them to me,' she said.

Fisher handed her the large envelope. She peeked inside. 'Thank God, thank God,' she whispered and then turned to him, threw her arms round his neck and kissed him a dozen times on his forehead, his cheeks, his eyes. 'Thank you, thank you,' she said and laughed wildly, tossing her head as though to rid herself of unpleasant memories. 'Please, please, come and help,' she said.

Obediently he followed her to a sheltered corner formed by the angle of two metal plates riveted to a leg of the crane. From her handbag she took a cigarette-lighter and asked Fisher to light it. One by one, she burned her letters to Gerald, she burned the manilla envelope as well. 'It's better to do this,' she said. 'There's no danger now.'

Observing her in the sudden flares of the burning paper, Fisher saw for the first time, as if he hadn't dared face her before, that she was wearing a long evening gown, her shoulders covered in a fur stole – imitation or real, he wondered? Around her neck, the gold cross on its chain and a more elaborate choker, a velvet band surmounted by a cameo which was matched to a pair of earrings. Her hair was swept back and to one side, kept in place by a comb. She looked aristocratic and handsome. Fisher could not reconcile the woman who stood opposite him with the writer of the letters, whose embers, caught in the cold wind, bounced along the quay and into the water. When there was nothing left to burn, she said, 'Let's walk.'

In silence they strolled along the road towards the berth where the ferry from Genoa was moored. The sound of a radio tuned to a frenetic pop group floated across to them, and even though the beat was violent and insistent it seemed to Fisher a sad, despairing tune. The wind grew colder and buffeted them as they walked farther and farther along the quay. Fisher turned up the collar of his jacket, thrust his hands deep into the pockets of his jeans and said, 'Can't we go back to the car?'

'In a moment,' she said.

He had the impression that she walked now in the cold night simply to have company, to alleviate perhaps the strain of secret mourning. Nothing about her was certain, fixed. It was as though he was meeting someone new for the first time: the nervous, frightened, silent woman whom he had met in the Suk – 'spiritual matters are important to me,' she had said – was someone else; this creature now was serene and stately, born, he speculated, because the concerns of the first had been assuaged, the letters discovered and destroyed, in need of sympathetic companionship; and there was the third Paola, the one he had not seen but read – 'a high-class whore,' Nash had called her, 'and sometimes not so high-class' – she, venting her crude sexual appetite, he could not fathom at all: yet, he was able to admit, it was the third who most intrigued him.

'Thank you,' she said, 'for what you've done. Knowing that my love for Gerald won't be dragged through the mud, makes certain things possible for me. It has taught me a lesson. I won't squander the experience, I promise you.'

'No more affairs?' he said not meaning to sound insolent but in his mind addressing the whore.

She shot a look at him, an enquiring, suspicious look. She said, 'Sometimes you remind me terribly of Gerald.'

'Isn't that painful?' he asked, wishing he could keep the disapproval of her from his voice.

'Why painful?'

'To be reminded of what you've lost.'

'I have to cry somewhere,' she said.

'But you're not crying now.'

'Oh, yes, I am.'

They had reached the ferry. A patchwork of light glowed in the stern. On the foredeck, someone explored by torchlight and, against the sky, Fisher recognised the stooping, hunched figure of the Captain, the ferryman, Charon.

Perhaps, Fisher thought, it was grief that had fractured her. He had no insight in that direction, no way of imagining a sorrow so deep and arcane it could not manifest itself in tears. Suddenly, he wanted to touch her, a gesture of sympathy and apology, not of lust, but when he glanced at her she was leaning over to adjust the strap of her evening shoes, and in the V of her dress he saw her breasts, could sense their weight and texture. To want her astonished him and in his effort to still his randiness, he turned away and watched the ferryman on his lonely rounds. He sensed her beside him and caught her appraising him in a disconcerting way as though she'd read his thoughts. The notion that, by her look, she was suggesting that she may in turn want him intruded; he allowed the fancy to linger, then dismissed it: he knew too well the danger of masculine assumptions.

Yet, when she next spoke, she echoed something of what had passed through his mind. 'It's been my misfortune to fall in love with complex men. I seem to attract them. Perhaps it's because I'm not really very clever. Are you complex? There are always dangers, even in grief.'

He laughed, not to mock her, but in surprise; and far away, as though on board one of the ships they, too, had been amused, Fisher's laughter was briefly answered. They walked back the way they had come.

They were both cold by the time they reached the car; her teeth were chattering. Once inside, she drained the last of the drink. She said, 'I've always been subjected to extremes, you know. I'm either extremely happy or extremely sad or extremely nothing. My first husband was horribly rich. Nigs is horribly poor. I used to have servants and houses, Paris clothes and champagne. Now look at me. I make my own clothes and I drink Hope's Peach Nectar.' She wound down the window and tossed the can on to the quay, clattering like a broken toy. She caused silence to come between them again, as she had in the café, long and ungainly. Then, she wept, though not with abandon : her body shuddered no more than it did from the cold. One eye filled with a huge, solitary tear. Fisher could not prevent himself from taking her hand, and she did not resist. He leaned towards her and cradled her in his arms. A reflex, he found himself gently and repeatedly kissing her forehead and his hand went down the V of her dress to her breast. She pulled away violently. 'I don't want your sympathy!' Her eyes were blazing. 'Don't treat me like a whore!'

She didn't allow him to apologise or explain. She started up the car and headed back towards the town, sitting on the very edge of the driving seat, her back unnaturally stiff and erect. They were just gathering speed when she said, 'You bastard! How dare you!' and then jammed on the brakes : Fisher was thrown forward, bumping his head against the windscreen hard enough to hurt. Paola turned on him and beat him with her fists. 'You did read the letters,' she cried, 'you read them, didn't you, you read them! That's why you think I'm a whore!'

He covered his head with both arms to ward off her blows, tried to open the door to get out but, abruptly, the attack ceased. She closed her eyes, leaning back, weakened by the effort. Barely audible she said again, 'You did read them, didn't you?'

Fisher hoped she would take his silence as an admission. He was alarmed by her, aware she was on a knife-edge, frightened of which way she might fall.

'I'll never be safe now,' she said, the tempo too fast.

'You've burned them. You're safe,' he said to calm her.

'No. Not with your knowing.'

'I don't matter. I'm leaving tomorrow.'

'You frighten me. Gerald frightened me, too.'

'I'm not Gerald.'

'He was sick, you know, a very sick man.'

'Was he? I didn't know –' He tried to sound sympathetic.

'Oh yes, very sick indeed. He had very great problems. Terrible, terrible difficulties. My mistake was to think that I was the cure.'

'The cure?'

'That I, me, personally, my presence, what I am, was the cure. Not the nurse, but the medicine itself, do you see? Do you see?'

'What was wrong with him? Tell me?'

'He was dead.'

'Dead,' Fisher repeated.

'Do you understand what I mean when I say dead? I don't mean spiritually, I don't mean intellectually, I mean physically dead.'

'No, I don't understand.'

'Impotent, not sterile, impotent. He used to cry tears of stone.' Her teeth chattered loudly. 'I wanted your brother. He just wanted. Expectation, I thought, would help him as it helped me. The letters, that's why the letters. Nothing helped. He couldn't give of himself. I behaved like a man.' She laughed emptily.

Fisher remembered Abdulsalaam saying he'd come upon them in the Ruins. *Ils ne baisaient pas ... Il pleurait.*

'At the end,' she said, 'he did a terrible thing to me. I gave him a gift, it was meant to be a parting gift and he knew it, but he didn't like letting go. So he told Aubrey we only went to his classes as an excuse to meet. He knew that would hurt me. I need contact with things outside myself. I need to be in touch. And Aubrey thanked him for being honest and scolded me for selling myself short. People have always said that. That I denigrate myself too much. I said to Aubrey, "Can't you see I'm empty, less than empty; and even less than that?" "You must take her away," he said. "I cannot bear blasphemy." '

118

'Why did you read that poem over Gerald's ashes?' Fisher asked gently sensing that to assert himself would be to intrude, but understanding that she needed to unburden.

The necklet went into her mouth. 'Gerald would have loathed me for that.' She looked to be smiling. 'Out of a kind of spite, I cried with relief, I thought I was free of him, but I'm not. He still *terrorises* me.'

No more was said; she reached into her handbag, found a small bejewelled pill-case and took out a capsule which she swallowed. She started the car and set off towards the town; when she reached The Square, she stopped and waited for Fisher to get out. He stood on the island of the shoe-blacks watching the car disappear at speed.

7

Even before he opened the door to the flat, Fisher smelled the insecticide; when he entered he saw the devastation and was moved to fury almost as if he himself had been attacked. The bedclothes had been pulled from the bed, the wardrobe emptied, the lid of the record-player unhinged, the records of Chopin, Rachmaninoff and Schumann ripped from torn sleeves: only the bust of the Colonel with the broken nose remained in place. Fisher stumbled over an upturned chair; he crawled to look under the bed: the briefcase was gone; the money was gone. Fisher shivered, as Paola had done, but with a kind of desperate, burning fever. And his forehead which he had struck on the windscreen of her car began to ache.

He fumbled in his pocket for the card with the Embassy's telephone number – would there be a Duty Officer at night? – but the telephone was dead, he could get no dialling tone. And, as he stood, gazing helplessly at the wreckage, he was conscious that the sense of loss had returned. He felt as though the room should be littered with corpses.

Someone knocked on the door and called his name. He heard a key inserted and the door opened. Julnar entered a little diffidently, like a hotel maid who'd come at an inconvenient moment, but Fisher was oddly reassured by her appearance as though familiar faces were always comforting. Behind her stood Mr Fawzi's chauffeur with the scratch down his cheek and in his hand the soiled handkerchief stained with congealed blood.

'You remember me, please. I am Julnar. This is Wanis. You must please to come with us, Mr Fisher,' Julnar said. She carried a handbag which looked out of place. As at the funeral she was dressed entirely in black; on her upper lip were beads of sweat. Fisher remembered her being sick in the boat.

'Where to?' Fisher asked. Why am I so docile? he wondered.

'Mr Fawzi wants please to see you.'

'Mr Fawzi?'

'Please to come.'

'Have you taken my money? Where's my money? I must have it otherwise I can't leave tomorrow –' he wished he could prevent himself from sounding servile.

'Please to bring your passport.'

Wanis said nothing but pointed to his cheek, then wagging his forefinger under Fisher's nose as a warning. Julnar spoke sharply to him; the boy, puffy like a school bully, lowered his eyes and rubbed his chin moodily.

In the street the black Cadillac waited. Julnar sat with Fisher in the back. Like being in a funeral procession, he thought: and he recalled again the last time he had seen Gerald, returning from the cemetery. (But, Gerald, I haven't any money.)

The car entered the gates to a house that Fisher vaguely remembered: was this not the place Nash had called the sewage farm? And when he was shown indoors the smell of flykiller was strong, and they seemed to follow it until they entered a large bare room, dimly lit by an oil lamp, where the smell was stronger still. There was no furniture but the floor was strewn with cushions and pillows. A tall, emaciated blond man, all eyes and nose, wearing a Mao Tse-Tung suit, paced up and down anxiously and was made more anxious by their entrance. Julnar disappeared through a door.

He said, bowing, 'Engineer Holmqvist,' and edged close to Fisher, whispering with some urgency, 'I have a terrible hotel. I'm sharing with two Germans. One of them's blind.'

Julnar was absent no more than a minute. 'Mr Fawzi is ready, Mr Fisher,' she said. 'He will see you now.' And as

Fisher turned, he saw, or thought he saw, in Fawzi's office, the dwarfish moathen disappear through a door behind the desk.

8

Mr Fawzi's office was littered with dead flies like stale currants, and the stench of insecticide made Fisher retch. Everywhere there were papers, books and files; a map of the world hung to one side of a curtained arch, photographs of the Colonel and the late President Nasser on the other. Two deep leather armchairs faced Fawzi who sat behind his untidy desk, and on the desk lay Gerald's briefcase, open. Beside it stood an aerosol can of fly-killer which Fawzi used often and with deadly accuracy, letting loose short, vicious bursts at any and every insect that came into sight. Lighting one cigarette from another he stared at Fisher with anxious, bulging eyes. Fisher noticed tiny nicks on his neck and chin from shaving carelessly.

He had forgotten how intensely the man stared, and how stricken the look, as though he'd just learned he'd contracted an incurable disease.

Fawzi rose and opened his arms in welcome. He said, 'I apologise from my heart for all the trouble you've been given. What you must think of us! Please, please accept my apologies.' The pleasantries were forced, spoken like protests, and the hoarseness, Fisher supposed, came from a lifetime of inhaling insecticide and cigarette smoke.

But it was the sight of the briefcase lying brazenly on the desk that rekindled Fisher's sullen anger. 'I want my money back,' he said. 'I want to get out of here. I want to take the first flight out tomorrow,' he said firmly, trying to keep fear from his voice.

'Don't be in such a hurry,' Fawzi said, clearing his throat of phlegm. 'Please, sit down, we will drink tea, we have many things to discuss, I owe you explanations.' He nodded to Wanis who disappeared through the door behind Fawzi's desk. Julnar stood beside Fisher and guided him into one of the armchairs as though he were an invalid; she remained at his back, on guard.

Fawzi took one of the envelopes from the briefcase and sat in the other armchair which he shifted nearer to Fisher so that their knees were almost touching. When Wanis returned, he served the glasses of lemon tea and honey, then set at Fawzi's feet the aerosol can and a lid of a biscuit tin for ash.

'Now, where to begin, where to begin,' he said removing papers from the envelope and shuffling them. A fly overhead distracted him: he grabbed hold of the aerosol can and opened fire wildly, shooting in all directions until the thing dropped to the floor. 'Ah, yes,' he said, 'now I remember. Look, it's like this. Your brother Gerald, half-brother, was my very close friend, my very close colleague. In this Ministry we deal in highly secret matters. Oil is now such a commodity that people in your country, in America, in other countries behave like men did in ancient times towards gold. Technical secrets, sources must be guarded and so on. Oil is the new reality.' Everything was said as though the man was in pain.

'Oil,' Fisher repeated, staring at an ashtray on the desk overflowing with butts and ash and dead flies.

Fawzi smiled: his teeth were yellow. 'I am a philosopher,' he explained. 'It is my metaphor.'

'For what?'

'Like with the best philosophers that is for you to guess. You are a teacher – you will know what I mean. I have lectured on oil or what I call oil. How slippery it is, you understand, how untrustworthy. I try to show it has no reality at all. It is a philosophical lecture.'

'How did you know I was a teacher?' Fisher asked.

'Yes, in Accra, am I not right? Sip your tea while it is hot.' He paused to light a cigarette. 'What a very uncivilised way they behaved towards you. Very puritanical, I think, to deport you for such reasons.' He made an expression of disapproval. 'Here such an immorality charge is impossible. For such an offence we would never deport a man. Half the male population would have to live elsewhere.' His laugh resembled an escape of fly-killer. 'But for drinking alcohol we may deport a man.'

Fisher remained silent and still: he felt as though the insecticide could, at any instant, be turned against him.

'But first things first,' Fawzi said. 'I was telling you about Gerald. For reasons that cannot be confided let me say at once that his death was an accident. And we had to, how do they say in America, make a cover-up?' He blasted at a mosquito before continuing. 'Believe me, if I knew – had known, d'you say? – that Gerald had a brother, a half-brother who was coming here, I would never have allowed the particular circumstance of suicide to be used as a camouflage. I am extremely sorry. I know what it's like to lose a brother. Or a son. That man Nash caused you a lot of unpleasantness, but I don't believe he will cause you any more.

'So, in this Ministry of ours, we sometimes have jobs, missions of a highly secret nature. For one such mission we required a British subject – I can't explain at this moment why – and I discussed the problem with Gerald. He said he had just the person in mind, but he didn't tell me who. You remember how secretive he was, how – do you say close to the breast? But he *did* tell me he was having a report made. Unfortunately, he died before he had time to have it decoded or to show it to me. Have a look –' and he turned one of the papers in his hand for Fisher to see: CONFIDENTIAL REPORT, it read and beneath the meaningless letters Fisher had seen before – AJLZ PTRY VIZX JKQW – was printed in pen: TO G. A. M. SUBJECT PLACED UNDER SURVEILLANCE IN ACCRA –

'You see,' Fawzi said, withdrawing the page, 'until we got hold of this document in the briefcase we didn't know of your existence. One of Gerald's little jokes. His own half-brother!'

The tear-sodden face of Anne burst into Fisher's head: the sensation of falling ended; he splintered into meaningless pieces. But he summoned all his strength so that Fawzi would not be able to see that he was no longer whole. Fawzi's attention, however, was not on Fisher: his starting eyes searched for victims in the air. Suddenly he stood, leaned towards the photograph of the Colonel and destroyed a fly in the vicinity of the left eye; when the vapour cleared it looked as though the Colonel was crying. Satisfied, Fawzi resumed his seat and leaning towards Fisher in an intimate, gossipy way, said, 'Tell me something, there's a point not absolutely clear from the report regarding the circumstances of the immorality charge and the subsequent deportation. Who reported you to the Headmaster? The boy? Or the girl you were living with, this woman, Anne?'

Fisher covered his face with his hands; his forehead ached and was beginning to swell.

'It was the girl, wasn't it?' Fawzi said regretfully. 'Not very understanding of her, but I gather from the report that it wasn't the first time. And yes, there's another thing I don't quite understand. The report says you have no political or religious views. Is that right? Can such a thing be possible? But now that I meet you and see you face to face, I think it's probably right. Fascinating. No principles whatsoever. Your tea is getting cold.' He stood once more and lifted Fisher up to embrace him warmly, pulling his face into his chest against the grubby maroon cardigan. 'Yes, yes, you will do the job well,' he said. 'It's not a difficult task, and don't worry, you will, of course, be well paid. There is much money in oil.'

Fisher reacted unexpectedly: the stench, the insinuation, the Arab's false, ingratiating manner caused a residue of anger to erupt. Fisher pushed him away hard with both hands. Fawzi reeled backwards, sitting unwillingly on the desk top, his eyes wilder than ever. Wanis and Julnar both stepped forward, ready to pounce.

Fisher said, 'Give me back my money. It's mine. You've no right to it. Give it back to me. I won't have anything to do with you.' And as the words tumbled out Fisher regretted them: he had shown how vulnerable he was, like a child putting on a front of useless defiance.

In anger, Fawzi's voice rasped. 'Don't talk to me like that. I treat you with the utmost courtesy and this is how you behave? You are beneath my contempt.' He stubbed out his cigarette. 'I have spared your feelings, but I'll tell you what it says here about you. It says you are a man without principle, without moral fibre. It says you are pathetic. I don't care what you do, whether it's women, boys, girls, or donkeys, but to leave this woman pregnant, that's a disgraceful thing to do. You are pathetic!'

'I didn't know she was pregnant –' Fisher protested feebly.

'Didn't you? Didn't you know she was bulging with your child when you were in bed with that boy? Didn't you? It's all here in black and white, so don't you try to be smart with me. You know what it says here? It says you have debts of two hundred and eighty-seven pounds and that if we pay you three hundred you will do anything. Gerald knew you well. You are like all your kind, you will do anything for money. You are a piece of shit and don't you forget it.'

From far off, through a honeycomb of walls, came the muffled night-summons to prayer. *God is most great. God is most great. God is most great. God is most great.*

Fawzi said, 'Take him out of here,' and after Fisher was led from the room, the Arab disappeared through the curtained arch.

PART FOUR

I

In solitude, Mr Fawzi prepared to face reality: his daily landscape was inhabited by shadows, but his reality, flesh, blood,
concrete, was Faith. He dwelt inwardly on a rarefied plane of
existence which his imagination likened to a perpetual
journey, a pilgrimage towards what he called the Eternal
Absolute. His life was submission to the Will of God. Allah was
the Ultimate Being, the Ultimate Reality, the rest of life, the
shadows, His fulfilment. Mr Fawzi thought in these terms; the
words had profound meaning for him.

From the mosques the call, the *Azan*, went out across the
city, over the outskirts and the army camps which ring the
place, out over the sands dotted with green scrub, out along
the coast and into the vast, empty desert. In darkness the final
call pervades the air and the faithful pray. *God is most great –*
four times; *I testify there is no God but God –* twice; *I testify
that Mohammed is the Prophet of God –* also twice. *Come to
prayer. Come to salvation. Prayer is better than sleep, God is
most great. There is no God but God –* four times.

Mr Fawzi had watched them take the European from the
room and then turned to pass through the curtained arch into
a small alcove which was his sanctuary. He had to rid his mind
of that useless, weak, failed man, that Al Ahram caricature
whose hair was too long and whose reality was money. They
are all the same, thought Mr Fawzi: they have no other
god.

In his sanctuary, following the prescribed order and using an
enamel ewer and basin, Mr Fawzi washed his hands, gargled
and inhaled water up each nostril; he doused his face, his arms
up to the elbows, his head, his ears and last of all his feet. He
faced the *Ka'aba*, the blessed stone in Mecca, and recited the
salat beginning, 'Praise be to Allah, the Cherisher and Sustainer
of the World, the Compassionate...'

After obeying the rules of prayer and the obligations of prayer, reciting the *Sûra* and the *Fâtiha*, he thanked God for sending him the European so that the mission which he had planned could now be undertaken, and he dedicated the mission to glorify Allah's name and he called it The Piercing of the Enemy's Heart.

For the fifth time that day Mr Fawzi came fully to himself, entering upon a vision of the infinite. The finite world, the hours between his devotions, what others may call reality, was the dimmer landscape where he encountered the shadows. Here, at prayer, his belief was in one God, in angels, prophets, in the revealed books, in the Day of Judgement and in Fate and in the piercing of the enemy's heart. He fell on to his knees, victim to a fearsome spacelessness as though the organs of his body flew from their moorings leaving him empty. A numbness set about his brain, a buzzing sound, a hiss of air escaping and he sensed the unravelling of knots, the lifting of a curtain, the submission to the Ultimate Will.

2

Harvey Nash emerged from the lavatory and washed his hands. Out of the medicine cabinet he took a bottle of Dettol and dabbed the scratches on his chest; he winced. In his room where he brewed the liquor he found a joss stick and lit it to cleanse the air of the smell of insecticide which seemed to be everywhere. He still trembled and had to return to the lavatory for the fourth or fifth time since Mr Fawzi's visit.

He examined the octagonal rosewood table in the hall. The magazines and newspapers lay scattered on the polished floor, and the table itself was horribly scratched, deep, venomous, irreparable scars made by the girl with the point of a scissors. They knew how to get a man, Nash thought. Oddly enough, the scratches she had made on his chest did not hurt him half as much as the damage to the table. He would have it dumped on the waste ground near the Afreka, he decided; it was worthless now.

He poured himself a large drink and gradually became calmer, or simply anaesthetised his pain and fear. He wondered why his bowels had been affected so by fright. He shambled into his office, drew the curtains and sat heavily at his desk. He wanted to escape the present, wanted to forget the threats and the sudden violence and the scratches on his rosewood table. He had his own way of retreating into himself; he thought of it as finding a second presence that shied away from light.

On his record-player he placed a recording of Schubert's Great C major Symphony, number 9. To the noble sound of the muted horn, introducing the heroic and sublime melody he wrote out what he had been working on all afternoon in a fair hand, before he had been interrupted:

> O Paola, Francesco's love,
> The whiteness of thy skin the dove
> Is pleased to emulate.
> Thy lustrous hair
> The Queen of Troy must envy.
> Paola, beloved, to the flowers of the field
> Comparison is bleak, for do they wield
> Thy power over me?
> Come, be mine, for I am doomed to wait
> Alone and loyal at thy gate.

The music gained in tempo and tension, an agitated rhythm in the strings signalling a warning, the trombones re-affirming belief in the power of beauty. There is a rising note, a questioning, lyrical melody that transported Nash into secret realms where, to the question, 'What is possible?' the answer comes, 'Everything.'

He wrote more:

I begin plainly like this, because no words are able to describe adequately how you should be addressed. The little poem I enclose gives you some indication that my feelings are in no way altered, but only some indication. I have not muse enough to express fully my deepest emotions. Please, please, don't return the poem as you've done the others. Keep it, I beg you. If you favour me in no other way, favour me with acceptance of this verse. A smile from you would mean much when we next meet. If we next meet. I sit listening to Schubert. The tunes, every one, say Paola, Paola,

Paola, until I think I shall go mad. You occupy my thoughts every hour of the day. I ask nothing but to be allowed to sit with you alone, to talk and gaze on you.

Yours with a true heart,

Harvey Nash.

P.S. I want you to keep my records – Schumann, Chopin and Rachmaninoff, I think I am obliged shortly to take a trip abroad. Please let us meet before then. Music is my chief solace.

H.N.

He laid down his pen and listened to the music. He rose once to turn over the record. In its finality which clearly spoke to him of the spirit's triumph over darkness, Nash cried. He could not ever remember listening to Schubert's Great Symphony without the tears streaming down his cheeks.

3

She drew circles, endlessly, one after the other, filling page upon page upon page; occasionally the circles overlapped or bisected each other; for the most part they were separate. The circle was Paola's image of self-containment; the drawing of them a kind of therapy. Each circle represented a life. She wished to draw one that would stand for her, but each time she said to herself, this is me, she was compelled to draw a second circle in collision, interrupting. When the final call to prayer went out over the city, she paused, confronted by a blank page: its very emptiness and whiteness hypnotised her. This is me, she thought. Gerald has done this to me. I have contracted his impotence.

She worked in what they called 'the spare room' though it contained no bed and was crammed with her canvases, sketch-books, paints, crayons, a large trunk and several suitcases. From the bedroom she could hear Nigel on the telephone.

'The Carsons want to know if we're going to hear Winzer on Thursday?'

'Who's Winzer?'

'The pianist. A Beethoven recital.'

'Can I make up my mind later?'

Later, her husband put his head round the door. 'Am I disturbing you?' he asked.

'No.'

'Do you want something to drink? Coffee? Tea? Cocoa? Milk?'

'No, thank you.'

'Are you going on working?'

'Yes.'

'I'll be doing my Arabic. Don't be late.'

'No.'

An hour passed before she decided she would wash and change into her nightdress, a long virtuous garment with frills; she took her third Valium of the day. When she passed the bedroom she saw Nigel in bed, listening through an earphone to a Teach Yourself Arabic cassette, following the lesson from a textbook on his lap and repeating 'La tit-akhar, don't be late, la tit-akhar, don't be late'; he smiled at her. She returned to the spare room, sat, folded her hands on her lap, stared into space and entertained a lengthy stillness in which no thoughts occurred, in which she welcomed nothingness. Her face washed clean of make-up, her hair loose, she looked like a lost child waiting for someone to claim her.

The tranquilliser did not entirely release the tensions within her, but rather distanced her from them, put them into another, more bearable perspective. With the gradual acknowledgement of this emptiness, she took up her sketchbook and with a red crayon began idly to draw, lines now, rectangles, graceful arcs giving them shape and form. The figure of a woman emerged, wrapped in paper tied with fancy bows like a Christmas present from a smart department store; in broad cartoon style she outlined another female body in a shroud, unwinding; she drew a drooping reed in water; with sweeping strokes she composed a pyramid of stones, one upon the other, like a simple monument; a supplicant hand appeared and, with her thumb, she smudged the colours to give the effect of decay; she drew a skull. The act of drawing slowly but surely released a flow of thought, tentative and circuitous, but one that gave her confidence to confront, however timidly, however briefly, her self. She believed the act of drawing kindled the inner process. The final sketch was of a child in school uniform, dead.

4

Nigel Wirrel watched his wife more diligently than any keeper. He invented excuses to look in on her in the spare room, to ask a question, to test her awareness. He could not bear the thought that she might be ill again and retreat into that dreadful, silent despair as she had after Mather's death. But for the past day or two he had been anxious: he knew too well the symptoms; he knew too well the cause. What had Mather done to her, he wondered?

He lay in bed, his knees raised to make a rest for his Arabic textbook, the earpiece from the cassette pressed into his ear. He did not notice that he had the textbook upside down. He ran the tape on, well past the lesson on reflexive pronouns, until he came to a gap in the tape, and then to Dr Swediq's toneless uninvolved voice:

'There is something planned for the day after tomorrow. They call it a Parade. As far as can be ascertained it has no other code name, so my belief is that it is part of a patriotic celebration of some sort. I am not able to confirm whether Fisher is a fully fledged member of the organisation. Certainly, he is spending tonight in the house I am reliably informed. The flat has been given to a Swede named Holmqvist who is, I have learned, G's replacement. I am given to understand that some pressure was brought to bear on Harvey Nash for asking too many embarrassing questions. He has been persuaded, I understand, to take a short holiday. To the other matter –'

Paola entered and he switched off the machine. 'All right?' he asked.

She nodded wearily and slipped into bed beside him. 'I won't be long,' he said. She did not respond but turned her back on him; he knew that her eyes were open, but gazing at what? He restarted the cassette:

'To the other matter concerning Fisher. It is more difficult for me since the death of my man, Kamal. Fisher recovered the briefcase from Abdulsalaam. He succeeded where I failed. I believe also that the woman, Julnar, also tried but,

134

like me, was unsuccessful. Presumably P's letters to G were in the case. I did not witness the handover in the Ruins because there were too many visitors present. Fisher then made contact with P using the same method as G, through Mrs Farhat, the receptionist at the hairdresser. The letters were burned on the Quay. No traces remain. I think that may be said to be the end of the love affair and that you need no longer be concerned that your official position will be in any way compromised.'

Paola turned to Nigel and closed her eyes; he put his arm around her and tenderly stroked her hair.

'After the letters were burned they strolled along the Quay. He made advances but they were rebuffed. She drove him home, stopping once violently. They talked. She dropped him in The Square. I will continue to probe Fisher's rôle. I am told he was deported from Accra but you could more easily check that out than I. He is not the best type. By the way, thank you for your help over the visa. Perhaps I shall see you at the Winzer recital. End. Cheery-bye.'

Nigel unplugged the earpiece and put the cassette and the book aside. He turned off the light and kissed Paola on the forehead. In the dark, he prayed for her peace of mind. He wished he could tell her that he knew about her affair with Mather; wished he could have helped her to retrieve the letters; longed to share in the relief that they were burned. He wanted most of all to comfort her. But circumstances made such human contact impossible.

5

Each evening for more than thirty years Aubrey Scott-Burrows and Abdulsalaam passed the hour before sleep in each other's company. When younger, Aubrey had read or recounted a story to his servant, but the custom had lapsed because the old man could not now concentrate for long on a printed page, nor could he find any more the energy to invent or remember tales simply for Abdulsalaam's benefit. All strength, the old man had decided, must be husbanded to maintain the daily classes, for the classes were their only income, and they required money not only for the necessities of life, but also for another, and to the old man, more important reason. And so, each evening, Abdulsalaam would turn back Aubrey's bedclothes, help the old man off with his white burnous, which was the only garment he possessed, and carry him naked to the bed. The pillows would be puffed and propped so that Aubrey could sit up, a single candle placed on his bedside table and a cup of warm milk, his supper, put into his hands. While Aubrey sipped his milk, Abdulsalaam would go into the kitchen and soak the burnous – at dawn he would rise and hang it on a line strung across the terrace so that it would be dry in time for class – and then return to the bedroom to fill and light Aubrey's pipe, to roll a Thai-stick for himself and to sit crosslegged on the bed facing the old man. They would allow some minutes of silence in which to savour the effects of their smoking before Aubrey asked the first question:

'How much did we take today, prettiness?'

'Deux livres.'

The old man became flustered, tetchy. 'Why so little? Are the disciples dissatisfied? We used to take more, a good deal more, why are they so ungenerous?'

Abdulsalaam shrugged, heaving his shoulders to his ears.

They smoked, each with his own tricks of inhalation to coax inner quietude: to Aubrey, mental clarity; to Abdulsalaam, absence of thought.

'I shall take the disciples to the Ruins,' Aubrey said.

'Mais chéri, you will be tired.'

'It has always produced a good reward. I will tell them the legend, if I can remember it.'

'You will be tired, *chéri.'*

The old man's hands nervously pinched the bedclothes. 'How much have we saved, what is the total now?'

From the bedside table, the servant took an abacus on which he did his sums, flicking the beads this way and that; he was inordinately proud of the speed with which he could calculate and his face showed pleasure when this moment was reached. He was able to announce that he had hidden beneath the floorboards of the black windowless van a little over twelve hundred pounds.

'We need more. A good deal more,' Aubrey said. 'Yes, I will tell the legend. I'm certain to remember it tomorrow.'

Then, like a catechism, the nightly ritual continued:

'The van has petrol?' Aubrey asked.

'*Oui.*'

'You know where to buy tickets?'

'*Oui.*'

'Where?'

'*Au bureau.*'

'Which office, prettiness?'

'*Près du quai ancien, chéri.*' Abdulsalaam sang his answers as the Christian Brothers had taught him to do at their school in Alexandria.

'And how many tickets will you buy?'

'One for me, one for the van.'

'Tell me the route.'

'Genova, Spezia, Piza, Firenze.'

'And what is the name of the Father Superior?'

'Sauleo.'

'And what will you give him?'

'*Toute la monnaie.*'

'All, mind. It is for your keep forever and ever.'

'*Oui, chéri.*'

'You will have paid for the petrol, paid for the passage, and whatever is left is for the Fathers to keep you.'

'*Oui, chéri.*'

'Good, that's very good, prettiness. And have you ordered the coffin?'

The question always upset Abdulsalaam. '*Non,*' he said, tossing the abacus aside.

'You must order the coffin, prettiness.'

'You are not ready yet, *chéri,*' Abdulsalaam protested, tears welling up in his eyes.

'It can't be long now,' Aubrey said, sinking back into the pillows. 'It *can't* be long now.'

The old man was drowsy; thought receded. In a fragile voice he said, 'Yes, order the coffin,' and a little later, 'It can't be long now.' And when he was near to sleep a faint memory of an ancient legend stirred, a sacrificial island; but the particular was never rooted and was quickly lost. Tomorrow, I'll remember.

Abdulsalaam gently removed the pipe from Aubrey's mouth; took away one pillow and laid the old man's head to rest, covering his wrinkled body with a sheet. He kissed the old man's smooth forehead. Then, the servant lay at the foot of the master's bed, like a watchdog, and slept, too.

6

Fisher was put into a small whitewashed room containing an iron bedstead, a chair, a jug of water and a bucket. The windows were painted black, and sealed. The door was locked. For much of the time Fisher cried, thinking of Anne and aching to feel the life inside her when it stirred. Early in the morning, or what Fisher supposed was morning, Wanis brought from the flat his suitcase, clumsily stuffed with his own clothes and a good many of Gerald's things. A little later he had another visitor, Brogan, the American.

Fisher, lying on the bed, asked, 'Why am I being kept a prisoner?'

'No, no, you've got it all wrong. You're not a prisoner. Far from it. No, they need the flat. They've moved someone in there. Holmqvist. Did you meet him? This is only for a very short time. You'll be out of here in a couple of days. You're not a prisoner, why, that's ridiculous. I slept here myself.'

Fisher turned his back on him.

Brogan said softly, soothingly, 'It's best to co-operate, Mr Fisher. You'll be doing an honourable job, believe me. And I want to give you some other advice. You're in a vulnerable position: the girl, pregnant, you know what I mean? Pretty high stakes are involved. I hate to say this but she's the one who'll suffer. She's the one that can be got at. Just go along with Mr Fawzi. You'll be well paid.'

And he laid his hand gently on Fisher's shoulder, then left. Alone, Fisher continued to cry.

PART FIVE

I

Julnar emptied the slops from Fisher's room. He heard her, somewhere down a passage perhaps, emptying the bucket and flushing a cistern. When she returned Fawzi was with her; his eyes were red-rimmed and he looked weary as though he'd slept little. He sat at the foot of Fisher's narrow bed studying his nicotine-stained hands; the girl leaned against the wall, cleaning her spectacles with the hem of her black dress.

Fawzi said, 'I owe you an apology. I was hard on you. But I have been waiting so long for you that I hoped for someone who would share my pleasure. Will you be so gracious, d'you say, magnanimous, to accept my apology? It would please me.'

Fisher lit a cigarette, saying nothing.

'What I most wanted,' Fawzi continued, also lighting up, 'was to make you feel welcome. Not only as Gerald's half-brother, but for yourself. I didn't make a good start, I know. But now I have a kindness to ask. There are many preparations. All must help. I want you to get acquainted with Julnar here. It's important to the mission. She has work to do today. I want you to accompany her, help her, get to know her. Will you?'

Fisher glanced at the girl: her head was lowered, her hands piously clasped, but she sensed his eyes on her and made a nervous attempt at a smile, though never looking at him. She seemed, as she did at Gerald's funeral, like a perpetual mourner.

When Fawzi realised that Fisher was not responding to his gesture of reconciliation, his weariness became more noticeable. He said, as though he were commiserating, 'I believe our American friend, Brogan, has had a word with you. He made everything plain, did he? About the pregnant girl, Anne?' His tone suggested he meant to save a life instead of threatening it.

141

He rose, and as he left the room, said, 'Get yourself ready. Julnar will call for you in half an hour.'

Fisher washed himself in the cold water from the jug; drowned flies floated on the surface. He wished he could gather the strength to act but he knew too well from experience what reserves had to be mustered in order to resist Gerald alive or dead. (He remembered the Court, and the swearing of the oath.) The strength it took: the thought itself drained him. And he was a boy then, and no one else had been in danger – only himself. Yet, he knew that somehow he had to find, for the second time in his life, a source of power stronger than Gerald's, a charge that was invincible. But where did the power lie? He did not have to think about the answer. In the same hiding-place where he had discovered it all those years ago: in himself. But the misgivings he had couldn't be explained: he believed, irrationally, that whatever courage he'd once possessed had long since been expended and was not to be renewed.

2

The day was the hottest since Fisher's arrival. There was little breeze to cool the city and he could feel the heat of the pavements through the soles of his shoes. With Julnar he tramped the streets; he kept silent as a way of making a timid gesture of defiance. She soon gave up trying to make contact; naturally reticent, she needed encouragement to be human. But Fisher could not help admiring her physical endurance and determination: not once did she tire, not once was she tempted to rest in the shade.

She had some sort of list – of schools, it turned out, and of various houses and shops. At each school they were treated to similar formalities: ushered into the Head Teacher's room to be given tea or a gaseous water called *Ben Gashir*, to discuss the heat, the humidity, a dozen other trivial topics. One of the teachers said that if the breeze dropped altogether they must expect the *ghibli*, the hot arid wind which blows with terrible force from the south: tomorrow perhaps, or the next day. At two of the schools Fisher heard 'Rule Britannia' being sung. To conclude each interview Julnar delivered a message in Arabic

142

Fisher had to fight himself not to ask for an explanation; she was elaborately thanked. And then the farewells:

'*Assalaam aleikum.*'

'*Wa-aleikum assalaam.*'

A shaking of hands, fingers pressed quickly to the heart.

They worked through the list. After the five schools had been visited, Julnar went into shops of all kinds, mostly in the vicinity of the old cathedral which had been converted into a mosque, the crescent moon and star fixed to the bell tower in place of the cross. (Even so, to Fisher it seemed a recognisable sanctuary.) They visited fruiterers, a bookshop, the hairdressing salon at the Palace, a leather shop and several cafés. In each Julnar spoke to women, the men were excluded. All appeared flattered and impressed; only one, the receptionist in the hairdressing salon, put up an argument; she followed Julnar into the street, burst into tears, pleaded. But Julnar was unmoved.

At one of the cafés, after delivering the whispered message – like busy female gossip, Fisher decided – Julnar laid a hand on his arm and said, 'Please, you want Pepsi iced?'

The action startled him: her touch was cold and, although brief, he felt the pressure of her icy fingers after she'd removed them to rummage in her purse for change. Like a deadly sting, he thought.

They sat at a table near the door, he with his back to the street. He avoided looking at her, but knew she was studying him while she sucked her drink through a straw. All he saw of her was the beads of sweat on her upper lip, and acne on her chin.

She said, 'Please, where you get that bag?' and instantly he was reminded of Kamal in the Damascu leaning forward to admire the flowers on Fisher's denim jacket. When he looked up, Julnar was leaning forward too, feeling the quality of his shoulder-bag.

'In Rome,' he said.

'Does such a thing cost much?'

'I don't remember.'

'It's more for a girl, no?'

'Perhaps.'

Kamal's face remained with him, smiling and handsome.

Fisher remembered the boy in bed, flaunting his youthfulness as he flaunted the lewd playing-cards; and Fisher also remembered the moment of the boy's death, the awful grey of Kamal's face. His thoughts were interrupted by a movement from Julnar, a wish to speak, a stifled sound that came to nothing. He glanced at her; she was wearing a crooked, tentative smile. Embarrassed, she said, 'Mr Fawzi wishes us be friends.' She could not hold the smile for long. Above her head insects danced.

'Why?' Fisher asked.

Again she exposed the brief, diffident smile. And then, she winked. At first he thought something was troubling her eye, but she did it again and he realised suddenly she was making an attempt to be frank with him, flirtatious, available. As if to explain, she said, 'It is more an order from Mr Fawzi than a wish.'

'An order?'

Eyes downcast she sucked slowly at the Pepsi and, like a child, she continued to suck after the drink was finished, making a hollow, bubbling noise like a death rattle. She said, 'I am not married. I am not knowing any man.' Was she offering herself or just trying to discomfort him? But having confessed she seemed relieved. She dabbed at her mouth with a paper napkin, a polite, genteel gesture. 'Mr Fawzi says it is important we are friends.' She could not hide the effort she had to make in order to speak.

'Important?'

'That is what he says.'

'I don't understand.'

'No,' she said, 'he did not explain,' and twisted feverishly the paper napkin in her fingers, trying to find the courage for what she was about to say: 'I have a room. In the Suk. No one will see. There is a bed.' The napkin was quickly in shreds.

To think of her naked, to imagine those droplets of sweat against his mouth, the acne brushing his chin, sickened Fisher. He shifted position and unexpectedly saw her reflection in a cracked mirror behind the L-shaped bar: the angle of her head, the tense muscles in her thin neck put him in mind of a stricken bird. But she did not engage his sympathy. He felt nothing but a vague disquiet as though to be near her was to be in some way at risk. Yet, he found himself saying gently, 'Why do you do everything Mr Fawzi tells you to when it hurts you so much?'

'Please to come,' she said softly, urgently. 'I will – I will be nice for you. It is important. Mr Fawzi says. For the work. There is a bed.'

'Did he order you to be friends with Gerald for the work?'

'Please to come now,' she said, half-rising.

'I've not finished my drink yet.' Deliberately he took his time and she sat again on the edge of the chair, her head once more tilted, her neck strained. Against his instinct he asked, 'How did Gerald die?'

'An accident,' she said, 'he was –' but she stopped herself. 'It's not allowed for me to tell. It was accident. I don't lie. Please to finish your drink. We must be friends. It is necessary. My room is not far.' And again: 'There is a bed.'

Addressing her reflection in the mirror he said, 'I have a girl. I don't want to be unfaithful,' and inwardly he cursed himself for being kind, but knowing by some curious instinct that he had spoken a sort of truth.

She let out a cry, a quiet, lost sound; he looked directly at her and saw that she was smiling. 'I understand,' she said, 'I understand. I will tell Mr Fawzi. Yes, yes, I understand.' She did not disguise the relief. And when they were out in the street she said, 'If you have girl you should not have such a bag.'

Shortly before noon, she summoned a taxi which she directed to a warehouse in the harbour: it stood on the quay where the Genoa ferry was berthed.

3

The warehouse was the size of an aeroplane hangar, cool as a cathedral. When they entered, most of the huge area was empty, gaping; only a tiny part, at the farthest end, was in use. Here, amidst scaffolding and wooden planks, a score of large cardboard packing cases of different shapes and sizes, the Japanese waited with Jorda, the Basque, and with Brogan. Julnar climbed a wooden staircase to an upper gantry which led to an office; behind wide glass panes Fisher saw Charon waiting for her.

The Japanese bowed, the Basque saluted with a clenched fist. Brogan said cheerfully, 'We've got to unpack and check all this stuff, then pack it up again. Like being in the army, I guess.'

'We start now?' the Japanese interpreter asked.

'No, we better wait for the go-ahead.'

Meanwhile, Wanis entered the warehouse, traversing the vast floor-space with all eyes on him; he carried wicker-work picnic baskets in each hand. Brogan said, 'The workers have gotta eat, I guess.'

Julnar and Charon descended from the gantry. 'Please to have coffee, first,' she said, 'then please to start.'

Without greeting anyone, Charon marched slowly the length of the warehouse, shoulders hunched, head bowed, hands clasped behind his back, like a traveller doomed to cross an eternal plain; he let himself out into the sunshine.

From one of the picnic baskets, Wanis produced a vacuum flask of warm water and mixed Nescafé into plastic cups. Julnar fished out a packet of dry bisuits, like Melba toast, and offered them one at a time with her fingers; her nails were long and dirty; Fisher declined and deliberately detached himself from the others, turning his back and sitting on a packing case bound with metal strips. He wanted to demonstrate, however feebly, that he wasn't one of them. He studied the light from windows in the high roof, well defined shafts which criss-crossed meaninglessly in mid-air.

'Have some coffee,' Brogan said.

Fisher didn't answer, but stared defiantly at the roof. He took out a cigarette.

'No. No smoking, please,' Julnar said.

When the others had finished their refreshments Julnar ordered work to begin. Fisher and Brogan were paired, and set about cutting the metal bands from one of the smaller cases, and after they'd removed a top layer of straw, Brogan reached in and withdrew transparent polythene bags which contained comic masks, some with moustaches and beards, some with rosy cheeks and bulbous noses, all with thin elastic to keep them in place.

'What in heavens are these for?' Brogan asked.

Julnar, who carried a clipboard, acted as overseer. To Brogan she said, 'There are to be one hundred masks. Please to count.'

While they worked, Fisher observed the others, to see what else was being unpacked; navy-blue trousers and tunics and plastic truncheons; there were whistles, toy guns and several pairs of white cotton gloves; the nervous laughter of the Japanese boy drew his attention to helmets of London policemen made from papiermâché.

Fisher made no comment, asked no questions. While he counted the masks, he was aware of Brogan watching him, waiting for something to be said. Fisher's silence began to irritate the American. 'Aren't you anxious what all this is for?'

Fisher said, 'I make it a hundred. Would you like to check?'

'Yeah, okay,' said Brogan, taking a pile from Fisher. 'I'm curious, that's for sure. Maybe it's for some fancy-dress ball, huh? Anyway, we'll know the day after tomorrow.' Still nothing from Fisher who began to return the straw to the packing case like an unwilling drudge. Brogan said, 'Did Mr Fawzi say anything to you about an outing? Something to do with schoolchildren, he told me. I guess it's a kind of party. Well, you know my motto: just do as you're told and don't ask any questions.'

After a pause, Fisher said, 'I won't.'

By lunch time, all the cases had been unpacked, their contents checked and repacked. The last to be uncovered were outsized enlargements, six feet by four, of the photographs Paola had taken of Fisher's school, grainy in quality, but you could now detect children careering in the playground, and Fisher recognised the windows of his old classroom. And he remembered unexpectedly Mr Wilkinson – Old Wilkie, never just Wilkie, always Old Wilkie – white-haired and florid, teaching English. He'd taught Gerald, too, but Gerald hadn't liked him. Old Wilkie, mad about choral music. (*Hearts of Oak* was his favourite, he said, words by David Garrick, music by Boyce, and putting Fisher in the choir not because Fisher could sing but because Old Wilkie liked him and said he must have at least one communal activity.) And the sing-songs in class. It was Old Wilkie who called him out the day Gerald was arrested, saying, 'Your mother wants you to go straight home, old son. The police are there. Gerald's in trouble. Something to do with throwing bricks at an Embassy, I think your mother said. Pity. He was a good student, you know, Gerald was. Always a bit of a fanatic, about everything, except singing.'

'I don't want to go, sir –' He remembered twisting his maroon cap in his hands.

'You must, old son. You're needed.' And tousling Fisher's hair like an affectionate uncle, or a father, 'You're needed.'

And then Julnar and Wanis covered the enlargements in cotton sheets: the memory receded.

Lunch consisted of bread, fruit and cheese. Fisher took his ration and again sat apart from the others, this time arranging one of the packing cases so that he sat facing a wall, but Brogan joined him.

'Make room for a friend?' Brogan said.

Fisher didn't move. Brogan said, 'C'mon now, Martin. You're not gonna do yourself any good with this attitude. Don't make trouble for yourself. Don't resist.'

'I've resisted all my life,' Fisher said.

'Resisted what? To do right? To do good? To stamp out injustice? That's not very smart. That's nothing to be proud of.'

'Could you let me eat my lunch in peace?'

'I want to know what it is you're resisting, Martin.'

'Gerald,' Fisher said as though swearing.

'But he's dead.'

'I'd forgotten.'

'Ah, c'mon, Martin –'

Fisher turned to him. 'I've resisted all my life,' he said again, deliberately. 'In childhood by instinct. In adolescence because I was naturally perverse. And because as a grown man I am able to make an intelligent choice.'

'Between what, for Heaven's sake?'

'Between life and death.'

'Oh, c'mon,' the American said, laughing.

'Don't laugh, Brogan,' Fisher warned quietly. 'I've been sucked dry.' The exchange gave the illusion of defiance. He ate greedily, tearing the bread with his teeth, to aid and abet the impression of belligerence. He thought: I'm not giving in now: Gerald has always stood for chaos and death, and I stand for something else. But for what? For what? He gazed into a void. Like coming to the edge of a chasm Fisher suddenly saw the futility of his posturing. Whatever struggle he'd put up those many years ago had sapped his vitality; his life had been an elaborate quadrille of evasion.

'Don't sulk,' Brogan said.

Fisher rose and began the walk across the empty warehouse. He felt as though guns were trained on him and he might be shot down at any second; an ant crossing a flagstone.

Julnar called, 'Please, where are you going?'

He walked on, hearing Wanis' heavy step catching up with him. Fisher turned sharply. 'I'm going to have a cigarette. Any objections?' He took pleasure in a kind of juvenile bluster.

Out on the quay, he sat on a bollard and smoked. Work in the harbour had stopped for the afternoon. Men lounged in the shade, eating lunch, brushing flies from their food. He could feel the sun burning his forehead. Like a wounded child he wanted to get his own back. He regretted his gaudy phrases: life and death; sucked dry. But they were true just the same. He had resisted Gerald for as long as he could remember.

The warehouse door opened and Brogan emerged, shielding his eyes from the sun. He said, 'I didn't mean to laugh, Martin. Please forgive me. But I wish I could make you understand that all this could be the making of you, Martin.' He came very close. 'Let me ask you something. Are you a God man?'

'A what?'

'Do you believe in God?'

'Go away, Brogan,' Fisher said wearily.

'All right. Omega point.'

'What?'

'No, c'mon, I want an answer. It's not a difficult question. Why do you look so hang-dog about it? All you have to say is yes or no.'

'Piss off.'

'You've lost your faith, I guess.'

'That implies that I had some to lose.'

'Why, everybody has faith one time or another. You weren't any different, were you?'

'Brogan, please leave me alone.'

'Indulge me, Martin. Just answer my questions. Was there ever a time in your life that you had faith, a faith in some being outside yourself? Just answer yes or no.' He wore his serious, boyish frown, caring, anxious.

'Fuck off.'

Imperturbable, Brogan continued, 'Okay, let's see what you do believe in. How about, oh, let's call it the orderliness of natural law? You believe in that? The sun will rise, the sun will set, there'll be spring and winter? You believe that, don't you?' He sat on his haunches looking up at Fisher. 'You know what? I guess you accept without question words and statements you don't have the ability or the least intention of testing. I mean, stuff like the power of the atom, the existence in other places of people you can't see. And you must've accepted the authority of those you figure know more than you do, and you probably believe in the decency of others and the reliability factor of the universe. Don't you?'

Fisher followed the patterns the gulls made overhead. 'Yes,' he said, 'and I've seen people, quite close to me, believe in systems which have never been tried but which are supposed to be universal panaceas, and for which they'll kill.'

'Right!' Brogan cried, springing to his feet as if he'd made Fisher see what he was getting at. 'That's what it's all about. So, c'mon now, Martin, gimme a straight answer: are you a God man, yes or no?'

Minutes passed. Brogan stood there, his face shining with expectation. Across the harbour a ship's siren sounded, and then they heard the approach of a truck, an army truck, a dull olive green. Two sliding doors to the warehouse opened and Wanis waved the truck inside. A driver and a sergeant jumped down from the cabin and presented papers to Julnar. She signed and said for Brogan and Fisher to hear, 'Please to load up.'

But Fisher remained where he was and did nothing to help. He felt he should have the courage to answer – but what? He gazed towards the ferry and watched Charon on the lower deck tossing chunks of bread on to the water for the gulls.

4

At dusk the *Azan* floated across the city. Mr Fawzi entered his curtained sanctuary, washed and prayed with what he called exultant serenity; to conclude his prayers he recited fervently 'Glory be to Allah,' thirty-three times, 'Blessed be Allah,' thirty-three times, 'Allah is the Greater,' thirty-three times, and to make the hundredth glorification said, 'There is no God but Allah, and Mohammed is His Prophet.' Then, he asked once more for a blessing on his mission which he called The Piercing of the Enemy's Heart.

When he emerged from the sanctuary, heartened and re-freshed, he heard voices in the next room – what Fawzi called the Outer Tent; his office he thought of as the Inner Tent. Julnar and the others had returned from the warehouse and Fawzi went out to welcome them.

In English he thanked them for their hard labour and apolo-gised for the heat. He said, 'Tomorrow, you will appreciate the value of the work you have done. Tonight, however, we are going to have a little party.' When this was translated to the Japanese, they applauded. 'It is a way,' Fawzi continued, 'of thanking you and a congenial manner in which to conclude any outstanding business. It is also a place to say *au revoir*, because soon, very soon, we will all be separated, d'you say separated or parted?'

'Parted,' Brogan said, laughing.

'So you see, there are many reasons for a party.'

A short while later, three cars drew up outside the house and set off in convoy. Fisher was sandwiched between Fawzi and Julnar in the Cadillac. Fawzi said, 'Julnar tells me you were not unco-operative. That's good. But you must learn to show more enthusiasm. Enjoy the party.' It was an order.

They passed through the arch of the Spanish Castle, parking near the shuttered Hall of the Carpetsellers. From there, Fawzi led them along secret and inner passages which existed behind the façade of the Suk; covered ways connecting one house to another, often without windows, always airless, intercom-municating tunnels, rooms, doors, staircases until at last they came on a small inside courtyard, open to the sky, lit by coloured fairy-lights, red, blue, yellow, green, strung in bisect-ing diagonals.

'Welcome,' Fawzi said, 'to the Café of September '72.'

Several guests were already present: Holmqvist sat in a corner with a middle-aged, Hitler-moustached black, and was showing him a book of green cloakroom tickets; a dozen or so young men whom Fisher had never seen before, and two girls who talked to no one, not even to each other. On Fawzi's arrival Holmqvist stood and applauded. The tango 'Jealousy' blared out of loudspeakers strategically placed at the four corners of the square. One of the Japanese began to take photographs of the guests.

Effortlessly, for no one paid him any attention, Fisher again detached himself as though he were compelled to make a symbolic act of separation. He sat alone under the night sky, twinkling with stars and fairy-lights, to observe the others as one might a shadow play, and what struck him first was the artificiality of the atmosphere, as though all the guests had turned up unexpectedly on the wrong evening. There was, of course, no alcohol, but a pair of waiters brought out from the kitchen Pepsis and orange juice, iced *Ben Gashir* and Hope's Peach and Pear Nectar made in Japan; on all the tables there were glass bowls overflowing with assorted nuts. Later, *kefta* were served, the texture and taste of burned bread.

Fawzi and Julnar introduced a formal note: they danced to 'Jealousy' like father and daughter at the girl's wedding reception, she with a proud smile, he self-conscious and a little clumsy. When a prolonged hiss signalled that the record had come to an end, Fawzi retired, beaming, to a side table and held court. Brogan was the first petitioner: from the way fingers were held up and notes taken, Fisher somehow assumed that financial matters were being discussed. Papers were signed and, in the manner of the Suk, a handshake sealed the bargain; then, Julnar asked Brogan to dance. Holmqvist took the American's place at Fawzi's table.

Fisher was reminded of Gerald's twenty-first birthday party: as a little boy he had stolen out of bed and stood at the door of the lounge to spy on the celebration. He saw his mother, smiling, showing her gums, dancing with each of Gerald's young male friends in turn and laughing too loudly; Gerald had shaken up a bottle of beer and squirted foam at her. Fisher had been frightened by that and wanted to go to her help.

He was, he knew, about to vomit. Thoughts, unconnected and illogical, filtered through his mind: Gerald in fragments like an exploding grenade, then dabbing his forehead with dragon's blood and glycerine; the view from the minaret;

Abdulsalaam pushing Gerald's white Mercedes and battered body into the sea; ash plummeting like a cloud. Nothing he'd ever been told was anchored; like participating in a nightmare without being frightened. He felt nothing at all except nausea, but the images continued at ever-increasing speed: Paola naked in the Ruins, Julnar scrubbing a tiled lavatory floor, Nash urinating from the minaret, the blind Günther feeling his face, Brogan licking lips. Fawzi spraying him with insecticide –

A waiter helped him to the lavatory where he vomited; the place was foul but Fisher welcomed it as if he acknowledged that he belonged there. When he emerged, he leaned against a wall and, after a while, noticed that either side of him were framed photographs: all taken at night of young men, some in Bedouin head-dress, arms raised victoriously, descending the steps of aeroplanes to be welcomed on the runway by Mr Fawzi: in one of the photographs Fawzi hugged a boy as Fisher himself remembered being hugged.

Unsteadily, he returned to the courtyard. Brogan was dancing to 'Lara's Theme' with one of the Japanese boys and Julnar, awkwardly, with the Basque. Holmqvist approached Fisher. 'Do you want tickets for a piano concert?' he asked; a lank strand of hair fell over his eyes and he flicked it back into place with a nervous jerk of his head.

'No,' said Fisher, 'I have some already.'

'Really? For the blind German?'

'Yes.'

'Really? Is he well known?'

'Famous,' Fisher said.

'Really?' Impressed, he rejoined his black friend.

Julnar came up behind Fisher. 'Please to dance?'

'I don't feel very well,' Fisher said.

'Please,' she said. 'You must. Mr Fawzi would be upset. It is the form.'

They took the floor, waltzing to 'Lara's Theme'. Fisher felt as though he'd made contact with the carrier of a dread disease and had been fatally infected: her hands were cold and damp, icy like a corpse. Gliding by, Brogan winked at Fisher over the shoulder of the Japanese boy; Fisher pretended not to see. Spinning, he noticed a newcomer join Mr Fawzi and sit at the table, someone Fisher recognised, Charon, the Captain of the

Genoa ferry, hunched, doleful, weary. In brief snatches, Fisher observed them talking earnestly, and just before the music stopped he was aware that Fawzi was pointing at him and jiggling his forefinger to include Julnar; Charon nodded as though Fawzi had just added to his burden.

Fisher returned to his table. To 'Jesus Christ, Superstar' played on a harmonica Holmqvist made an exhibition of himself which was much appreciated, gyrating and snapping his fingers like a marionette out of control; embarrassed, Julnar stood in awe of him, her eyes fixed on his industrious feet.

The black came to Fisher's table. 'Excuse me, master, are you important?' he asked.

'No,' said Fisher.

'May I sit, please, master?'

'Yes, please do.'

He was dapper, his moustache slightly comic as though it hadn't been stuck on straight. His brow was perpetually furrowed which gave the impression that he was peering at some far point on a distant landscape. He said, 'I am not important, either.'

'Where are you from?' Fisher asked.

'South, master.'

'What's your name?'

'My name is John, master.'

'Mine is Martin.'

'How do you do, sir,' John said, bobbing.

'How d'you do. Have you been here long?'

'No, master. Only two days. Only.'

'And do you like it?'

'Well, master,' John said after a moment's hesitation, 'they could be more helpful, these people.'

'In what way?'

'All the time they are asking what my organisation is. I am saying I have no organisation. I have people, master. I want money, master, to make the organisation. But all the time they shake their heads and say, "We must look for return on investment." What's that mean when we are talking about slavery?'

They were interrupted by the Japanese youth with the neighing laugh. He bowed low to Fisher and held out his arms.

'You dance, yes?' He whinnied nervously.

The song was called 'Downtown'; they trotted around the floor: the Japanese put his cheek against Fisher's chest and Fisher felt him shudder as though the laughter had turned to tears. But the dance and the music was brought to a sudden stop by Brogan. He stood on a table, his eyes blazing with fervour and sang in a forced, throaty tenor:

'Glory-o, glory-o
To the brave boys who died
In the cause of long down-trodden men ...'

One hand on his heart, the other outstretched, his voice grew in confidence:

'But the bravest of all
In the fight for the free
Was Kelly,
The pride of Killarn!
Glory-o, glory-o ...'

Mr Fawzi tugged at Fisher's sleeve and said, 'Sit down a moment, I want to talk to you.' With a bow, the Japanese youth retired. Brogan continued to sing lustily. 'Are you enjoying the party?' Fawzi asked.

'Are you?' Fisher replied, envying Charon in the shadows drinking from a flask.

Fawzi said, 'I will let you in on a secret. This party is really in Gerald's honour. I don't tell the others because they wouldn't understand. But you, you understand. Here, I've kept this for you. I found it when I was searching the flat.' He handed Fisher a shiny black notebook. On the first page Gerald had written 'Pensées by G. A. Mather'. Inside there were only five sentences:

1 Out of what we do something new will be born.
2 All a man needs is the belief that to his ideals all other living things are subservient.
3 Kill but be not killed, for we are few and they are many.
4 The new infidels are the men who condemn terror who never condemned war.
5 To succeed make use of the enemy's virtues, not his vices.

Applause greeted Brogan's song; now, two of the Japanese circled each other warily: one mounted a formal attack, hands cutting through the air like scythes, the other countering with great hooking movements of the legs. Their harsh, guttural cries reminded Fisher of the Ruins. The inmates entertaining the inmates.

Fawzi said, 'You, I think, are a follower of the second proposition, d'you say proposition or postulation?'

Fisher read again Gerald's words. 'No,' he said. 'I don't believe in anything that strongly.'

'Of course you do,' Fawzi said, patting Fisher's knee to reassure him.

'Do I?'

'Certainly. You believe the most important thing is getting through from one day to the next without anybody noticing.' He laughed with rich enjoyment; the laugh turned to a wheeze, the wheeze to a cough, the cough brought tears to his eyes. He lit another cigarette.

The Japanese gave way to the Basque who mounted the table and sang a plaintive lament, clapping his hands from time to time, stamping his feet; once, he almost overbalanced.

'But I think,' Fawzi said, 'that the most beautiful postulation is the first.'

'Violent births often produce deformities,' Fisher said.

'You have a way with proverbs, too,' he said and smiled with his mouth; the rest of his face remained serious. 'Is it a family trait?'

'What is the mission you mentioned?' Fisher asked.

'You'll find out.'

'Why do you want me to sleep with Julnar?'

'It was not my idea,' Fawzi said, 'It was Gerald's. It would have been appropriate, or do you say apt? But tastebuds are a man's own. I cannot tell how peppermint is in your mouth. Yet, you have such wide fancies. Kamal, Anne, who knows what? I thought perhaps Julnar would amuse you. But I am not a whoremaster. I do not insist.'

'What is the job you want me to do?'

'You ask too many questions which I'm not prepared to answer. And for security reasons, Mr Fisher, you will remain silent about all that you have seen or heard. You won't write letters, or telephone anyone, or go running to your Embassy. You will just do as you're told.'

'And if I don't?'

'The point is you will. Remember Kamal. Think of Anne. Which reminds me. I have something for you to sign.' He reached into his inside pocket.

'For me?'

Fawzi laid three pieces of paper on the table and smoothed out each copy with the palm of his hand; he offered Fisher a pen. 'Just sign all three at the bottom, if you please. It's a standard form. All the foreign nationals who work for me have to sign them. We don't want Embassies asking any unnecessary questions. Just in case, you understand. Julnar and I will be witnesses.'

And while Jorda sang of lost lands, of hopes, of promises, and of painful longing, Fisher read:

> I, Martin Fisher, wish to be cremated and
> my ashes are to be committed to the sea.

PART SIX

PART SIX

Early the following morning, bright and unusually hot, Abdul-salaam carried Aubrey Scott-Burrows in his arms into the Roman Ruins. They were accompanied by a group of disciples which included Ella Carson, Dr Swediq and a party from Tunisia. Clustering around servant and master, they clambered over the stones listening to the old man who had, when young, helped to uncover the streets and houses, the basilicas and temples.

The town the Romans built, however, now interested him little: the past to which it belonged was too recent, Aubrey told the disciples. Stendahl's provision that a landscape needed to possess some history or human interest, Aubrey accepted only in an eternal perspective. He dismissed Rome querulously. 'Who is interested, I ask, my dears, in clever things about architecture and drainage? Are we to tremble when we gaze upon the Forum and the courtroom? What are they, after all? Monuments to what? To the passage of time, that's all.'

One of the disciples asked, 'Does it not tell us, maître, about life in a previous time?'

'Yes, it tells us that man hasn't changed much and that we must look beyond, far beyond.' He pointed vaguely to the sea. 'This was a provincial place, like any provincial place, self-assertive and complacent.'

'But is it not on a human scale, maître, a scale we are able to embrace?' asked another.

'Certainly it is, which makes it for me uninteresting. I agree the public buildings are not intimidating or overpowering like their paradigms in some great imperial metropolis. And, my dears, if you are captivated by the thought of small town politicians scheming away in the Curia, or of modest spectacles presented in the amphitheatre, or of the gossip in the seaward baths, then this is the place for you. Or any similar place which flourishes now in Lancashire or Michigan or Tuscany or Puy-de-Dôme. But I have brought you here for something else, not to marvel at archways or pillars, at conduits or window frames, not to show you where laws were discussed and made, sometimes quixotic, sometimes whimsical, sometimes sensible, not to tell you that the laws were passed, the laws upheld, the lawbreakers punished. What is that to us? There is no meaning in it. Our task is to discover meaning in ourselves, not in our monuments.'

Abdulsalaam, who smiled proudly as though he were a parent or in some way responsible for the old man's vigour, carried his master to the northern point where the Byzantine Wall meets the sea. Here, Aubrey closed his eyes, held out his brittle arms like a sorcerer preparing to conjure spirits from the deep. 'What, we must ask, of us? What of our inglorious fate, our destiny, our eternity?' His voice became more frail, caught on the wind and taken out to sea, returned by the waves breaking on the rocks. And when he next spoke, he asked the gathering to clear their minds of stones and weathered columns, to think, if they could, of a time long before the Romans built their town, of an ancient, primitive time when there were but few men and women on earth, when to walk for a single day was to travel to infinity.

Then, he said, there lived here a people whose gods had deserted them, who were plagued with pestilence, with famine and sickness, and in the hope of divine reconciliation, a human sacrifice was made. A young girl and boy, their names are lost, were chosen from the populace, bound together, hand and foot, placed in a boat and the boat pushed out to sea. All the people gathered on these shores to watch the passage of the boat carrying its human sacrifices. And only when the boat could no longer be seen did they retire to their homes. One man, the father of the girl it is said, remained to watch until the sun set, and into the night. When, at dawn, they found him gazing out to sea, they questioned him and asked what he did there. He answered that he could still see his daughter but when the people looked into his eyes they discovered he'd become blind. This man, this father was revered thereafter as a seer and he recounted the journey of the sacrifices, of the boy and of the girl who was his daughter.

From his grief a legend arose. He told that these children did not drown, were not devoured by monsters or consumed by the angry gods, but that they were guided by invisible hands to an uninhabited island where they settled and produced children.

The legend grew, was elaborated, embellished. The Island of Sacrifice was endowed with beauty, happiness and perfection. And so, when the gods were next capricious, the Elders here no longer had to select from the youth the sacrifices to the gods, had no need to bind them hand and foot, for the fate awaiting them was now clothed in such splendour that there were instead volunteers. To be sacrificed for the greater good, to sail eventually to the unknown island was the goal, the ideal.

Then there came a time, Aubrey said, when even the Island of Sacrifice was not immune from pestilence, famine and sickness. The islanders were conquered and enslaved, carried abroad, dispersed among the peoples of the Earth, lost. Yet, it is said, that even now, in every generation, their descendants are born or reborn, and in times of great pestilence, of great human suffering, will willingly sacrifice themselves, even knowing there is no island, for the general good.

PART SEVEN

In the privacy of the bedroom Abdulsalaam informed Aubrey that the collection had produced seven pounds.

'Ah,' sighed the old man, 'then it was well worth the effort, prettiness. A goodly haul. The legend has always been a little silver-mine. They liked it, I think. They were attentive.'

'*Mais oui, chéri. Reposez-vous, maintenant.*'

'Yes, yes, yes, don't bully me. And why are you so excited this morning?'

'*Non, pas du tout.*' He pouted crossly.

'Yes, you are, prettiness. What is it?'

'*Rien.*'

Aubrey became agitated, fussed with the folds of his bed-clothes, hummed tunelessly. 'Give me Dhammapada,' he said.

'But you must sleep, *chéri.*'

'I wish to read first.'

Abdulsalaam handed him the book and, half-closing the shutters, left the old man to read. The servant ran out on to the terrace and, shielding his eyes, peered out at the western head-land, the twin to the one on which the Roman Ruins stood. The old man had been right to detect excitement in his servant – Abdulsalaam was hoping for more fireworks.

All the previous night he had heard and seen the activity: a monotonous tenor wailing had drawn him at midnight out on to the terrace: across the bay he had seen two fires burning like tigers' eyes, had heard men's voices floating across the narrow strip of water. And, then, the most thrilling of all, a firework, a rocket whistled into the sky and burst into a fountain of tiny luminous beads; and laughter; and a Roman candle lobbing at short intervals coloured spheres which pop-ped like pricked balloons before falling into the sea; then, fire-crackers and more laughter. Now, by day, he could, through the heat haze, dimly discern activity: soldiers and something being built at the edge of the sea: a house, was it? or a tent?

'What can you see, Abdulsalaam?'

The servant spun round to find Dr Swediq dressed in shades of fawn and carrying a binocular-case over one shoulder standing on the terrace.

'There is no class today,' Abdulsalaam said. 'Not after the Ruins. He is tired.'

'I know that,' Swediq answered irritably. 'That's why I thought I would look in on him, in case it was too much for him.'

'He's not ill.'

'But just in case. So fascinating what he had to tell us this morning. But so tiring.' He took out his binoculars and focused them on the headland. 'What's going on?'

'Soldiers.'

'Soldiers?'

'Yes, they are building something.'

'A-ha. What?'

'*Je ne sais pas.*'

From the bedroom a handbell sounded. 'Is that *le maître?*' Swediq asked. 'I will see him.'

Abdulsalaam led him into the bedroom. Aubrey lay supported by pillows, a sheet barely covering his waist, his flesh pink and almost transparent. Half-moon glasses perched on the tip of his long nose. Seeing Swediq, he said, 'You look like a racing-tipster.'

'Thank you,' Swediq said, flattered. 'And how are you, *maître?*' he asked, unhooking his binocular-case, sitting close to the old man in his best bedside manner.

'Encouraged,' said Aubrey.

'Oh, for what reason especially?'

'I meet new wisdom daily.'

'Will you share it with me, *maître?*'

Aubrey read from the book. ' "He abused me, he beat me, he defeated me, he robbed me – in those who harbour such thoughts hatred will never cease. He abused me, he beat me, he defeated me, he robbed me – in those who do not harbour such thoughts hatred will cease. For hatred does not cease by hatred at any time – this is an old rule." It may be an old rule to Dhammapada, but not to me.'

'It is indeed very wise, *maître*,' said Swediq who had not really listened. 'And your lecture this morning was supreme.'

Aubrey removed his spectacles to study Swediq's face. 'You are nervous today,' the old man said.

'Am I?' Swediq took the fawn handkerchief from his breast pocket and mopped his brow.

'Decidedly.'

'I think not.'

'And I say you are.'

Swediq, who was adept at turning an attack, said, 'Perhaps I am making *you* nervous, *maître*?'

'Yes, you are. So is Abdulsalaam.'

'Would you prefer me to leave you?' he said, taking up his binocular-case.

'Yes, I would.'

'Then I shall.'

'Do.'

Swediq re-entered the living-room where Abdulsalaam had remained, and was now on his hands and knees scrubbing the tiled floor. The doctor said, 'Watch him carefully, Abdulsalaam, I think he's sickening for something.'

The servant sat back on his haunches. 'Is he ill?'

'No, no, but very bad tempered and that's always a sign.'

Immediately Abdulsalaam rose and disappeared into the bedroom. Swediq returned to the terrace, withdrew the binoculars from their case and trained them on the headland, across the inlet from the Roman Ruins, to the west. At first he saw only trees and rocks, shingle and sand. Then, he detected movement: a vehicle flashing between the trees, an army truck, well camouflaged olive-green and khaki. The truck came to a halt near the water's edge. Figures appeared and began to unload from the back: packages, scaffolding, planks. When the task was completed, the truck moved off, returning the way it had come and was lost to sight.

Although there was nothing more to see, Swediq kept his glasses trained on the headland. He was puzzled. What were they doing out there? What was this Outing he had heard so much about? The bazaar was full of it; something to do with children. A half-dozen schools had been given a holiday; coaches had been ordered; mothers told to bring food.

Ordinarily, Swediq would have ignored the rumours, but several times he had heard Fawzi's name mentioned, and so he knew there was more to it than just an indoctrination picnic for the young. Now, he had seen an army truck with his own eyes. Wirrel ought to be told.

He lowered the binoculars and replaced them in their case. When he turned to leave the terrace, Abdulsalaam barred his way. In his hand the servant held the wooden begging-bowl. 'Pour le maître,' he said.

Swediq put one coin in the bowl; another he gave into Abdulsalaam's hand. 'Keep an eye on what's happening out there,' he said. 'And I shall be back in the afternoon to give you another.'

Abdulsalaam went out on to the terrace, crouched still as a statue, looking out across the bay. He did not hear the bell ring a second time; he did not hear the noon summons from the mosque. He was too fascinated by the distant sound of children singing and of a voice droning and of clapping, to be aware of anything else. Only when silence fell did he remember that he hadn't given the old man lunch. When he re-entered the bed-room with a cup of hot tea and honey he saw that Aubrey had slumped forward in his bed, twisted at an ugly angle, the eyes open and staring. The old man made no sound, but saliva trickled from the corner of his mouth. And even then Abdul-salaam did not fully appreciate what had happened; or didn't want to; his mind was elsewhere, out there across the water where he thought he heard the sound of guns firing.

2

That morning there was a festive atmosphere on the coach leading the convoy. The children sang patriotic songs and one of their teachers, a robust young man with short-cropped hair, stood in the centre aisle conducting them. The adults, all women, clapped in time. Fisher sat at the very back next to Brogan, but the American never once looked at him, as if it was his turn to use silence as a weapon: he kept his face pressed to the window studying, Fisher guessed, his own re-flection.

Shortly after they passed the Roman Ruins and the turning

to Aubrey's house, the four coaches swung off the main road and travelled down a tree tunnel coming eventually to a halt at a roadblock guarded by armed soldiers. Here, the passengers dismounted. The children, almost two hundred of them, lined up in smart, disciplined ranks: all wore identical uniforms, white shirts and long navy-blue waistcoats that reached to the calves of their matching trousers; the girls sported white head-scarves. A sergeant inspected them, pausing now and then to ask a question or make a joke; when he was satisfied he marched them off under escort through a juniper wood; they sang as they marched.

Meanwhile, the women – the children's mothers, grand-mothers, elder sisters, aunts – began to unpack baskets of food. One of the soldiers beckoned to Fisher and handed him two carrier-bags containing bottles of *Ben Gashir*. By then, some of the women had set off in the direction the children had taken, but they did not sing.

Fisher found himself walking alone. The path through the juniper trees was surprisingly wide, wide enough for the coaches but for some reason they had not been permitted to go further than the roadblock; no one complained. The sun beat down on them. When Fisher strayed to the right to take advan-tage of the shade, a soldier ordered him back into the heat; he trudged on down the hard-baked mud track and presently he heard and smelled the sea; behind him a long, straggling line stretched back to the coaches: like pilgrims, Fisher thought, ex-cept that the women laughed and chattered gaily.

A few yards ahead of him a row erupted: two women, one middle-aged and dignified, the other young and rather beautiful with a modish hairstyle, had downed their carrier-bags and were squabbling. By the time Fisher drew level, a soldier had ordered them on their way. Fisher fell in beside the older woman who was plainly upset. He recognised her as the re-ceptionist at the Palace Hairdressing Salon who had argued with Julnar.

'Do you speak English?' Fisher asked as they walked. She nodded, but looked cautiously from side to side in case anyone was near. 'What was the trouble?'

Before answering she again glanced about nervously. 'Who are you?' she asked.

'A friend.'

'To who a friend?'

'To you, if you like.'

'You are English?'

'Yes.'

'Why are you here?'

'As an observer,' he said.

She seemed satisfied. 'You do not work for them?'

'No.'

'I don't work for them. But I am ordered.'

'I understand.'

'That young girl who shouts at me. She works for them.'

'Why did she shout at you?'

'These young ones. They know only how to make trouble.'

'In what way?'

'They can lie, they can cheat, they can behave like prostitutes; but if you complain, they make trouble.'

'You complained, did you?'

'Of course I complain. I have a job. My daughter and her husband are in Cairo studying. I look after their son, my grandson, for them. I have to work. Today these people tell me no work. I have to bring my grandson here. No work, no pay. Who will feed him? Who will pay rent? Who will buy clothes? The school is there to teach him, that is why I complain.'

'What did the young girl say?'

'She says it's for the Revolution. For the Colonel. But we have also our lives. I know that girl. She is a bad daughter to her mother. First, she should be good daughter, then she can tell me it's for the Revolution.'

They rested while the woman wiped her brow and changed her packages from one hand to the other. She said, 'I have a nice job. Good pay. Nice people. I'm receptionist. All foreign people I deal with. English, American, *corps diplomatique*, the wives, you know, salon for hair and nails. I don't want to lose job.'

'Did you know Kamal – who was killed?'

'Oh yes, poor boy. He used to sweep the hair up and sell it to a wig-maker in the Suk. He was always cheerful. A good son to his old mother. You knew him?'

172

Fisher detected the suspicion, the slight disapproval in spite of her sympathy. 'A little,' he said.

'Poor boy.'

'But you won't lose your job if you miss one day.'

'Plenty women want my job.'

'Yes, but you're not missing work because you want to.' They resumed the walk.

'Who will tell them that? If I complain they will say shut up and be proud you are helping Revolution, and I will still have no job.'

'It hasn't happened yet,' said Fisher.

'That's what my husband said before the Revolution. It hasn't happened yet. Now, it's happened, and he's dead. He was importer. Spirits and fine liqueurs. In one day, no business. In one year, no money. In two years, dead. I had a life, now I have no life. It is Fate. It is God's Will. Also it is hard.'

'What is to happen today?' Fisher asked.

'My grandson says they are to march and sing. For this I must lose money.'

At the end of the path they came to a clearing bordered by the sea: a large gravelled area without shade, like a parade-ground. To the right, by the water's edge, a modest, roofless grandstand of a dozen tiers had been erected out of the scaffolding and planks Fisher had helped unpack the previous day; the spectators were to sit with their backs to the sea; the base of the stand was covered in hessian and sheets and daubed with slogans; on each side stood the two larger than life colour photographs of the Colonel, dazzling, bemedalled, staring at the opposite end of the parade-ground where the children were forming up into lines, and where military bandsmen were receiving their instruments from the back of an army truck. Near by, a section had been roped off for the adults: parasols and sunshades sprouted like wild flowers in front of a tent where the food was being laid out. As more and more people arrived on the scene, so the chatter and laughter swelled, a fête-champêtre beneath a blistering sun.

'I hope you observe well,' said the middle-aged woman drily, and walked towards the tent. A trumpeter practised a flourish, and a drummer beat a repetitive tattoo.

A soldier took Fisher's carrier-bags from him and directed

him towards the grandstand. When he drew near he noticed the black scars of two burned-out bonfires and the shells of spent fireworks. Behind the grandstand, several motor-cars, including Fawzi's Cadillac, were parked. In knots the familiar figures huddled in murmured conversation: Holmqvist and Jorda, the Japanese, Mr Fawzi with two military officers and an important civilian; Wanis and Julnar stood apart dressed in uniforms similar to the ones the children wore. There was no sign of John, the black from the South who had talked to Fisher at the party; Brogan arrived when everyone was beginning to take their seats in the stand.

Fisher chose a place on the topmost tier, separate from the others. Looking down to his right he saw in the shadow of the stand, the cardboard boxes containing the comic masks, the truncheons, the police uniforms and helmets; the photographs of his school lay flat on the ground. To his left, across the narrow stretch of sapphire sea, he could just make out Aubrey's villa perched, unsteadily, it seemed, on the outcrop of rock; still farther off, he could see the outer limits of the Roman Ruins, the tip of the Byzantine Wall.

Engineers were fixing a microphone in front of Mr Fawzi who sat flanked by the officers on the middle tier. A camera team were photographing the activity on the sand. Later, Fisher learned from Holmqvist that they were his compatriots, but the Swede chose not to talk to them and, whenever their camera pointed even remotely in his direction, he ducked nervously, turned away or covered his face.

Mr Fawzi opened the proceedings with a speech. His voice, occasionally distorted by a sickening screech, echoed through loudspeakers around the ground. He spoke in Arabic; he spoke for more than an hour. Towards the end, in an emotional passage, he introduced a relay of young men, in twos and threes, whose faces were oddly familiar to Fisher. The recognition of one brought the memory into focus; he had seen him being embraced by Mr Fawzi in a photograph in the Café of September '72. Fisher thought he heard Munich mentioned when this youth was presented: he received a raucous cheer. The others Fisher also recalled from the photographs.

After Mr Fawzi at last sat down there was generous applause, and then a hitch: signals were waved to the band but without effect: the bandmaster was missing. Ten minutes passed before he was found, apparently in the food tent. He ran across the ground carrying his drum-major's baton like the Olympic torch and eating a sandwich. The children jeered.

The band played for a further hour what, to Fisher's ear, sounded like the same marching tune, repeated. He nodded off but was woken by a soldier issuing black umbrellas to the guests. It was nearly eleven, and the heat suffocating. Fisher thought he glimpsed a flash of light from the direction of Aubrey's house – a mirror, perhaps.

For the hour before noon the children performed. They sang, they skipped, they danced. They formed themselves into letters, and recited in unison. They marched past the grand-stand. The officers saluted. Mr Fawzi waved and smiled. And then, when their display was over, one of their number – or what looked to Fisher like one of their number – shuffled forward, small, hurrying steps. Only when the figure was quite close, did Fisher recognise the moathen from the harbour mosque. With Fawzi's help the old man clambered on to the stand. The microphone was lowered to accommodate him but he waved it aside. In his resonant, high-pitched voice he uttered the call to prayer beginning *God is most great*. Across the inlet, from the mosque behind Aubrey's house, the call was echoed.

Presently, the congregation, for that is what they had become, faced east and knelt. Only the foreigners were left on the stand. Once, during the prayers, Brogan looked over his shoulder and briefly, shyly, caught Fisher's eye; the Basque, Fisher noticed, was telling his beads. The Japanese took photo-graphs.

It was an impressive picture – women, teachers, children, soldiers, had become one worshipper, prostrate, submissive, seeking audience before God – marred only by the Swedish camera crew rushing up and down the rows of prone bodies, recording, in minute detail, the faces, hands and feet of the faithful in prayer. And when the final '*amin*' was voiced, and all began to rise, the director, who looked like an overweight Don Quixote, charged up to Fawzi and pleaded with him urgently; Fawzi, in turn, talked to the moathen who bellowed once more to the assembly. Instantly, everyone again knelt;

the director returned to his crew: the camera had evidently run out of film and they were obliged to re-load. The '*amin*' was repeated. The director called 'Cut!' It was time for lunch.

3

The middle-aged receptionist sought out Fisher and sat to eat lunch with him in the shade of a red and yellow striped beach umbrella. They introduced themselves and she told him her name was Mrs Farhat.

'Are you a chosen one?' she asked aggressively.

'How d'you mean?'

'They have chosen thirty children and my grandson is one of them.'

'To do what?'

'To stay behind this afternoon.'

'But what for?'

'They don't tell. Something to do with a mission. I don't understand. I have to wait in the coach. I am not allowed to watch. No one is. Only children. But I have to stay. I am not allowed to go. I have to miss work.'

They sat in the area surrounding the food tent. The older children handed out packed lunches – two or three sandwiches, dried-out *brik*, an orange – and poured *Ben Gashir* into paper cups. Several transistor radios, each tuned it seemed to a different station, accompanied the picnic with deafening cacophony. To be heard one had to shout. Of the foreigners Fisher alone ate with the crowd; the others were Fawzi's guests in one of the larger tents. He was annoyed with himself for noticing his exclusion.

Mrs Farhat complained more or less continuously, but Fisher didn't catch all she said. Suddenly, she rose on to her knees, waved excitedly and called.

A boy of seven or eight years old came charging towards her; he was dark and vigorous with bright, mischievous eyes. His mouth was circled with the remains of ice-cream. 'This is my grandson, Habib,' she said. Almost at once he began to pummel Fisher's arm, as though it were a punchbag. Mrs Farhat for the first and only time laughed which encouraged her grandson to pummel Fisher harder; when he tired of Fisher, he pummelled Mrs Farhat. She scolded him; he stuck his tongue out at her and ran off.

'He is full of fun,' she said loudly. 'Also very clever. You must hear him add up. And he is – he is – we call it *shoo-jaa.*'

'Shoo-jaa?'

'Brave, you can say.'

While she continued to extol her grandson's virtues, Fisher saw Wanis, with a loudhailer, make his way to the centre of the picnic area. He began to issue instructions. There was an immediate response: the transistors were turned off and people began to pack away their belongings. Boys collected refuse into large polythene sacks. From nowhere, Brogan appeared, eyes downcast. 'We can go back to town now. It's over,' he said hurriedly and continued on his way.

Mrs Farhat said, 'You are not one of the chosen ones.'

The soldiers started to chivvy them. In twos and threes the adults and a good many of the children made their way once more along the path through the juniper wood. Looking back, Fisher saw Wanis leading a crocodile of boys and girls, which included Mrs Farhat's grandson, into one of the larger tents. And he saw Fawzi bidding farewell to his guests: with each, he shook hands and tapped his heart. Only Holmqvist remained by his side.

Brogan and Jorda walked together, the Japanese just ahead of them; Fisher waited for the group to pass. 'What's going on now?' he asked Brogan. Jorda shrugged but the American responded not at all.

Suddenly, Fisher realised that he was behind everyone else, and isolated. The soldiers were supervising the boarding of the coaches. The Swedish camera crew packed their equipment into a mini-bus. No one was looking at him. Presently, the convoy began to move off slowly, nosing its way towards the main road. He did not really have time to make a decision: out of sight of the soldiers, he simply ducked into the juniper wood and found himself stealthily making his way back towards the grandstand at the edge of the copse, as though he had rediscovered a spirit of childhood mischief, or resolve.

A soldier, meant to be guarding the approach to the grand-stand, was asleep, leaning against the trunk of a tree, legs out-stretched before him, a rifle by his side. Fisher made a loop to the man's right, putting as much distance as possible between them. Twice, stepping on dried twigs, Fisher halted in his tracks, but he did not disturb the sleeping sentry, and he saw no one else about. The scented juniper berries, like incense, the heat, the tranquil sound of the sea coaxed a feeling of well-being which Fisher had to struggle to resist. He remembered the day he gave evidence in court was fine, too; he'd been sweating then. (He thought, I am taking the Book in my right hand.)

He came to where the motor-cars were parked at the back of the stand, and he crouched at the side of the Cadillac, listening. He heard Fawzi's voice droning on: it sounded as if he was some distance off, perhaps in the vicinity of the tents; nearer, at short intervals, came the sound of metallic hammering. Slowly, he edged his way along the length of the car until he was a few feet from the canvas skirt that covered the base of the grandstand. Dropping on all fours, he crawled the short remaining distance, ducked under the canvas and was inside the grandstand.

It was a cool hiding-place, but neither dark nor airless: the afternoon sun on its westward course found gaps between the rises of the tiers and slashed the place with chequered light. Fisher made for the left-hand corner where the shadows were deepest and from there he looked out at the parade-ground.

There were two areas of activity. Immediately in front of the stand soldiers had hammered four iron stakes into the ground to make a rectangle about twenty feet by fifteen. Be-tween the stakes they now strung strands of rope so that it began to look like a boxing-ring. Into the ring others were carrying school desks and setting them up in orderly rows; an easel holding a blackboard was put in position to face the desks. Farther off, near the tents where the picnic had taken place, Fawzi stood between two soldiers, who held the en-larged views of Fisher's school to which he pointed with a stick. Grouped on the ground in front of him, their backs to

Fisher, were the men whom he had recognised from the photographs in the café, together with Julnar, Wanis and Holmqvist. The children were nowhere to be seen.

Perhaps half an hour passed. Fawzi finished his lecture and came striding across the parade-ground to inspect the preparations within the boxing-ring; satisfied, he marched on, clambered up the stand and sat half-way up, to Fisher's right. In one hand he held a loudhailer; in the other flykiller. Looking sideways Fisher could see his legs, the trousers pulled half-way up his calves: grubby black socks with holes, and little screws of hair, like dead spiders, against his sallow skin.

Holmqvist, gripping a small round object the size of a walnut, mounted the stand and sat next to Fawzi. Fisher heard the Swede ask:

'Will she be wearing a belt?'

'I'll find out,' Fawzi said, and through the loudhailer called, 'Julnar!'

She ran from the woods. She was differently dressed now: instead of the navy-blue uniform she wore a tweed twin-set with pearls and a beret. She looked ridiculous. Fawzi and Holmqvist came down to ground level to meet her. Fisher could see the small object in the Swede's hand, like a miniature telephone dial, which he appeared to be adjusting, but where to attach it was the problem. They settled finally on her handbag: it seemed to stick magnetically to the metal rim, and it was hardly noticeable.

Holmqvist asked, 'You know how to set this type of detonator? It is remote control, ja?'

'I know,' she said.

'And remember, if you have to use it then it must face the explosives. You understand, ja, it must point at the explosives. And be careful, once it is set it is very sensitive.'

'I know,' she said again.

'Yes,' Fawzi nodded sadly, 'she knows all right. She was with Mather when he had the accident. She's lucky to be alive.' He took a step towards Holmqvist and asked anxiously, 'That can't happen again? Go off unexpectedly like that, like it did with Mather?'

'Mather dropped it,' Julnar said. 'He was upset that day. I won't drop it.'

179

'Don't let anyone jog the handbag,' Holmqvist warned. 'That also could be dangerous.'

Dismissed, Julnar trotted to the rear of the stand. Fisher watched her climb into the back seat of one of the cars, a black Fiat; a soldier joined her; before taking the wheel he fixed a card under the windscreen wipers: it read, TAXI.

Meanwhile Fawzi and Holmqvist had resumed their places on the stand. Fawzi blew a whistle and from a tent the thirty school-children emerged in crocodile. They, too, had exchanged uniforms: the boys for maroon caps, blazers, shorts and knee-length grey socks; the girls for gym-slips. Fisher caught his breath: they were wearing the uniform of his school, the uniform he had worn as a boy. He began to feel a pain in his chest, a pinprick at first but growing deadlier, like a lump of indigestible food burning him. And he remembered the walk from home across the Common: the intensity of childhood emotions: fear at being caught out for work neglected warring with a rush of freedom at being shot of his mother's house. Why, he asked himself, were these children out here in the cloying sun recreating the damp, fog-soaked memories of another time, another place?

Into the roped-off area the children marched and took their places at the desks, sitting with arms folded. A teacher – the man who had conducted the singing on Fisher's coach, was wearing a blue serge suit – came to the head of the class. He chalked something up on the blackboard, too far away for Fisher to read. Then, turning to face the boys and girls he raised his hands: they sang 'Rule Britannia'. It should have been 'Hearts of Oak', Fisher thought. He knew the classroom; Old Wilkie; the singing; as though Gerald and he were talking of old times. Fisher's pain was more acute.

Again Fawzi blew his whistle. An astonishing sight greeted Fisher's eyes: from the tents and from the woodland, came a procession that looked like a *mardi gras* parade or a students' rag: policemen led the way, followed by an assortment of figures: young women pushing empty prams, bicyclists, pedestrians, all came forward and lined up in front of the stand for Fawzi's inspection: all wore comic masks. They talked and joked among themselves, one of the policemen kept raising his mask to stick his tongue out at his neighbour. When Fawzi was satisfied, he waved them away and they began to mill about the roped-off class of children at their desks who began again, in sweet sopranos, to sing of the azure main and guardian angels.

From behind the stand, Fisher heard a car engine start; a second later, Julnar's black Fiat – TAXI – nosed into view and, gathering speed, headed for the classroom. None of the other participants paid any attention to the car; they wandered around senselessly while the children sang over and over 'Rule Britannia'.

Julnar emerged from the black Fiat. She was carrying her handbag in one hand and in the other a leather grip; and she was walking away when Fawzi barked at her through the loudhailer: she acknowledged the order, turned, went back to the car and, juggling with her handbag, opened it and pretended to pay the driver. The car drove off. Now when she turned, two men, neither wearing a comic mask but both carrying similar leather grips, detached themselves from the rest of the crowd and fell in behind her. They took stocking masks from their pockets and pulled them over their heads. They marched into the classroom of singing children.

What followed happened at speed: from their leather grips Julnar and her cohorts took automatic rifles. The two men faced the class; Julnar threatened the teacher, ordering him to join his pupils. Then, she took hold of one of the girls, talked sharply to her and pushed her out under the ropes. At once, the girl ran this way and that screaming, 'Police! Police! Police!'

The crowd were now activated. They gathered round the classroom and one of the policemen went forward cautiously. When he neared the ropes, Julnar let off a short burst of automatic fire: the man fell backwards. Several of the children screamed. The wounded policeman crawled away and two of his colleagues carried him off. A little later, he joined Fawzi and Holmqvist on the stand and received from both a pat on the back. When he removed his mask, Fisher recognised one of the men in the café photographs.

For a long while, nothing seemed to happen. Julnar and the two armed men held the children captive: four or five were crying and the teacher was doing his best to comfort them.

Policemen, in comic masks, kept the crowd outside well back. Two army trucks were brought up, disgorging armed soldiers who took up positions in a wide circle around the area. The officer in charge conferred with the police. The whole operation had the feel of a well-planned charade.

Then, Mrs Farhat's grandson, Habib, made a dash for it. He tried to slip under the ropes but the teacher caught hold of his leg and dragged him back. To Fisher the incident appeared unrehearsed: Julnar swung round; the two comrades raised their guns more threateningly. The little boy began to cry and Julnar marched up to him, struck him hard across the face and, with a wagging forefinger, issued a warning. The boy continued to cry, his face buried in the teacher's neck; the other children cowered but one, a girl, older than the others, crawled among them to give comfort where she could.

Outside the classroom, two policemen came forward to within a few feet of the ropes; one removed his mask and helmet; the other, his arm upstretched, held a white handkerchief. It hung limply; there was no breeze. And only then did Fisher realise how unbearably hot it had become.

Julnar faced the policemen; she said in a loud voice, 'Before we talk, I am telling you that we have explosives in the classroom. I have in my hand –' she showed them the dial which had been attached to her handbag '– the detonator. One mistaken move and we will blow up the children and ourselves. Now –' but she got no further. This time Habib escaped. He was under the ropes and away before the teacher could reach him. The boy ran directly towards the grandstand, making for the corner where Fisher hid.

Fawzi stood and screamed an order through the loudhailer. Julnar swung round, only then sighting the fleeing child. Again Fawzi shouted, his hoarseness resounding like a monstrous whisper.

Julnar opened fire aiming at the boy's back. The boy, by then, was yelling continuously and he fell to the ground rolling over and over until he reached the stand and blindly, wildly scrambled between the seating until he had crawled face to face with Fisher.

The two stared at each other. For an instant the boy caught his breath with the shock of seeing a man there, but then renewed his terrible cries, his face blue and contorted with fright.

Fisher's first thought was for himself: he heard Fawzi and Holmqvist stamping about above, was aware of activity around the stand, running steps, shouts, some laughter. He grabbed hold of the boy by the arm, dragged him to the canvas skirt which he raised and then pushed him out. Fisher felt as though he'd rid himself of a bomb that was about to explode.

Fawzi did his best to comfort the boy. Peering through the slats, Fisher saw them no more than two feet away: Fawzi held the little boy in his arms, rhythmically turning in a sort of dance and patting the child's back. Alternately, Fawzi's face was presented to Fisher, then the child's; Fawzi, soothing and fatherly; the child hysterical from terror.

Holmqvist said, 'It's only a game, ja?'

A quarter of an hour or more passed before Habib became calmer. And then, Fawzi, with a mischievous look, said, 'I've an idea. I'm going to send him back into the school.'

'Send him back? Why? She shot him. If that happens in London he'd be dead.' Holmqvist simpered with amusement.

'I know. But this is only a rehearsal. We are permitted to experiment. You know what my idea is? To this boy, Julnar must attach the explosives. That puts a strain on the other hostages. If there is an explosion it is their responsibility not ours. There will always be one who is nervous and frightened' – he continued to pat Habib's back, soothing him – 'there will be such a one in the school. Mather told me in that school all are frightened, all are cowards.'

Fawzi lowered Habib to the ground and taking his hand led him back to the classroom, leaning over a little to talk to him. For a moment the tension inside and out of the roped-off area relaxed. Fawzi returned the boy to his place and gave Julnar fresh instructions; then he came trotting back to the stand, wheezing from the exertion. In the classroom one of Julnar's accomplices took packages from his hold-all and began to tape them to Habib's body.

To Holmqvist Fawzi said, 'We will go back to where she demands the freedom of our two men from police custody.'

'Before we talk,' Julnar said again to the policemen, 'I am telling you that we have explosives attached to one of the children. I have in my hand the detonator. One mistaken move and we will blow up the children and ourselves. Now, I will give you the terms for the release of these children.' And she handed to one of the gaily masked men a sheet of paper and quickly returned to the classroom where her two companions, their faces covered in stockings, stood guard, guns directed at the frightened children who had made a circle around Habib. He sat quiet and shocked, occasionally looking down at the packages taped to his chest. Outside, men wearing the uniforms of London policemen and comic masks conferred with soldiers and watched cautiously.

Fawzi said, 'She is an amazing girl, that Julnar. Wholly dedicated. We are lucky she wasn't killed in the accident with Mather. Poor Mather. He would have enjoyed this.'

'Ja,' said the Swede on an intake of breath. 'She is a good shot, too.'

When darkness came, powerful arc lights were brought into position and trained on those within the ropes. Later, Julnar and the two men each took hold of a child and held guns to their heads while food was brought in.

The hostages and their captors ate. Holmqvist said, 'What will you do if they do not free your two men?'

'We will blow up the school,' Fawzi replied.

'Will you? Will she have the courage for that? For the sake of two comrades?'

Fawzi raised his voice angrily and turned on the Swede. 'It is not just for the comrades. She does this because for all we have suffered. Are suffering. If it was not the comrades we would find another reason. You Europeans are too literal. This is something else. Terrible wrongs have been done to our people, her people.' He paused and was silent a moment. 'Do you say wrongs or wrong-doings?' he asked.

Fisher ached. Again the words My Dear Gerald ran through his mind. It's a charade, he tried to tell himself, but the thought carried no conviction. It is no charade. In a day, two days, when? Julnar would stand in a classroom he had known and could remember. The bullets she fired would be real. And another, not Habib, would have the explosives strapped to his chest.

The wind started to blow from the south. The canvas skirt

184

flapped like distant thunder. Bits of paper and tin cans flew across the parade-ground. The juniper leaves hissed. But still, in the brightly illuminated ring, Julnar and her comrades stood guard, like a tableau from some barbaric pageant.

Holmqvist said, 'The British will not give you back your men. That is the new technique. The waiting game. To wear down Julnar, that is what they will do.'

The remark irritated Fawzi. Fisher saw him impatiently tapping his feet. 'I know the game, I know the game,' he said. And later: 'Curse the wind. I hoped we'd go another twenty-four hours at least. Then straight from here on to the ferry.' And later: 'All right. The waiting game is over.' He raised the loudhailer to his mouth and barked instructions. Julnar went to the ropes and called out, 'If my brothers are not here in half an hour I will blow up the school.'

Fisher glanced at his watch. The seconds – hours, days, years – passed. And when there were only two minutes left, Fawzi said, 'Now we shall see.' He kept his eyes on his watch. '*Ashraa, tis-aa, tamanya –*' and the Swede said more quietly, almost to himself, 'Ten, nine, eight –'

The simultaneous countdown continued to its conclusion: '– *ta-laat, et-nain, WAHED.*' – three, two, ONE.

Julnar spun round to face Habib. There was a flash of light, a deafening crack; a heavy pall of smoke belched into the sky, caught by the rising wind and like a curtain obscured the arc lights. There were screams and cries. Fisher recoiled, falling backwards. The Swede slipped, too: his leg dangled momentarily through the gap in the seating.

And then Fisher became conscious of other sounds, of applause and cheers and singing. Looking once more out at the parade-ground, the smoke beginning to clear, he saw Julnar lifted on to the shoulders of her comrades while those who had been outside crowded round to touch and congratulate her. Even one or two of the children joined in. But not Habib. He sat on the ground while others jeered at him, mocking him for his fear, pointing at the packages which were still intact and strapped to his chest. He cried again, an awful wail, a lament.

But Fisher knew that in the classroom where he himself had often cried the children would be dead.

5

In the dark, Fisher made his way along the outcrop of rock that bordered the inlet. The sea was beginning to swell and with increasing regularity threw itself at the rocks. In a short time he was soaked. When he looked back he could see the incandescent glow of the arc lights; before him, like a beacon, a solitary light in Aubrey's house. The wind was fierce and made the going even more dangerous; at intervals, Fisher rested, crouching on the rocks trying to duck from the force of the wind. And although the wind buffeted him and the sea crashed around his feet, all he carried in his mind was the noise of the explosion and the premonition of the children's death.

The wind fanned the heat; Fisher tasted sand on his tongue, and his eyes smarted. There were no stars to be seen, but on the headland the faint light from the arcs reddened.

Aubrey's house was in darkness; the place appeared deserted; the terrace windows were shuttered and locked. Then, Fisher heard the starting of a car engine at the front of the house and ran round to investigate in time to see the black windowless van gathering speed. But it had not gone very far when one of the rear doors flew open and the van screeched to a halt. It was too dark to see what was inside. From the driver's seat, Abdulsalaam, wrapped in a blanket secured round his waist with rope, trotted to the back, banged the door to several times until it held; satisfied, the servant resumed the journey. Fisher could hear the engine long after the van was swallowed by the darkness.

Fisher discovered a window near the carport open a crack; he forced it wider and struggled through into the small kitchen. He did not dare to turn on lights in case he drew attention to himself, but he lit matches and made his way into the main room: it was undisturbed, or so it seemed. He found a candle and lit it. He called softly Aubrey's name, but there was no reply.

The bedroom was in disorder, and there was a sweet, unidentifiable smell like marzipan: the bedclothes lay strewn across the floor, the cupboards were empty. Fisher stumbled over an open book and, by the light of the guttering candle, read the place which someone had marked:

'When a mother cries to her sucking babe, "Come
  O son, I am thy mother!"
Does the child answer, "O mother, show a proof
That I shall find comfort in taking thy milk?"'

The almond-scented smell drove him back into the main
room; there, he arranged cushions on the floor, removed his
soaking clothes and lay down to sleep. Relentlessly the wind
attacked the house but Fisher felt safe. He welcomed the
wind: he believed it gave him protection.

For hours he lay without sleeping. Habib's frightened face
appeared before him like a mirror image of his own. Why me?
he asked, why did I have to be a witness? And later: in what
rôle am I to be cast? What part am I to play in the slaughter?
In the coming of sleep his body and his mind spiralled round
and round, like a man drowning in a whirlpool.

He dreamed more or less continuously, confused and wild
visions. One remained with him when he woke: a sloping,
hilly landscape; a barbed wire fence dividing the hillside in
two; he dwelled in a wooden shack on the lower slope, alone.
A girl, wearing a freshly laundered peasant costume – he did
not know who she was, had never seen her before – came towards him on the opposite side of the fence. She peered at him
through the barbed wire; instantly he was attracted to her; she
invited him to slip under the wire and to visit her home which
somehow he knew to be beyond the crest of the hill; he refused, feeling fear; again she invited him, saying that she
would help him, but again he refused. She asked why. He said
hopelessly, 'Because there's nothing there, is there?'

He woke to the sound of voices. It was still dark and the
wind howled. Keeping down, he went to the windows and saw
on the terrace two soldiers trying the doors. Fisher knew they
were searching for him. They were making their way round
the house when he remembered the open window. He charged
into the kitchen and shut it a second before the soldiers
approached. They tried the window but it was secure.

When they had gone, Fisher searched the cupboards and
drawers in the house until he found a pair of baggy trousers, a
blue smock and a cap, a black *taghira* that was a little too large
for him but which hid his hair.

187

Leaning into the wind, fierce and unbearably hot, he struggled towards the main road. There was no one about. The sun rose but the sky was already red and remained so. He thumbed a lift from a passing lorry and when it reached the city, he hopped off the back. By then, Fisher had decided he needed help to prevent something terrible from happening.

PART EIGHT

The cuts Julnar had made with scissors to hurt and frighten Harvey Nash throbbed. An ugly scar of congealed blood in the shape of a Y disfigured his flabby, hairless chest. The freckled area surrounding the wound he dabbed with cotton wool on which he poured from a bottle 190° proof *Flash*; what was left in the bottle he poured into himself; he did not feel like eating breakfast.

From his illicit still he staggered into the bedroom to continue his packing. In a sort of trance he piled clothes into a suitcase. His servant had not turned up for work that morning. It would be the same all over the city. Nash was fond of quoting the proverb that in the *ghibli* only the diligent and guilty venture abroad. In a way he welcomed the wind: it delayed his departure – the airport would be closed; he had gained time and perhaps opportunity to do what he most wanted which was to call on Paola Wirrel before he left. But the problem was to decide whether Mr Wirrel was diligent or guilty?

At half-past eight that morning he had tried to telephone the Embassy but the line was unobtainable, so he had dressed and then walked the short distance. Outside, he had seen the familiar black Cadillac with Wanis at the wheel, talking to a policeman. They seemed to be watchful and suspicious. At the desk he saw the porter.

'Your telephone's not working,' Nash said.

'No, sir. Out of order, sir.'

'Is Mr Wirrel in this morning?'

'Yes, sir.'

Diligent, Nash thought, then pretended he had forgotten his passport. He trotted back to the flat, satisfied the ruse had established that Wirrel was at work and his wife probably alone.

Nash's hand trembled too much to risk shaving. Instead, to cover the heavy reddish growth of stubble, he sprinkled on his face Johnson's Baby powder : he looked as though he had some awful disease of the skin. He doused himself in Italian cologne, dragged a brush through his greying hair. 'I might kiss her,' he said aloud and washed out his mouth with a rose-scented gargle he had bought years ago in Jermyn Street. He dressed in a pale blue linen suit, and tied a silk cravat of red and white polka dots round his neck. Appraising himself in the mirror he thought no one would know I was drunk. Aloud he said, 'Go to it, Harvey.' Yeah, yeah. To complete his preparations, he put on dark glasses and wound a broad length of muslin round his nose and mouth. He shambled out of the flat, down the wide marble staircase into the street. The wind propelled him forward, his bulk seeming to rotate on its own axis as he was buffeted along the road.

Paola, wearing her dressing-gown, her hair loose and untidy, opened the door, saw what she thought was a sinister apparition, caught her breath and tried to keep it out. Nash put his weight against the door and she retreated, stumbling back along the passage and falling into bed. She pulled the sheets up about her neck and watched Nash swaying on the threshold of her room, smiling foolishly. She said, 'Go away. Please, go away.'

'I'm sorry if I frightened you.' He removed his glasses and the muslin mask spotted with grime. 'That's the last thing I meant to do, frighten you, I mean.'

'I'm not well. I've taken pills. I can't see anybody. I –'

'Aren't you well? What's the matter with you? Not serious, is it?' He lurched forward and sat heavily on her dressing-table stool. His head to one side, he gazed on her with gross tenderness. 'You look fine to me,' he said. 'But then you always do.' Yeah, yeah.

Her voice was weak; she had no energy. She said, 'If you don't go, I shall – I shall telephone my husband.'

'Don't, don't do that.' He edged closer to the bed. 'Please don't do that. I've only come to say goodbye. I won't keep you long. I'm off for a few weeks, did you know? Not something I want to do, but certain people – no names, no pack-drill – certain people want me out the way for a bit. I've been a naughty boy. Asked questions I shouldn't. Thought I could make a few bob. Not very terrible, but you know what they're like. Look what they did to me –' He unbuttoned his shirt and showed her the scar on his chest. 'We all know what goes on, don't we? God, you look beautiful –'

She moaned softly.

'Don't let me upset you. Oh dear me, I'm not here to upset you. On the contrary, very much on the contrary. Would you like some *Flash*? I always carry some in my hip-flask.' She closed her eyes. He swigged from the flask to gather courage. 'Tell me – this is a very delicate matter – tell me – and probably embarrassing – tell me, did you by any chance receive my poem? I suspect you did.' He drank again. 'I know people think I'm coarse and vulgar, Paola. I know I drink too much and swear too much, but it's pleasant to have feelings that no one knows anything about. A secret with yourself. Do I make myself clear? Probably not. But that poem – it probably embarrasses you, I know it embarrasses you – that poem is nearer to what I'm really like.'

'Mr Nash, don't go on, please, I'm begging you –'

'Harvey! Why so formal? Harvey. Paola.'

'Don't –'

'I have to see you, to talk to you, to be with you –' The words tumbled out at increasing speed.

'Don't –'

'No, no, let me finish. I had a miserable marriage. Neither of my sons like me. Well, the younger one perhaps a bit. But the older one – he's the psychiatrist in Wolverhampton – he really despises me. Well, I am what I am. And I think we have something in common, you and I, Paola. We've nothing to do with this sordid, squalid little place. We're here by accident, you and I. I hate the place, every square, diseased inch of it. People ask me if I condone what goes on here. Do I know, they ask, that the Government gives money to all manner of criminals in every corner of the Earth for what reason nobody knows? And I tell them I don't know and I don't care. How can you worry about criminals when the Government's the biggest criminal of all? It's too big, my dear. It's not to be bothered with people like us. We don't belong here.

'I'll be fifty-five next January. I'm of an age now, Paola,

when I need companionship and affection. God knows I've been short of them all my life. But, you and I, Paola – I've always thought we understand something about life, hold a similar view. It's not just blank and meaningless. Is it for you? I don't think it is. And don't you feel as you get older, that something marvellous is just – that it may be – age has nothing to do with it. Life doesn't just stop. We all need a bit of luck finding the person to share our lives with. Things can be full and wonderful, don't you feel that?

'If only they'd let us live our lives. If only they'd let us live our lives.

'I've got to say it, Paola. I love you. I've got to say it. I love you. If I'm making a fool of myself you'll tell me, but I've got to say it: I love you. I love everything about you. Your eyes, your lips, your nose, the way you walk, the way you smile, and laugh, everything, everything, everything. I love you, love you, love you –'

'You mustn't, please, stop –'

'I've a little money. We could keep a little nest in Paris or Rome or Vienna or London. Nothing that'll bring unhappiness to anybody. Just the odd day or two, or week, whatever – will you consider it? Will you? I know people said dreadful things about you and Mather, but I never believed them. I've always thought well of you. I'm a vigorous fellow. A rogue male' – he dropped the flask, tried to retrieve it and, in doing so, slid to his knees, his face flushed, his speech slurred – 'it can't be much fun for you with a husband as wet as Nigel. There's no cure. Poor devil. No cure –' He sat back on his haunches, smiling forlornly. 'What's your answer, Paola? Be mine? Yes? Be mine? No?' He gazed at her, palms upturned in modest supplication. 'If only they'd let us live our lives.'

Nothing passed through Paola's mind except a deep embarrassment and when that subsided, the question what do I say, what do I say? She did not dare look at him. She said to herself: as long as the wind blows I shall be all right, like a childhood game.

He said, 'Rome's convenient. A stone's throw.'

She wanted to scream but the sound stuck like a bone in her throat.

'Oh, Paola, Paola,' he moaned, laying his face on her legs: he felt them stiffen and gently stroked them with his cheek, smearing the blue blanket with powder. 'Shall it be Rome?' he asked, and began to rise, putting one knee on the bed, one hand across her, his face as close to hers as he dared. He could not believe that anyone could be so beautiful.

She did not move. She stared at him, mouth open in the hope the scream would somehow escape.

Gently, he lowered himself on to her and just lay quite still. She thought his weight would crush the life out of her body. He said, 'Oh God, Paola, let me hear you say something kind to me. Tell me there's hope.' Yeah, yeah.

Anything, she thought, for respite. The scream escaped. 'Yes, yes, yes, there's hope, yes, yes, yes, there's hope.' Had it not been the same with Gerald? Anything for peace, anything. What difference did it make? To acquiesce was always the easiest road.

For what seemed an age, Nash lay on her without moving. When he rose at last from the bed his face was stained with tears. In a whisper he said, 'I'll find us somewhere in Rome,' and pressing his fingers to his lips clumsily blew her a kiss. He stumbled out of the flat, leaving the door open. He ran against the wind as though he were a boy again. He had forgotten his mask and glasses: the sand in the air blinded him, he coughed and spluttered but nothing seemed to matter except for a kind of elephantine joy that possessed him; reaching home, he bounded up the wide staircase, past the statues, and came face to face with Fisher.

Fisher had been sitting on the top step, waiting. He rose and stood looking down on Nash.

Nash said, 'What are you doing here?'

'I have to see you,' Fisher said, 'I need help.'

'You're bad news, Fisher.' He pushed past and started to fumble with a bunch of keys.

'Please, I need help, urgently –'

'Not from me. You've caused me enough trouble,' he said, and baring his chest showed the scar. 'That's what they did to me because of you –'

'Because of me?'

'Because of your sodding brother. Just go away, leave me in

peace. I've got my own life to lead.' He found the right key and inserted it in the lock.

'Just let me use your phone. I have to talk to Wirrel at the Embassy –'

'You can't. Their phone's out of order. You'll have to go round and see him.'

'I can't do that either. They've got people there watching for me. A man called Wanis, and the police –'

'Too bad. I can't help you,' Nash said firmly, opening the door.

At once Fisher lunged forward, pushing Nash into the flat and following after him. 'I'm sorry but this is too important to wait for an invitation. You've got to take a message to Wirrel.'

'How dare you push your way in?' Nash demanded, spinning round.

'Just do as I tell you. Go to Wirrel. He's got to come here and see me –'

'Don't talk to me like that –'

'Children are going to be killed. You've got to help –' As he said the words he realised how ridiculous they must sound.

'Don't start on me,' Nash said and shoved Fisher back against the front door. 'Get out of here, this is private property –'

'Did you hear me? Children are going to die,' Fisher said, beginning to weep. 'I know where, I know how, I know who's going to kill them –' He wished he could stop himself from being so desperate – how could he make it sound reasonable?

Nash said, 'I don't want to listen. You're raving mad. I've got to go on living here, you know. My living depends on it. My whole life –' Again he pushed Fisher hard.

'I've got to use your phone, Nash. I don't give a fuck what you say –'

'It's out of order, it's out of order!' Nash screamed. 'Get out of this flat, d'you hear me? Get out! This is private property! *Private!*'

Awkwardly Nash grabbed him by the folds of the smock and at the same time tried to open the door to throw him out, but Fisher jabbed his elbow into Nash's face. Nash let go and cried out in pain.

'I'm sorry,' Fisher said, 'but where's your bloody phone?'

Whimpering and coughing, Nash scampered down the passage with Fisher in pursuit. 'You're not using my telephone,' he said. 'They'll trace it back to me here and I'll be for it. Haven't you done enough to me?'

'Children are going to be murdered. Something terrible is going to happen.'

'So you bloody say!'

He burst into the illicit still and grabbed the telephone wire to wrench it from the wall, and Fisher grabbed hold of Nash. In the struggle, an inane tug-of-war, Nash kicked out wildly and both men fell to the floor pulling the telephone lead out of its socket. Fisher stood first. 'Now look what you've done,' he said. 'I just wanted to telephone.'

'Oh Christ!' Nash said scrambling to his feet. 'I'm going to be sick,' and he rushed from the room, a hand covering his mouth. Fisher heard him retching in the lavatory down the passage.

Helplessly, Fisher stood staring at the severed lead. Then, he saw on a low table a black leather book: in gilt on the cover was the word ADDRESSES. He opened it and tore out the W page. As he was leaving, Nash called, 'Fisher!' Fisher turned. Nash was leaning against the lavatory door; the colour had drained from his face. He said, 'We've got our own lives to lead –' And as Fisher opened the door, added, 'And you're an unspeakable little shit.'

Out on the landing, Fisher paused. And after a moment he thought he heard coming from Nash's flat, a strain of music.

2

The first two men whom Fisher asked to direct him couldn't read. The third took him by the hand and led him into the old Cathedral square. As they walked Fisher felt a compulsion to tell what he had witnessed even to this stranger: the need for help was great. But the moment passed, and he found himself crossing the square alone, going around the back of the cathedral-mosque and ascending a gentle hill. The wind was heavy against him and the sand stung his eyes: he walked with his head down, pausing every few steps to make sure the way was clear. Half-way up the hill he heard a tapping sound and glanced up to see a lone figure coming towards him. It was Günther Winzer with his short white stick.

Günther paused, sensing somebody was there. He said sweetly, 'Do I know you?'

Fisher said, 'From the Afreka.'

Günther recognised the voice. 'You have not gone? You will come tonight to my recital? My girl Zubaydah will be there. We are in love.' He beamed.

Again the compulsion swept over Fisher. He said, 'Have you got a moment? I need help –'

Immediately Günther started on down the hill. 'I have to practise on the piano. Come tonight. We will talk. I hope the wind drops. Helmuth can't go out in the *ghibli*. The *ghibli* was made for the blind.' Tapping his way, he chuckled as he went.

Fisher plodded on upward and saw the disturbance as he turned into the appointed street. A uniformed man – at first, Fisher thought he was a policeman – struggled with a woman who broke free and began to run in Fisher's direction. She stumbled and he went forward to catch her. She smelled of Nash's cologne. He said her name, 'Paola,' but she didn't seem to hear.

She wore her dressing-gown but nothing on her feet. Her hair was dishevelled and her eyes red from the stinging wind. The uniformed man turned out to be the porter from her apartment block, and he was distressed and anxious.

'I phone Mr Wirrel, but phone no good. She ill. Very ill.'

'I'll get her back to the flat –' Fisher began to say but Paola shook her head violently, her hair flying in his face. He said, 'I'll take care of her –' though he didn't know what he could do. The caretaker shrugged dispiritedly and turned away.

Fisher led her into a small bus shelter protected on three sides. On the long bench were four Muslim women covered from head to foot in spotless white linen, like bundles of washing drying in the wind; each had an eye visible. Fisher and Paola sat in the corner. He put his arm protectively around her. The affinity he felt he knew was the bond that Gerald had forged between them, the bond of those who have known the same suffering; his helpless, massive sympathy was as much for himself as for her. They did not speak. The four eyes watched suspiciously.

At last he said, 'Won't you let me take you home now?'

She said or sounded as if she said, 'No, no, I –' But she may only have been moaning, impossible to tell.

'Where were you going?' he asked.

She began to whimper, then to cry but noiselessly.

'And I,' he said, 'was coming to you for help.'

'Help?' she repeated as if it was a foreign word.

'Something terrible is going to happen,' he said as though there were a tune running repetitively through his head.

'Oh,' she said, a long-drawn-out note which sounded to him like one of enormous relief. 'You know then.'

'Know? Know what?'

'About the school.'

'The school?' he repeated dully.

'Your school.'

'Mine.'

'I took – I took the photographs. I knew something terrible –' She didn't finish.

'Yes.'

'Gerald made me. I had no choice. I couldn't say no. The letters, you see. I shouldn't have written –' She broke off. He heard the sucking noise she made and guessed her necklet had gone into her mouth. After a long pause, she said softly, 'Once, he urinated on me.'

A bus drew up at the stop. The four women remained seated, their eyes, like strange insects, fixed on the couple.

Fisher said, 'Will you come with me?'

'Where?'

'We must warn your husband. Come. We'll go together.'

The bus moved on. Paola said, 'I haven't the strength. I haven't anything. He terrorised me.'

'Please come with me.'

'I haven't the strength,' she said again. 'Have you?'

'I don't know.'

'Why, do you know why we can't just go on uninterrupted? Why do they want to trample on us all the time?'

'Because they're so certain, and we're so full of doubt.'

'He always said he would win. He's always won.'

'Not always,' Fisher said after a moment; and later: 'You asked me if I had the strength. I don't know why we should need strength. But there's a feeling, isn't there, that no one else cares? I don't know why that is. I don't know why one feels so alone, but one does. Someone just said to me he'd got his own life to lead. And in a way I understood that, but God knows why we should be the ones who have to stand up. I've known it before, you see. I've had to fight it before. And ever since I've had this awful feeling of loss. A loss of everything. And I've often wondered whether it was worth it.' And when he began to tell her of the past he talked for his own benefit not for hers, a hope that the act of remembrance was in itself a source of courage.

'We had different fathers. His was a war-hero. The Spanish war. Our mother used to keep a photograph of him on the sideboard. He had watery eyes, a walrus moustache and a bald head. I once told Gerald I thought he looked more like Dr Crippen than a hero. I paid for that. Gerald loved him. He never did any work as far as I know. But he used to speak in Hyde Park on Sundays, I believe, and take Gerald with him. And Gerald used to look up at this fellow on the soap-box, and I suppose he believed every word he said. In those days they'd have called the old man a crank. Nowadays, he'd be an extremist.

'Well, he was killed in Spain, a member of the International Brigade, and left his wife and son with nothing but a proud belief in his heroism and a loyalty to his ideals. And they were ideals, you know. And he'd laid down his life for them, and that takes some doing. But somehow I think mother and child felt they'd been cheated by his death, and, almost as if they were erecting a memorial to him, continued to serve the causes in which he'd believed. They were poor, of course, and poverty's progressive. So, she married again, to give Gerald a home, I believe she said. Certainly not to have me. I was an accident.

'My father was quite different from Gerald's father. He was very English, although his grandfather, I think, was German or French. He always stood for the King's speech on Christmas Day. Respectable, respectful. Ran a little tobacco kiosk near Blackfriars Station. Strict, but kind. God knows why he married mother. I think she must've deceived him in some way. She used to buy her cigarettes from him and I suppose one thing led to another. And perhaps when they were first married he used to be amused by her activities. But when I remember him he wasn't amused at all.

'He gave Gerald a home all right. A decent home. He had a little money. Not much. He made a fair living, and he saved. A prudent man, you'd call him. Gerald called him a bourgeois cunt. My mother called him other names which I was too young to appreciate. I remember him angry and weary and beaten. For all he'd given them, they condemned him day in and day out. Hated him for it. Hated him for taking the place of Gerald's father and for being conscientious and patriotic and worthy.

'Just before my tenth birthday he found he couldn't stand it a moment longer and ran away. I think he tried to join the army but he was too old or unfit and he went to live in Coventry. He wrote me a letter, a sort of apology, but I never saw him again. Perhaps he got bombed. One thing's certain, he ran away because he couldn't take the hatred any more. Couldn't bear his wife siding with her elder son, couldn't bear the bitterness that was in the two of them which spilled out over him and me like caustic soda. Couldn't bear the meetings in the front room, the seedy little men coming and going, idle little men who never did a day's work, who looked at my father with contempt but accepted his hospitality just the same and never said thank you. He grew tired of the petitions, the marches, the banners stretched out across the kitchen floor, the yards and yards of red taffeta cut into letters and stitched into slogans. But you know what I think he was tired of most? Joylessness.

'And so he ran off. There was no photograph of him on the sideboard. Funny thing, I can remember Gerald's father better than my own. He left mother all his savings, the kiosk and a note saying, "You'll need this more than me. I can always make a living. And anyway, I want you to accuse me of being true to my class." I used to puzzle over that. And even now I'm not absolutely sure what it means, but I think he wanted them to condemn him for seeing that they were taken care of, that he hadn't run off and left them penniless, that he'd taken his responsibilities seriously. He never explained why he didn't take me with him. Mother's loving care and all that, I suppose.

Yes, you could say he was true to his class. A kind of decency.

'A few years later, I was thirteen, Gerald would be in his early twenties. One day, I was called out of school. When I got home the police were in the front room. My mother was crying. Gerald stood between two officers. Mother made a great deal of noise about me being a minor, but the police questioned me just the same. A brick had been thrown into an Embassy. Harmless stuff by today's standards but rather serious then. Gerald had done the throwing and he'd been shopped by one of his comrades. From mother's looks I knew what was expected of me. I was Gerald's alibi. "Yes," I lied, "Gerald was with me all last night. I never let him out of my sight, officer." They took a statement from me but they charged Gerald just the same. And when the case came to court, I, of course, was the chief witness for the Defence. I went into the witness-box. I took the Bible in my right hand and swore to tell the truth, the whole truth and nothing but the truth. Gerald's lawyer rose and told me to remember I was on oath. I promised I would. "Where was Gerald Mather on the night of the 15th?" he asked. "Take your time before answering," he said. So I did. And when I was ready I said, "I've no idea where Gerald Mather was on the night of the 15th," which was the truth. I wanted to lie but I couldn't. Mother screamed. Gerald screamed. The Clerk of the Court screamed. In the papers next day they said it was pandemonium. Gerald was given nine months. He said to me, "You always do the right thing." That evening two of his comrades knocked the shit out of me. Or into me.

'I've often wondered why I did what I did. I had an immense feeling of power standing in that box. I'd built a tree-house Gerald had once destroyed and perhaps I was getting back at him for that. Or perhaps I thought if he goes to prison I'll have mother to myself. Or perhaps I didn't know what I was doing. Or perhaps I took the oath seriously.

'Mother never talked to me again. Except on her deathbed. I was sent away to live with her sister. Aunt Rosa. She was childless. And kind. "You're better off without her," she said, but I didn't think so. When mother was dying, Aunt Rosa took me to see her. Mother said she hoped I'd repented for what I'd done. For telling the truth, I suppose she meant. She bequeathed all that was left of my father's money to Gerald. Yes, it's a feeling of loss.'

When he had finished and the only sound was the sound of the wind, he noticed that the four women had gone and that he and Paola were no longer observed.

She said, 'Yes, but I haven't the strength. Have you?' as though she hadn't heard a word he'd said.

3

The wind was dying. Fisher hid in a small storeroom stacked with German guidebooks of the city. He could hardly see: his eyes were swollen and painful. There was a sink in the corner and he'd tried to wash out the sand with cold water, but he had no relief. From time to time, he heard the piano in the louder passages, and the applause. He delayed and delayed: he did not know if he had found the strength to speak out.

The cries of 'Bravo' and 'Bis' told him that the time had come; it was now or never; the recital must be over or nearly over. He stepped out into a wide corridor and feeling his way, he made towards the noise of applause.

He came to long silken curtains and peering through discerned that he was behind the piano, but facing the audience. Two enormous crystal chandeliers, alive with light, dominated the room which danced before him. Everything was blurred and hazy. He thought: shall I step out now, take the Book in my right hand and swear to tell the truth? Ladies and gentlemen, children are to be murdered. When, when would he say it? Now? Now? When?

Günther Winzer spoke first in German, then in English. 'Ladies and gentlemen, as encore I wish to play the last sonata of my fellow countryman Ludwig van Beethoven, opus one hundred and eleven in C minor. For a reason unknown he did not make this a dedication to some special person. So, I am wishing to make a dedication myself of this great piece. I am dedicating this performance to my companion, Zubaydah.'

Now should I stand? Something terrible is going to happen. Children are going to be murdered. We must act together to prevent indiscriminate slaughter. Now?

He was arrested by the two dramatic notes with which the

sonata begins. His mind went back to the sight of Günther playing silently in the hotel room. Was the mood of the piece sombre, he wondered, or was it a warning? He shut his eyes. Anne, pregnant, burst in his head. It was hopeful. But something in the pace of the music shattered his mood, a sudden crescendo and unexpected acceleration. He tried not to listen. He wanted no misgivings to enter his resolve. When the movement ended, he thought, I'll cry out now for help.

Like the stately progress of a pilgrimage, the slow movement began. Fisher rubbed his eyes in the hope of resisting its sadness. But the music had a strange effect on him, not its power or its purity, but what it released in him, an unasked-for response: the sound removed censure.

He peered through the curtains again and saw a little more clearly the audience. Who were they? Forty were there? Fifty? Five million? What did it matter? Here they sat, each unique, individual, solitary, complete, a universe with particular responses, memories, influences. He saw Nash, a crumpled handkerchief in his hand trying to hide, what? His tears? Wirrel, inscrutable; Ella Carson, leaning forward as though she was afraid of missing something; and Brogan, bored; Swediq, beatific; Holmqvist, head bowed, hair over his eyes; Helmuth, seated beside the pianist, a proud guardian angel; in the front row, Zubaydah, her mouth open in wonder. Like unhappiness, Fisher discovered that joy could be unexpected, too: he felt suddenly and unaccountably inestimable pleasure at being alive, and of this varied company, of all the others he did not know and could not see, each their own universe. The music embraced him and he believed he had found the strength.

When the last note ended he stepped forward. At the sight of him, the applause stopped abruptly. Fisher said, 'Ladies and gentlemen, something terrible is going to happen.' He wished he could get the tune out of his head.

Someone sniggered.

'Children are going to be murdered.'

'He's drunk,' another shouted.

'Are you crazy?' Helmuth asked, coming up behind him, angry and intense. 'You're ruining the recital.'

'Ladies and gentlemen, please, do listen to me. I –' But he got no further. Brogan took one arm, Holmqvist the other. Brogan said, 'I apologise for my friend. He's as drunk as a lord. Heaven knows where you get liquor in this town.'

Cheers, applause and laughter.

Fisher said, 'Won't anyone help?'

'Come on, old buddy,' said Brogan.

'Wirrel,' cried Fisher, 'I must see you.'

'This way,' Holmqvist said.

Fisher broke free. He scrambled back to the curtains, down the wide corridor and found the storeroom. He heard footsteps, doors opening and Brogan saying, 'Tell Fawzi we've got him.'

He had no sense of time. Ten minutes may have passed or twenty. He opened the door a crack: he could see no one, but when he stepped out, there was Helmuth Winzer standing in the corridor with a bewildered, baffled look on his face. 'What did you do? What did you do?' he cried wildly. He grabbed hold of Fisher and shook him as though he were a recalcitrant child. 'Have you seen him?' he asked. 'Have you seen him?'

'Who?'

'Who? Who? Günther, of course! He's run off! While you make disturbance he ran off with that cross-eyed harlot! He's left me! He's gone! My own brother!'

Behind Helmuth's back a door opened. A finger urgently beckoned Fisher. A solitaire ring sparkled. Fisher pushed aside the German, was about to run when he saw Swediq. 'Here, here,' said the doctor, beckoning. 'I'm here to help you.'

Fisher went through the door into an empty room. Swediq, resplendent in a white tuxedo and huge velvet bow tie, said, 'Tell me, my dear friend. Tell me all. I know you're not drunk. I know you have information. I saw you from Aubrey's terrace, through the glasses, hiding in the grandstand. I am your ally, believe me. I will get the message to Wirrel. Life is not all mucus to me.'

Fisher told him what he had seen. He could not stop himself from crying. Swediq made hurried notes with a slim gold pencil on the back of a cigarette packet. 'Don't worry,' said the doctor. 'Trust me. You had better wait here. I'll go and find Wirrel. Cheery-bye.'

Fisher sank to the floor and hugged his knees. He wept with relief. When the door next opened, Brogan and Holmqvist entered. Fisher did not resist. He'd been helped, and that was enough.

4

Fawzi waited for him in the Outer Tent. He slapped Fisher hard across the face. They returned him to the room with the bed and the whitewashed walls. He slept in profound peace.

Julnar appeared at intervals with food; at her third appearance – he guessed it was evening – she spoke for the first time, ordered him to follow her. With Wanis one step behind him, and sometimes deliberately treading on his heels, Fisher followed Julnar up two flights of stairs. He smelled ether and antiseptic.

They entered a room with a hospital bed. Fawzi stood beside it. In the bed, a man lay sobbing. Fisher did not recognise him at first but coming round to stand next to Fawzi, he saw on the bedside table a solitaire ring.

'Show him,' ordered Fawzi.

The doctor, who was shuddering with fear and pain, raised his right arm. The hand had been amputated; the stump was bandaged; the bandage was bloodstained.

Fawzi said, 'That's what we do to criminals.'

PART NINE

The *ghibli* had blown itself out. The last summons to prayer was heard across the land. At midnight Fisher was taken aboard the ferry for Genoa. The motor-cars, the vans, the monstrous container lorries stretched out along the quay: one by one their contents and documents were checked by slow thinking, over-zealous officials; one by one the vehicles were driven up the ramps and secured by chains to the cavernous lower deck.

Mr Fawzi's Cadillac did not join the procession. Wanis parked the car in the forecourt and took his farewell of Fawzi and Julnar – a handshake, a hand tapping the heart:

'*Assalaam aleikum.*'

'*Wa-aleikum assalaam.*'

To Fisher he nodded, and then watched the three travellers enter the Immigration shed.

Brogan, Jorda and Holmqvist were seated side by side on a bench, each clutching a briefcase. At Mr Fawzi's appearance they rose as one, and followed him into an office behind the cubicles. Passports were quickly stamped. Again the greetings were exchanged:

'*Assalaam aleikum.*'

'*Wa-aleikum assalaam.*'

Charon waited for them at the head of the companionway. Although the night was warm, he wore a greatcoat and his hands were thrust deep into the pockets. He led them along ill-lit corridors to cabins where the stench of oil was noxious, and the throb of the engines being made ready, insistent. Fisher was given a two-berth cabin with the Basque.

Fawzi said, 'Get some sleep. We sail at five. At seven your work will be done.' He wheezed with enjoyment.

Fisher lay on his bunk, but sleep was impossible. He was encased in the noise of the ship, the roar of each vehicle boarding, the clank of chains, the shouts and swearing, and the engines, throbbing; only the Basque, it seemed, was silent.

What work, Fisher wondered? What work had they in store for him? And, more insistent, what work had he in store for himself? He dreaded the sweetness of Gerald's revenge. He longed to write to Anne, but what would he say? The one line that came into his head was 'If I should die think only this of me ...' but that made him smile. His fear was not of the unknown, but of the known: of Gerald.

Obstinacy, learned in childhood, encouraged Fisher: a part of him, a small part which, perhaps, he pretended was the whole, refused to allow Gerald a final victory. A voice against which he was powerless, commanded him to resist. There was no rational reason, just a feeling, and that was sufficient. The memory of watching his mother, framed in the kiosk, brought an odd and unexpected comfort, like an acceptance of death. He remembered her, too, in the courtroom, with that awful cocky smile of encouragement to lie, showing her smug pink gums. He had wiped that hope from her face, but not from Gerald's: neither disappointed nor shocked, but knowing; you always do the right thing. And thinking of them, his mother and his half-brother, Fisher felt in the pit of his stomach the cold sickly sensation he associated not with death itself but with dying, and he knew that that was to be resisted also. In the grave it was to be resisted; in the furnace, as ash; in the sea it was to be resisted.

He wished he could pray. How pleasant, he thought, to subscribe to the infallible order of things. How more courageous he would be now if he was able to rely on the well-trodden path of doctrine, worship, entreaty, reward and punishment. His cowardice, he acknowledged, sprang from a lack of trust in his own resources, to discomfort the presence within; to doubt his own existence. Why was it so hard to stand up and confess I am something more than a scavenger microbe fouling the Earth? And he understood dimly that he had never fully entered another's life only because he had never entered his own.

And even the children, the object of his concern, were abstract. Perhaps they did not exist at all. Perhaps they were a fantasy of Fawzi's creation in which Fisher had come to believe. Perhaps their non-existence was Gerald's revenge: to push Fisher to the point of danger in the cause of spectres. But Fisher knew he was avoiding the issue: he knew because he was a student of the pattern of things. Was the murder of children possible in the name of a cause, any cause? Had children not been murdered in Rama? With Gerald you did what you could to prevent the possible, not the reality.

Fisher resolved: in me lies the answer; mine is the kingdom.

He must have slept because he dreamed: a strange and terrifying episode that seemed to separate mind from body. He dreamed incestuously of Gerald. When he woke he was conscious of being shocked, but also experienced a feeling of heady elation which had no connection with the senses or with sexual pleasure, yet somehow strengthened his will to resist. Long after the images had receded, he continued to grow in confidence and determination. I must do what is necessary.

The ferry had passed the breakwater. Jorda was not in the cabin. Fisher opened the door to find a young Italian sailor barring the way. As though he was sad to be on guard, he pushed Fisher back and shut the door. Through the cabin window there was only the calm sea and a pale, promising sky.

Mr Fawzi came for him shortly before six.

'You must follow me now,' he said.

They went deeper into the bowels of the ship; along the way Julnar joined them and, presently, they paused at a door and without knocking entered the Captain's cabin.

Charon stood. Fawzi tossed a passport on to the table; it was Fisher's. From his breastpocket Charon took a pair of gold-rimmed spectacles and slipped them on to his nose. Julnar moved to Fisher's side.

Fawzi said, 'What Gerald had planned is this: the Captain will perform a wedding ceremony, as he is empowered to do under Italian maritime law. Julnar will be on your passport as your wife. It will give her easy entrance to your country. There are some formalities you have to undertake before the consul in Genoa –'

Fisher ceased to hear Fawzi's voice. He looked at the girl who smiled her tentative smile as she'd done in the café. Seeing her, in black, sweating, the rash on her chin like a scar, remembering her in the open-air classroom firing her gun at

Habib, Fisher understood that she was not the carrier of a disease but the disease itself: he was to be the carrier, the means of infection. I must see you, I *need* to see you, ran senselessly through his head. He knew he must act. He knew he must again take the Book in his hand, but aware that now he put all in hazard. No one in this world could prevent something terrible from happening except him.

Fawzi snapped his fingers in Fisher's face and brought him back into the stuffy cabin, to the bride, and to Charon who held in his hands an open book on which he placed a gold wedding ring. You always do the right thing. Fisher grabbed the girl, pushed her at Fawzi and then ran from the cabin. He heard Fawzi say in a calm, matter-of-fact way, 'Where's he going?' and call, 'Fisher, don't be a fool –'

2

Before long they were hunting him. Fisher kept to the lower decks, trying to find somewhere to hide, an empty cabin, anywhere. He came face to face with Holmqvist in a narrow triangular space near the Engine Room, but managed to flee up a spiral staircase that led to an empty corridor. He heard Holmqvist come after him and the Swede said, 'I've got a gun, Fisher, be careful –'

There were cabin doors either side of the corridor. He tried two but they were locked, the third opened and Fisher stepped inside a space larger than he expected: he thought it empty at first, but to his left, before a table on which stood a silver cross, was Brogan with his back to Fisher; and Jorda, kneeling, his hands clasped in prayer. Fisher would have run had not Brogan turned: he wore the surplice and the stole and the collar of a priest; there was something shiny in his hands. Fisher thought it was a gun and thrashed out wildly knocking the object from Brogan's hands. Jorda cried out '*Madre de Dio.*' Fisher stepped back feeling for the door knob. But Brogan, for a frozen instant, did not move. Then, he dropped to the floor and, crying like a wounded dog, licked the carpet and Fisher saw the silver chalice, shiny; it rolled first one way, then the other with the remorseless pitching of the ship.

A hand caught him by the ankle. Fisher, half-way up a narrow chute, thought he was safe when the hand grabbed him and pulled him down. A sailor, a boy with greased hair and a gold ear-ring in his left ear, leapt on him and, in a confined space that led to the car deck, they fought, the boy easily the stronger. Fisher gave up more or less immediately, pulling free and holding up his empty hands to show he meant no harm. The boy grinned nervously and produced a gun and even as he thrust it forward into Fisher's face, Fisher, by reflex, kicked upwards and caught the boy in the groin. He howled and dropped the weapon which fell like a stone into Fisher's lap. In the same movement the boy lurched forward and Fisher caught him round the neck in a stranglehold and put the gun to his temple. My only chance is to kill him, Fisher thought. I must pull the trigger and kill him. Who is he? What is he?

Shouts and answered shouts sounded overhead; and men running, a hoarse command from Mr Fawzi.

The boy stared in terror and pain at Fisher. Fisher thought: kill him, you have no alternative. But the question came, what right? Anonymous or known he is a universe, unique and entire and inviolate. Fisher shoved him aside, dropped the gun and made for the car deck.

The boy, trembling, pounced on the gun and fired, hitting Fisher in his left shoulder.

Fisher was too weak to stand. He crawled slowly and painfully along the car deck, between the vehicles, searching for a place to hide. And then, to his right, he heard a voice.

'Quack-quack-quack-quack.'

Abdulsalaam sat in the back of the black, windowless van. He had dyed his hair black, and the dye had run on to his forehead giving him a second fringe.

Nearby Mr Fawzi said. 'He must be somewhere here. Search the cars.'

Fisher pulled himself towards the van and Abdulsalaam helped him into the back. 'Quack-quack-quack-quack,' he cackled quietly and smiled at the sight of Fisher's blood. And Fisher saw for the first time Aubrey's coffin.

Holmqvist's voice: 'Start at this end. Every car. Every truck. We have to find him.' The order was relayed in Italian.

Abdulsalaam peered out through the back doors: the sailors were beginning their search, looking under the cars, trying the doors, hopping into the backs of the lorries to pull at ropes and to test tarpaulins.

'They are looking for you?' asked Abdulsalaam. 'Shall I tell them you are here, *chéri*?'

'No. Hide me. Please,' Fisher said, holding his wound so that his fingers slipped in the flow of blood.

'Hide you? Why should I hide you?'

'I'll pay you,' Fisher promised, 'I'll pay you.'

The sailors were two, three cars away. One shouted and the others ran to him, but it was a false alarm.

Abdulsalaam crawled to the coffin and by loosing a catch, opened the lid. Fisher could not breathe. He whispered, 'No, not in there.'

'There is nowhere else. They are searching everywhere. They won't search in there.'

The voices were close. Fawzi said, 'We must find him,' and Holmqvist answered, 'Don't worry, we'll find him, ja.'

'Will I be able to breathe?' asked Fisher, steeling himself.

'I dunno,' Abdulsalaam said. 'I have not tried it,' and hissed like a snake.

Fisher thought of Gerald. 'You bastard,' he said and, gazing into the crate, he saw the dead body of Aubrey Scott-Burrows dressed in his white burnous.

'Try the van,' said Holmqvist.

Fisher said again, 'You bastard,' and plunged.

Fawzi pulled open the door of the van.

'Hissssss...'

'Tell them to search,' Fawzi said, but the sailors crossed themselves and refused. 'Holmqvist, you do it.'

The Swede, giggling, climbed in, sniffed, poked in the corners and said, 'No. He's not here.'

No scream would escape his mouth. He lay with his face against the cold brittle flesh, smelling the sweet smell of corruption; after a while even that ceased. They lay like two petrified stone effigies.

He had no thoughts except that every sense seemed too acute to bear, yet, he could not smell or feel or taste or hear or see. He wanted to cry, he could not. He wanted to escape; he could not. Every muscle tautened to resist the embrace. Blood dropped on the white cowl and, in moving, Fisher disturbed the corpse so that one eye opened and stared at him. The corpse smiled.

He was victim to the sensation of falling from a great height, tumbling through an infinite void. He lay with all his weight on the dead man, feeling the face against his face. In that moment, Fisher submitted to a soaring vision. 'Save them,' he said.

Abdulsalaam could not stand the screams coming from the coffin: one continuous petrified scream. He sat on the lid and bolted it. The scream continued like a perpetual echo. The sound pushed all thoughts from his mind. He tried to remember where he was supposed to go – Spezia, Firenze, Sauleo – but he could remember nothing, not with that awful, agonising noise.

He peered out of the van: the sailors had finished their search. Abdulsalaam jumped down to the deck, reached in and dragged the coffin forward. Crouching low, he manoeuvred it on to his back and finding the proper balance weaved carefully between the rows of cars, came to an oblong opening and slid the coffin off his back into the sea; plummeting with a great crash it hit the water and the darkness.

7

At the docks in Genoa they searched all the vehicles again, except the van. The Customs Officers crossed themselves, and removed their caps as it passed. Charon ordered a further search of the ship from stern to prow, but no trace of Fisher was found. Fawzi paid the Captain and the crew their bonus. He paid the Customs Officers, too.

And when Abdulsalaam reached Florence and the monastery where Aubrey's friend was buried, Father Sauleo said, 'I thought Mr Scott-Burrows wanted to be buried here.'

'*Mais non*,' replied the servant. '*Dans la mer.*'

8

Wirrel read to Paola what Harvey Nash had sent from Rome:

'Forlorn! the very word is like a bell
To toll me back from thee to my sole self!
Adieu! the fancy cannot cheat so well
As she is fam'd to do, deceiving elf.
Adieu! Adieu! thy plaintive anthem fades
Past the near meadows, over the still stream,
Up the hill-side; and now 'tis buried deep
In the next valley-glades:
Was it a vision or a waking dream?
Fled is that music: Do I wake or sleep?'

'Isn't that nice of him?' Wirrel said, closing the book and turning to her. She gazed at the ceiling, entombed in silence. He said, 'Do you hear me? Do you know I'm here?' She gave no response. He said, 'I'll write to him for you. I'll give him all your news.'

And he left her on her bed not knowing whether she knew what he had said. He wrote to Nash and told him of Paola's illness, and that he would be taking her home for treatment. He wrote that Fisher had disappeared off the ferry; no one quite knew how. 'But he'll turn up again, I imagine. A frightful type. But a survivor if ever I saw one.'

9

'Touch and go,' the doctor said.

She lay as still as she could, feeling the life stir, not daring to hope that it would survive; but there was life, however precarious. She would do what the doctors ordered.

She wished she would hear from Martin.

In the evening she saw a television film, shot, they said, in secret by a Swedish camera crew: children marched up and down, and the people prostrated themselves in prayer. Dedication, they said, terror, reprisals. And then, she thought she saw Martin, seated apart from the others, on the grandstand, but it was too quick to be certain, and the film shuddered as though someone had pushed the cameraman. Perhaps she'd been dreaming.

'Touch and go,' said the nurse.

In his sanctuary, within the Inner Tent, Mr Fawzi could not pray. Knots, like stones, weighed him down. He was empty, deserted, cheated. Submission came hard. He had sworn to pierce the enemy's heart. But the enemy had found a defender. O Lord, give us your favour in this world, he cried, but the words were bitter. Protect us from hell's pain and anguish: hollow, the prayer. Grant us your mercy: the plea went unanswered. He squirted in the air: two flies copulating, twitched and died in ecstasy.

He lifted the telephone and reported to his superior.

'Excellency, we must postpone,' Fawzi said.

Must we?

'I'm afraid so, Excellency. We may have lost the advantage of surprise.'

Explain.

'That man Fisher, he knows too much. He can warn. He can point the finger. And we can't get the girl in. We need another way.'

But the others have the money?

'Of course.'

So we cancel?

'No, Excellency, we postpone.'

Until when?

'Until we find out what's happened to Fisher.'